the bargaining

Also by Carly Anne West

The Murmurings

the bargaining

CARLY ANNE WEST

simon pulse
NEW YORK LONDON TORONTO SYDNEY NEW DELHI

SIMON PULSE

An imprint of Simon & Schuster Children's Publishing Division

1230 Avenue of the Americas, New York, New York 10020

First Simon Pulse hardcover edition February 2015

Text copyright © 2015 by Carly Anne West

Jacket photographs copyright © 2015 by Trevillion Images (woods and girl),
and Getty Images (cabin)

All rights reserved, including the right of reproduction in whole or in part in any form.

SIMON PULSE and colophon are registered trademarks of Simon & Schuster, Inc.

For information about special discounts for bulk purchases, please contact
Simon & Schuster Special Sales at 1-866-506-1949 or
business@simonandschuster.com.

The Simon & Schuster Speakers Bureau can bring authors to your live event. For
more information or to book an event contact the Simon & Schuster Speakers Bureau
at 1-866-248-3049 or visit our website at www.simonspeakers.com.

Jacket designed by Jessica Handelman

Interior designed by Hilary Zarycky

The text of this book was set in New Baskerville.

Manufactured in the United States of America

2 4 6 8 10 9 7 5 3 1

Library of Congress Cataloging-in-Publication Data

West, Carly Anne.

The bargaining / Carly Anne West.—First Simon Pulse hardcover edition.

pages cm

Summary: Grieving and guilty over a friend's death, Penny is not surprised when
her mother sends her to live with her father and stepmother, April, but when
April takes her to help restore an old house in a dense forest, weird occurences
connected to missing children threaten Penny's safety and fragile mental health.

ISBN 978-1-4424-4182-8 (hc)

[1. Supernatural—Fiction. 2. Missing children—Fiction. 3. Forests and
forestry—Fiction. 4. Dwellings—Conservation and restoration—Fiction.
5. Stepfamilies—Fiction. 6. Horror stories.] I. Title.

PZ7.W51733Bar 2015

[Fic]—dc23

2014014866

ISBN 978-1-4424-4184-2 (eBook)

For Matt, always

"Do not despise the lore that has come down from distant years; for oft it may chance that old wives keep in memory word of things that once were needful for the wise to know."

—Celeborn, *The Fellowship of the Ring,* by J. R. R. Tolkien

Prologue

2004

THE FIRST THING I SHOULD see is Pop with his belt. He called me from the top of the stairs, so that's where he should be waiting, leather and buckle in hand, knuckles bulging against his grip.

Instead, he's in the living room, standing by the door, his hand in his pocket jingling the keys to the car I didn't leave a scratch on, so how the hell would he know? I consider telling him the side of the story he won't care about, but I know it's useless.

I'm taller than most kids my age. It's not like I can't reach the pedals. A real dad would have taken me out by now, nudged me with his elbow and tossed me the keys with one of those Don't Tell Mom winks. But Pop's not that kind of dad, so that's how I know this whooping is going to be the worst

I've ever had. I had a full day of knowing how it felt to be in control of something bigger than me, and I think I'd trade my whole life just to know what one more day would feel like.

"How's about we go for a ride, boy?" Pop asks, leaning toward the door.

Pop isn't known for asking. And I know this isn't really a question, either. He only ever calls me "boy" when he's ready to put his fist through something. It almost makes me glad that's the closest he's ever come to giving me a nickname.

Still, his asking makes me nervous.

"Where're we going?"

Pop shrugs, his shoulders the only parts of his body that are fluid. Everything else stands at attention. His stiff spine and locked knees fight against the way he rocks on his heels, back and forth like one of those toy birds that bends for water over and over. His hands are uneasy, searching for places to go.

"Just a drive," he says.

I look around, still not used to the new silence of our house, the way the walls even seem to hold their breath now.

"Where's Miller?" I might have guessed the minute he saw me slip Pop's keys into my pocket this morning that Miller would tell. He was born that way, his mouth wide open, ready to spill every truth that isn't his. But because I'm the only one who ever teaches him a lesson, he never learns. Lessons are what big brothers are supposed to teach, not that anyone ever did that for me.

"Never mind Miller," Pop says.

He always criticizes Mom for babying Miller, but Pop treats him like he's made of glass. We'll see how breakable he is later.

"What about Mom?"

"So many goddamn questions," Pop says and opens the door. "Get your jacket."

I pull my coat from the hook by the couch and shove my hands in my pockets, thumbing the pencil stub and loose button floating around in the left one, remembering again to tell Mom before she asks me about it. I could lose an arm, and the first thing she'd notice is the string on my coat that used to hold a stupid plastic button.

In the car, I rehearse the usual debate before I open my mouth. If I tell Pop everything now, maybe he'll keep the whooping to a minimum. But if I don't say anything, he doesn't have to know everything. The wild card, as always, is not knowing how much Miller spilled.

This time, I decide to go for broke.

"I bet you'd have let *him* drive it."

I see Pop's fingers curl tighter over the steering wheel.

"Don't talk about him," Pop says.

"And I didn't do anything to it," I push on. "I even put the seat back where it was."

"Stop talking," Pop says, his growl crackling under some internal fire.

"Why can't I just—?"

It's dark out, and it's even darker in the car, so I don't see his hand leave the steering wheel until it's inches from my face, and by then I can't duck. Light enters the car in one hot flash. I cover my mouth with the back of my hand, pushing in on the part of my lip that split on my tooth, forcing back the wave of pain that'll roll in soon.

"You never listen. It's like nobody else is even there. Like you're alone in your own little world, and to hell with the rest of us," Pop says, his reasoning a familiar epilogue.

Pop's never needed a location for my whooping before. The living room or the bedroom or the garage has always sufficed. The clock on the dash reads 6:32. Mom will be putting dinner out any minute. She's probably asking Miller if he wants milk or water right now. I smelled pot roast in the slow cooker this afternoon.

When we hit the fork in the road, Pop takes the path to the right, the one that isn't paved.

He's taking us into the woods. Which means Miller told him everything. Not just the car. He told Pop about the old house. The spiders. The shed. All of it.

I watch as the remaining light from the outside gets swallowed up, and pretty soon, just the shadows of evergreens my pencil's drawn a million different ways fill the spaces in the car between Pop and me. The wheels struggle over chunks gouged from the makeshift road.

"Where are we going?" I ask, knowing I've used up all my questions and fully expecting another crack in the mouth.

But Pop doesn't say anything. Just grips the steering wheel, his face fighting some sort of battle with itself.

Branches are slapping against the car I was so careful to keep from damaging, and I grip the handle on my door to keep myself from flinching at each smack.

After we've gone as far as the trees will let us, Pop stops the car and opens his door without a word. I'm supposed to follow, but all I can do is grip the handle. When he opens my door from the outside, I'm still holding it, and he wrenches my hand away and yanks hard enough for me to hear a pop somewhere near my shoulder. I stumble out of the car and look around, telling myself the usual things.

The sooner it starts, the sooner it'll be over.

He'll break skin if you swear. Don't swear.

You'll teach Miller a lesson later. Later.

Biting your lip just makes your lip hurt.

But as I wait for Pop to rip a switch from one of the hundreds of trees eating up all the light, I run out of things to tell myself. And he's just standing by the car, looking at me like he's trying to figure out what I am.

I'm your son.

It's in my throat, and I open my mouth to release it, but a puff of white air is all that escapes.

I've never waited this long for a whooping, and maybe that's Pop's new form of punishment. Making me wait. Except that now he's getting back into the car.

I blink for a second. I missed it somehow. I blacked out. The whooping came and went, and I'm stunned or delirious or whatever. I take a step toward the car, but Pop says something that stops me where I stand.

"I'm sorry."

They're words he's never said before, not that I've ever heard, and I put my hand gingerly on the backs of my thighs, my lower back. I feel for the welt marks that should be there, but all I can feel is the sting of cold starting to seep through my clothes.

I take another step toward the car, but I hear the locks drop, their heavy thud echoing through the doors' metal.

Pop looks straight ahead.

It's not about the car. This is my punishment for going

into the woods. He wants to show me I'm not such a big man. He wants to scare me. But the woods don't scare me. They scare him, but they don't scare me.

They don't scare me at all.

I shove my hands into my pockets, the detached button cold against my skin. I turn it around between my thumb and forefinger, hating my hand for shaking.

"So leave then," I say, maybe loud enough for him to hear me through the glass. Maybe loud enough for me to believe I want him to.

As if he was waiting on my command, Pop throws the car into reverse and backs down the narrow road, bumping his precious car through the holes and cracks, keeping his eyes ahead of him like something out there is going to tell him this is okay.

My feet betray me, running for the road toward the car, my hands stuck in my pockets. Something else is in my throat now, something that dislodges against every effort to keep it in. Something infantile, cracking the hard surface it pushes against in my mouth.

"Don't!"

Then I can't see his car anymore, and I know he really left me.

Part of me wonders why I'm so surprised. But I am, and

for a second, I can't breathe. The air is right there, but I can't remember how to use it. And when I do figure it out, all of it hurts. Inhaling. Exhaling.

He left me.

The woods start their creaking. That's what I remember from last time, and nothing has changed since then. I read in some story when I was little that it's the sound of trees counting their leaves. I don't know why that always stuck with me. It's not like I believed it. I guess I didn't like the idea of trees counting anything.

Or maybe I've just been listening too much to what people around here say about what the trees do in these woods.

The longer I stand here, the colder I get, and I think about following the road back out and walking the rest of the way home. But it's colder than balls out here, and besides, maybe Mom will freak when Pop comes home without me, and good. I hope she suffers a little before I finally do show up. It's not like she was there to stop him. It's not like she's ever there anymore, even when she's standing right in front of me.

The branches snag my jacket, and I push them away too hard, earning a couple of scratches. The trees in these woods hit back. I'm sweating a little, and only when my lungs start to ache do I notice that I've been running this whole time.

The roof of the old house is low, but the trees clear enough of a path for me to see just above their tops by the time I get to the outskirts of the drive.

The air feels thicker here, and I wonder how that could be with the trees finally giving me some breathing room. I listen for the creaking again, but this time all I hear is the sound of my own breath, the back of my throat clicking the way it does sometimes when I'm . . .

Quit being a pussy.

But I can't tell if those are Pop's words or mine. He's probably halfway home by now.

I walk around the back to the kitchen door and wedge through the crack I made last time, the bar locking it from the inside groaning against the strain.

It smells the same. Like sewage and absence. But this is closer than the shed, and besides, I think I'm done with that place.

I take the stairs two at a time to the upper level, breathing into my hands. Maybe I can dig up an old blanket or something. The last owners left pretty much all their junk.

I pull a mattress down from its place against the wall, and when I realize I'm not tired at all, I pull a few more down, and before I know it, I have a shelter even better than this pile of firewood that used to be a house, a tunnel starting at the wall with the window, leading all the way back to the closet on the other side of the room. I haven't built a fort in years, and it feels good to do it without Pop telling me to grow up. I slam one more mattress to the floor and scoot it to the back of the tunnel. It fits almost perfectly in the closet once I move the rest of the garbage from the floor. My hand brushes a little box in the farthest corner of the closet. I know what it is before I even pick it up. I'd know that rattle anywhere.

Matches.

It's like nobody else is even here. Like you're alone in your own little world.

"And to hell with the rest of you." I finish Pop's thought.

I slide the box open and lay down on my bed for the night, rolling the thin sticks between my fingers.

The worst whooping I ever got was the night I set the lawn on fire. I cried so hard my throat burned for three days afterward. But that's what Pop never understood. It's not about doing whatever I want. It's about control.

And even he can't control fire.

Now I let myself light just one match. There are only four, and I don't want to burn through them all. Not if I'm going to be here all night.

The house leans against a stiff gust of wind outside, its frame crying out, and I remind myself I'm the only one in the woods.

I'm alone.

I curl up with a moldy sheet and think about my brother. I don't mean to, but he drops into my brain before I can make him go away, and all I can do is stare at his face until he finally opens his mouth.

"I shouldn't be here," he says to me, and I try to remember him ever actually talking to me that way. Like I was ever somebody he would talk to at all.

"So go home then," I say, just wanting to sleep. "You're the only one they care about anyway." Dreams never end well for me. They just waste good hours of nothingness.

"I can now," he says, giving me a look like he's . . .

"Sorry," he says. Like he's sorry.

I try to ask him what he means, but he turns around and starts walking away. The back of his head and everything below it are covered in mud and leaves, like he's been snoozing in the dirt for the last six months.

He's walking toward a road overgrown by shrubs and tangled branches. Just before he rounds the corner, he turns back to me, his face flat and pale.

"I think this is where loneliness grows," he says, and makes it to the last tree in the road before turning one more time.

"It stops hurting eventually," he says.

And he disappears behind the last tree, the road swallowing him up.

Then the trees fold over themselves, erasing the road and the light that shone down on it, their branches tangling and writhing like snakes lunging for the last remaining rat, thickening the air and knotting the ground until they're at my feet, climbing beneath the legs of my pants, binding my arms and my chest and prying my mouth open, piercing my eyes and devouring me where I stand.

I wake under the moldy sheet in the old house, the light from the moon finding the tiny moth-eaten holes and spilling silver rays on the mattress.

Dreams. Such a goddamn waste.

But my heart is still acting like it wants out of my chest, and maybe that's because I can barely breathe under this stupid sheet.

I start to pull it away, but when I hear tapping on the window, I stop.

A branch.

But that doesn't make me feel better, the memory of my dream too close to the edge of my waking mind.

Then the tapping sounds more like thudding on the glass. More like a sharp knuckle rapping.

I hold still, warning my heart against abandoning me.

When I hear the window slide open, my stupid heart stays where it is, and at first I think it's playing dead, a possum behind my ribs.

But then I hear dragging, and my heart beats back to life long enough for me to drop the sheet and strike one precious match to burn the sharp, dragging knuckle straight to hell.

Before it takes me.

1

Spring 2013

THE INK ON THE BATHROOM stall door is a rainbow of degradation.

"Amanda and Jay 4Ever" in purple.

"Amanda Ziegler is a str8 up SLUT!" in blue.

"U don't even know her!" in green.

"The whole basketball team knows her!" in orange.

Amanda Ziegler was before my time, so I only know her as the third stall from the left. She might have been a math genius. A prodigy. A jock. A tortured artist.

She could have been my best friend.

But her legacy is str8 up SLUT, sealed in blue ink, written into the record forever. Or until they renovate the girls' bathroom.

The bell rings. The sound of thirty doors opening at

once, the sound of a thousand pairs of rubber and cork soles squeaking and thumping against the linoleum in the hallway. I count time this way now. Mom says I'm languishing, but she has no idea how much work it takes to account for all that movement around me. Two pairs of feet approach the door to the bathroom.

One two.

One two.

Then they push inside.

"But do you think she was high when it happened?"

"Of course she was high. Major tweaker. You know how I had biology lab with her my sophomore year? She told me she'd sneak into my house and stab my eyes out with a scalpel if I looked at her. I swear to God. I wasn't even looking at her! Well, a little, but you know, when you act like a total psycho, you really just want attention."

"You're so rude."

"Whatever. I'm just telling the truth. I'm not going to be all fake now and make her out to be some misunderstood saint, like some people."

"You know Alex's cousin, C. J.? The smart one who goes to Truman? He was there. He told Alex all they found was one of her shoes."

"Shut up."

"There was, like, a coyote den nearby or something."

"Gross!"

"And apparently there was some major drama going down before she wandered off."

"If Rae Fenwick was involved, there was definite drama."

"Yeah, but I guess she totally threw down with that girl, Penny."

"No way . . . I thought they were all besties forever."

I can only seem to focus on one sense at a time. Watch this now. Listen to that later. Too much, and I'll experience massive sensory overload, and wouldn't that be horrendous? For my brain to explode? For me to be found in the very same stall where Amanda Ziegler was immortalized as the tragic slut she maybe never was, beneath an air conditioning vent that's sputtering to its breaking point?

I watch these girls I've never even met as they devour each new revelation, drops of my life smeared across their lips.

I watch their mouths move through the crack in the door, how they form my name, form Rae's name. Only after they've stopped moving do I hear what they say.

Air pants through the vent above me like a protective dog trying to drown out the sound of their talking. But the air conditioner coughs a dying breath before quitting, and sound reaches me eventually.

"You lying heifer, there's no way that's true."

"I swear to God. Dragged off by wild dogs. It's maybe, like, the worst way ever to die."

I push out of Amanda Ziegler's stall and move to the sink, washing my hands even though I don't need to. I only came in here for a little quiet, and now this place is louder than the halls outside. I'd rather count a million steps from a million feet than listen to one more word in this tiny room.

One of the girls clears her throat, and I can feel them both staring at me in the mirror, waiting for me to give them something more to snack on.

It's what I'm supposed to do. Girls like me feed conversations in bathrooms.

I shake the water from my hands. I focus on my own reflection. Same charcoal sweater I put on today, slouching off my shoulder, a neon yellow bra strap exposed, skinny gray jeans. Short brown hair, gray eyes, Asphalt Magic eye shadow. It's still me.

Except that I can't recognize the girl behind all those pieces. I blink back the memory of the last time I felt this way.

The air conditioner above Amanda Ziegler's stall coughs back to life. And in that second—under cover of fresh sound—the girl closest to me laughs. It's tiny, hardly detectable if not for the fact that I can see her face in the mirror, the way her mouth distorts as she tries to mask it. It's obvious she's nervous, that the act wasn't entirely voluntary. But the other girl doesn't know that, and she picks up the laugh where the first girl dropped it.

I let my hand connect with her blushed cheek as many times as I can before her friend pulls me off her and some teacher pulls her friend off me.

Deep red spots decorate the front of my gray sweater. Asphalt Magic smears from eye to temple. But I don't care. For the first time in months, a new sense has made its way into my body's vocabulary. I have regained the sense of touch.

And it feels amazing to smack the shit out of this girl I've never met.

I wonder if Amanda Ziegler ever bloodied a girl's nose. I decide that maybe she did. I only come down from my new high when I realize how proud Rae would have been of me.

One large Rubbermaid bin with a matching blue lid is all I bring to Dad's house. Mom kept rolling suitcases into my room, shoving clothes I didn't need and yearbooks I didn't care about into them.

"You're going to want them once you're up there," she kept saying. And when I didn't say anything, she just kept packing, which was maybe her way of apologizing for being so utterly wrapped up in everything except the unraveling life of her daughter. Or maybe it was her way of clearing out my room so she didn't have to do it after I left. Ever since the capital D-Divorce, she's been very focused on a career she never cared about before.

Not that I was really up for hearing "Quit feeling sorry for yourself," her unique brand of comfort, or how hard this was making *her* life. So when she acted so surprised that I only loaded the Rubbermaid into the car, I finally did say something.

"If you want to get rid of me so badly, why not just leave me on the curb with the rest of my stuff instead of shipping me off to Seattle? It'd be a lot cheaper."

We didn't talk for the entire three-day drive to Dad's. It's not that I didn't have more to say. It's that I knew she wouldn't hear anything but the sound of her own wounded feelings crying out, and nobody could be heard over that.

Besides, it's going to be nothing but noise the minute we get to Dad's.

"I'm not saying that, and you know it. Why do you always do that? You twist everything I say."

"I don't know, Dale. I'm just evil, I guess."

"And there she is. Passive-aggressive Natalie. I was wondering how long it was going to take before she showed up."

"Oh grow up, would you? Christ, I can't say two words without you—"

"What about that doctor you were taking her to?"

"It didn't work."

"And that Pax, Zylo, whatever, what about that stuff she was taking?"

"It. Didn't. Work. How many times do I have to say it? Nothing is working."

I lift the lid from the Rubbermaid and pull out the pad and paper I packed last. I want to write a letter to Rae, but it's the wrong time. I set them aside and pull Troy from the box next. Considering I won him at the Maricopa County Fair three years ago, it's a wonder he's still in one piece. Everyone knows how crappy those stuffed animals are, and Troy the Miraculous Pink Unicorn has defied the odds by at least a year. His horn is bent and there's more than one bald patch exposed, but he's otherwise in decent shape. I won him after shooting the hat off a plastic cowboy with a water gun. Rae always used to tell me she was the one who won it. Like I wasn't there.

"It's just that we should have talked about this more. You know how nuts my schedule is going to get this summer with that job up in Vancouver starting in a couple of months."

"Well I'm sorry the timing isn't convenient, Dale. Exactly how many more conversations were you hoping to have?"

"Don't do that. You don't have the monopoly on parental concern. You treat your custody like a trophy, lauding it over me whenever you've decided maybe, just maybe, moving her to Phoenix on your own was a bad idea."

"Don't you dare blame me for this. And keep your voice down, for God's sake."

I've heard some kids with divorced parents say they hated it when their parents would hide stuff from them, all that whispering behind closed doors before they finally put an end to it all. But I would have been fine with a little bit of secrecy. I feel like I know more about why my parents got divorced than they do.

"She just needs more time."

"It's been five months."

"Which is nothing considering what she's been through."

"She's getting worse, Dale. She's adrift. Your daughter is completely untethered. I can't be the only one anymore who thinks that matters."

When I was little, we learned that people from Seattle were called Seattleites, which always sounded like satellites to me. But in the whole time growing up here, Seattle never felt like my city. It didn't actually start feeling like it was until we moved to Arizona. Now that I'm back in Seattle, it's supposed to feel like I've found my orbit again.

"What do you mean 'What about school?' I know I've been gone for a few years, but I wasn't aware they'd done away with public school in Seattle."

"You just expect her to drop into a new school? Jesus, Natalie, you think that's going to make things better?"

"Frankly, I don't know how it could make things worse."

I abandon my box on the bed that isn't mine. It's the guest bed, the place they've semi-decorated for me now that I'll be here for more than two nights over Thanksgiving or a few days over winter break.

"She barely knows Rob. It's not exactly fair to either of them. And you know how she gets around April."

"Right. You're right. I completely forgot to consider how this would affect April. Let's all think about the impact this will have on poor April."

April bought a few black pillows covered in faux fur and a mesh laundry hamper from Target for the room. She's plugged an air freshener that smells like juniper into an outlet I can't find. I'm guessing she thinks this will make up for the fact that Mom is trading me in for an easier life.

My mom, who is following through on her threat, which still manages to stun me even though she has, in every living memory, followed through on every threat she has ever made. This time, she has brought me to live three states to the north in a house I have set foot in a total of five times with a family that is entirely whole without me.

I take my pad and paper, tuck it under my arm, and stop at my dad's and April's bedroom, and with the same hand that reminded me of my sense of touch a week ago, I smack the closed door until it rattles in its flimsy frame.

"You both make excellent points!" I shout. "Congratulations on another stellar debate!"

I slam the front door behind me, wishing I had engraved a congratulatory plaque to chuck at each of their heads.

2

I'D FORGOTTEN HOW COLD SEATTLE is in March. Summer won't finally arrive until July. It's already eighty degrees in Phoenix.

My hand and its pen shake under the chill. Or shake under something, anyway.

Dear Rae,

There was this girl who transferred into my fifth grade class named Lenni Hollingsworth. She used to say that she could tell if someone wasn't from New York by the way they'd wait at the edge of the street for the Walk sign to turn. Real New Yorkers, she said, would just walk when the coast was clear.

I found out later that Lenni actually grew up on Staten Island and only went into the city when she needed to buy new shoes.

Here's how you knew I wasn't from Phoenix: I was so fucking lonely that all I wanted was to be alone. When real, achy loneliness kicks in, this is the kind of self-fulfilling destiny that ensues. The kind that makes you want to wrap yourself in a tight ball and imagine the world moving past you, unaware that the curled up thing in the corner is alive and has a name. That same achy loneliness is probably what first made you notice me. People like you have senses specifically tuned to people like me. And they have talents to make people like me decide we don't actually want that balled-up-tight isolation after all.

You saw me get off the bus, hydraulics sighing like their job was really hard. You watched me until I saw you, then you smirked and kept walking. You just wanted to make sure I saw you see me. And you did it again at lunch two days later. I had a mouthful of ham on rye, and you laughed at me. Not exactly in a mean way. More like in that way that says I'm stupid for being self-conscious about everything. I was sure everyone was noticing what you'd just confirmed in one little laugh. That whatever I was doing was out there for the world to see. You knew that new kids fall into two categories—new and interesting or new and anonymous. I dropped into the anonymous pile. And you reminded me that sometimes the anonymous category gives way to the category of weird new girl from that place where it rains all the time, a world away from the desert.

So when you finally said something to me—in the gym, underneath the basketball hoop where girl after girl attempted half-hearted layups and we dodged errant basketballs—you said, "You're already a freak. So you should decide right now which sort of freak you're going to be. The kind people talk about or the kind people are afraid to talk about."

It wasn't that you were telling me something new. It's that you were telling me something at all. Someone had said something to me besides, "Can you move your bag?" or "What's your name again?" I wanted, just once, for someone to ask me a follow-up. "Is Penny short for something?" So then I could tell them no, it wasn't, and they could tell me they didn't think so, but it sounded like one of those names that should be short for something.

*I didn't care that you sounded like you were full of shit
half the time. Because you seemed proud of having me for a
friend, and that was enough.*

Love,

Penny

"It's strange, isn't it?"

She's maybe a foot from me, sitting with her knees under her chin in the cold sand.

Her head is tilted toward my pad of paper. She's been reading over my shoulder.

"When you're little, you can't see all the walls, you know? You just see acres and acres of space, and it's all yours to run. You can do cartwheels and build forts and bury treasure to find later. But something happens when you get older. You start to see the walls. Maybe it's because you get taller or something. And then you see the cracks, you see how unstable it all is. And you try to test the walls' strength, and you pull a little chunk of it out, and pretty soon, all the sides tumble down, and then you're buried under all of it."

I look at Rae now.

"Buried alive," she says.

As usual, I expect her to look like a monster, like something that crawled out of a sewer or my nightmare. But if this is my nightmare, she looks remarkably the same as she always has. Cherry-red lipstick and purple hair rolled into Vargas Girl curls, diamond labret that I used to think was sort of cool in a modern glamour kind of way. Now I think it looks contrived, like whatever she just said to me. She's the perfect contrast to my undyed hair that's cut in slants to point at my neck, my cheekbones, my forehead, the star tattoo tucked behind my ear, just enough to see one green tip to hint that there's more behind what my hair covers. The ring through my nostril is so thin it takes some people a second to see it, even though it took my mom no time at all. Rae is the vividness that's missing from me.

"Nothing?" she says, a response to my nonresponse. "I just laid the meaning of life at your feet, and I get nothing?"

"You're not here," I say.

"Believe me, I wish I wasn't. It's freezing as fuck here, and look at us. Both without jackets." She puts her arm across my shoulder and squeezes. "Just like your mom to send you north without one. Guess she really didn't want to deal anymore, huh?"

In biology, we learned about all the different species of animals and insects that eat their young. There are tons of them.

Way more than I ever would have thought. And when we talked about why, inevitably the conversation turned to evolution. There was just something that seemed to work in the practice. Otherwise, why would it continue to happen? Or maybe that's the reasoning that keeps wolf spiders and finches and voles licking their lips when they cozy up to their trusting offspring.

Rae tightens her grip on my shoulder briefly before releasing it.

"I'm done reading letters," she says.

"Then don't read them," I say.

"See, that's the thing, though. I have to. I have to because that's the only reason I'm here. And believe me, I'd rather be anywhere else but close to you."

I take the beating of her words as best as I can, deflecting what doesn't puncture. And then I look into her eyes. The normally cold stare of her blue irises. I've never been able to get past the color. But now I catch a glimpse of something else, something that sends a fresh wave of guilt over me.

She looks confused. Confused about how I could cut off our friendship like a dead limb. Quick, one snip of the garden shears on a rotted stem.

For a second, it all falls away—Rae's exterior of hair dye and red lips and piercings. I see a girl who thinks she'll be alone without the person she's made her friend.

I see the bruises of companionship deflected one too many times. Then, as quickly as her armor drops, she raises it back up, and her shell is thicker than ever.

"I'm sure I'll be seeing you soon," she says.

Then she gives me a slow wink and slips away. I only watch her go for a short time, and then the sight of her hurts.

I walk home the long way even though I'm freezing. I keep thinking I should be feeling something more, but maybe the brain stops making the body and the heart feel anything after a certain point. Maybe it has some sort of automatic shut-off after it hits its trauma limit for one day.

I look around at the brightly painted bungalows lining the streets of my dad's neighborhood and pick out pieces of their yards that might represent this sensation. Because I'm done with words for a while, and I think it might be nice to find a picture like I used to do.

I suddenly regret leaving my camera in Arizona.

The first place my gaze lands is on a garden gnome crouching between two dying rose bushes. Passing the bushes, I look back at the gnome and realize he's crouched because he's pulling his pants down, exposing his bare ass to whoever approaches from the other direction.

"Almost perfect," I say, framing my hands and snapping an imaginary picture.

When I get back to my dad's house, I see that Mom's car is gone.

I didn't want it to be here when I got back. And even still, I can't manage to catch my heart before it drops, a heavy weight suspended above my stomach. Not adrift. It's still secure. The only thing that's still secure, maybe. And the one thing I wish I could detach.

Rob's shifting the soccer ball between his feet on the front lawn.

"Sounds like peace negotiations went great as always," he says, pausing his dribbling to swipe the curtain of blond hair from his forehead.

He might be able to pull the look off better if his hair was wavy, but it's stick-straight and cut at odd angles, which is why he's constantly moving it out of his eyes.

"Oh yeah, they're on their way to an amicable treaty," I say.

It's maybe the only thing we share as stepsiblings: the unsuccessful dodge of parental conflict. We both know that even after the gunfire ceases, the tinnitus rattles your brain until you want to stick a screwdriver through your ear. I'm willing to bet Rob talks about his dad as seldom as I talk about mine.

And I wonder for the first time if that's something I'll have to change now that I'm living with the man I don't ever talk about and the stepson he lets call him Dad.

Rob stops kicking the ball but keeps looking down at it. "So this is for real then?" he says.

I nod because I can't make myself say the words. I want to be casual about this, but it's hard to make light of the knowledge that you've been deemed hopeless by one of the only two people who is never supposed to give up on you.

"I'm really sorry," he says.

It's getting noisier again. The sounds of all those fake apologies, those shoulder squeezes, that static sympathy that isn't meant to actually move anyone toward healing.

A black truck with glittering flames rounds the corner, and I see the wrong person behind the wheel before I have a chance to assess the truck with my usual eye roll. I would think Rob was being ironic with the unmistakably eighties paint job, except that I know when it comes to his truck, Rob is deadly serious. Not even the landscape of a wolf howling at an honest-to-God full moon tinted into the back windshield can make him crack a smile.

"Rob, you were supposed to call me!" April scolds from the open driver's side window. She throws the emergency brake before shifting the handle at the wheel into park, swinging her tiny legs out of the raised cab.

"Mom, Jesus, the transmission!" Rob runs to the truck's side, absently extending a hand to help his mom down while keeping his full focus on the truck. He's looking for damage, but Rob's one of those rare breeds who possesses a thoughtless chivalry. In the midst of his panic, he wouldn't let a lady jump from the cab all on her own.

"Well I'm sorry, but you know the big signs don't fit in my jeep." Then she turns to me. "Penny, we are so, so sorry for all you've been through." She envelops me in a hug I never once indicated was welcome.

Even in heels, she barely matches my height. She's maybe a size two at her most bloated, her shiny blond hair trying to make her look older in a loose bun, but she still looks all of twelve.

"If I'd known you were here already . . ." she shoots Rob a look, but Rob is stroking the top of the steering wheel.

"What'd she do to you, baby? Did the mean lady hurt you, Alfredo?" he says.

Alfredo is of course Alfredo di Stefano: history's most transcendental soccer forward ever, at least according to Rob. He could name his precious truck after no one else. Thus completes the vaguest of pictures I have of my stepbrother: a soccer ball, long arms and legs to match the rest of his Gumby body, and a 1993 black Ford Ranger pickup, his pride and joy for no good reason.

April extends her arms to take in the sight of me. "I would

have come home right away," she says, finishing the thought I'd forgotten she started.

"I just got here," I say.

"Well, I've got dinner planned," she says, then squeezes my arms. "Things are going to get better now. I have a very strong feeling."

"Because of dinner," I say, and the corners of her mouth twitch.

"That's typically where it starts," she says.

April releases me and trots inside with Rob close behind, her sandwich board and rolling briefcase filling his arms.

"She's making chicken Kiev," he says.

"I didn't know she cooked," I say.

"She doesn't," he says.

I've never really been susceptible to the discomfort of silence. People talk about that awkwardness that follows long breaks in conversation, but I've never seemed to notice them.

Until now.

"Could you pass the salt?" my dad asks, his water glass lodged firmly in his paw, his lumberjack body hunched in an effort to make up for his size at such a small table. He sips from it every few seconds. My mom used to tease him that no one was going to steal his water. And he would laugh and keep holding on to it. Clearly, there were things she said that Dad never fully believed.

"It's good, Mom," Rob says. He's lying, of course. We're all lying just by eating it. We're only encouraging her to keep doing this, but it's obvious none of us is going to be the first to get honest.

"I never realized how relaxing cooking can be," she says, her face still glowing and damp from the steam of the kitchen.

"Mmhmm," Dad says behind his water glass. I can't tell if it's agreement. Dad's one of those men who would be horribly intimidating to a guy I brought home. If I were the type to bring a guy home to meet my dad. If I were the type to have a dad at home at all.

"And it's so simple when you have a recipe," she says.

I suspect it's even simpler when you follow the recipe, but I don't dare thicken the silence by bringing that up. I just shove my plate away instead.

Dad notices, but his eyes don't get past my plate. I try very hard to remember the last time he looked at me. Not at my arm or my sweater or the hair caught in my earring. At me.

"We had a great turnout for the broker's open today," April says to the table, but the only one really listening is Rob.

"Cool," he says.

"Yeah, it is," she agrees. And her enthusiasm is genuine, which is what has always puzzled me. Not because she loves her job. It's great she loves buying shitty houses and fixing them up and selling them for tons more money. It actually sounds more exciting than Mom's job, which has something to do with surveys. What surprises me about April's enthusiasm is that it's everywhere. She gets excited about lots of things.

When my dad dropped the bomb that he was getting remarried, and that The Other One had a son a year younger than me, a ready-made family for Dad to plug right into, I thought I'd hate them all. It was easy to hate from a few states away. Dad had already given me ample reason, and April made it pretty simple with her birthday cards signed "Your Evil Stepmother"—as though she *got* me. I suppose her being a mere seventeen years older than me lent some credibility to that assumption. And then there was the replacement kid—Rob. April's son that she had super young, so Mom says, who never made an appearance in my life outside of the annual family picture they'd send me, with Rob always looking a little confused.

"I have some other news," she says.

None of us asks her to share it because we know she's going to anyway. My dad is still staring at my plate in the middle of the table.

"My bid on the Carver House was accepted!"

April slaps her hand down on the table in victory, but she only succeeds in jolting Dad and me out of our respective meditations.

"Hot damn, it feels good to win!"

"Is that the one near Tacoma?" Rob asks her, and I hear his teeth close around something crunchy. I don't know much about chicken Kiev, but I know it's not supposed to be crunchy. He seems to know that too, because I can see his hand curl around the napkin by his plate.

"I wouldn't call it near, but yeah, it's south of here. My first historic project. If I can flip this sucker into a bed-and-breakfast, oh the investment potential! It's a little off the beaten path, but I'm thinking it should appeal to the out-doorsy types."

"You don't know anything about historical renovation," Dad says. A statement of fact that should be discouraging, but April just shrugs.

"It can't be that much different than what I've been working on," she says. "Pull out old plumbing. Put in new plumbing."

"Right. That's all there is to it," Dad says, and now he pushes his plate away too.

"Oh, don't get surly. I know you know everything there is to know about HVAC and heating and cooling," April says, making my dad's business sound somehow adorable. "But I'll never learn if I don't try. And I've wanted a historical project for ages. I can't wait to pick out light fixtures! I'll have to do some serious antiquing."

Every time she starts a new sentence, April lifts out of her seat a little. I keep thinking she's going to stand up and start running laps around the table, but she stays put for now.

"That's great, babe," Dad says.

Babe? I can't . . . I just can't.

"You don't do fake enthusiasm very well," she says, but smiling. Because nothing bothers April.

I see Rob take advantage of their exchange to spit his last bite into his napkin while April stares at my dad the way Mom never did.

As though summoned, my phone lights up, rattling the whole table while my mom's picture adorns the screen. In front of the empty chair at the end of the table, she looks like a dinner guest arriving late, after everyone had given up hope she was ever coming.

We all stare at the phone until it stops buzzing, the missed call indicator the only thing left when she's done interrupting.

April picks up where she left off, some of her earlier enthusiasm diminished, but the breath behind her voice is still electric, as though she's talking on top of a layer of carbonation.

"Renovation starts in June."

"What?" my dad says.

"Cool," Rob says.

I say nothing.

"I know. I know. You have your big job in Vancouver, so you're defecting for the summer," she says to Dad.

Then she turns to Rob. "Soccer clinic goes until August fifth. You'll leave before we do and come back after we come back."

We?

She turns to me. She smiles. She knows I have nothing. "Which is why Penny will be coming with me to Point Finney."

And now it's my turn to answer.

"No."

"Now before you say no—" she says.

"No," I say again.

"You think you can renovate a place in two months?" Dad's eyes bulge in that way they used to when my mom would correct his grammar. "Anyway, you and I should be the ones talking about this, not you and Penny."

"Seriously?" And now I see, for possibly the first time ever, a pissed off April. "So when you said to treat her like family, you meant treat her like *your* family?"

Dad leans in. Finally, a familiar look. I actually find a little comfort in the recognition. "We'll talk about it later."

"See, that's where I think you're wrong. We won't talk about it later. We'll kill the conversation right here, at least if you have anything to do with it," she says, skirting dangerous territory with Dad. If I learned anything from his fights with my mom, it's that he doesn't respond particularly well to being told what he's doing.

The tinnitus is creeping in again.

Rob leans over to me. "Do you like soccer?"

"Nope," I say.

"Do you like soccer better than being in here right now?"

Outside, we kick the ball back and forth on the grass with the soundtrack of Dad scrubbing dishes vigorously and April nagging him to the brink of his demise.

"You know she's gonna win, right?" Rob says.

"She's never gone toe-to-toe with me before," I say, already losing faith in my dad's prospects. "I'm like this super hybrid between my mom and my dad. She doesn't stand a chance."

Rob stops the ball under his foot. "When I was little, I hated chocolate."

"God, you were one of those kids?"

He holds his hand up. "Spare me. I came around

eventually, but that's totally a product of my mom's determination. She made me a chocolate cake for my fifth birthday, and I flat out refused to eat it. I sat there and stared at it until the candles burned down. She left it on the table the rest of the day. I didn't know she threw it away that night, though, because for every day that summer, there was a chocolate cake sitting in the middle of the table, untouched. She baked a new cake every day and left it there for me, but I thought it was the same cake she just left sitting there, waiting for me to eat it. I couldn't understand why she was so determined to make me like chocolate until I started going to all kinds of birthday parties the next fall."

"And they all had chocolate cake," I say.

Rob kicks me the ball. "She didn't want me to be the kid who wouldn't eat the chocolate cake. I don't know. Maybe she thought that was the harbinger of death or unpopularity."

"Maybe she didn't want you to be an ungrateful little snot," I say.

"Same thing," he says. "Either way, you're going to Point Finney in June, so be ready to get your hermit on. I heard it's got a population of, like, five."

"That's comforting. Thanks, Rob."

"She's also going to make you take up an extracurricular at school between now and then. She's big on extracurriculars. They build character or something. She's already started talking about it to Dad, so it'll seem like it was his idea. But that's all her."

This I can't bear. I'm already being hijacked to the Pacific Northwest backcountry for the summer. By my dad's—excuse me, *our* dad's—teenager of a second wife. She's in there with him right now, talking about me like I'm hers to talk about. And she's choosing my hobbies, too?

"She can try," I tell Rob. "She can sure try."

NEWS TRIBUNE | TACOMA, Feb. 22, 2004—Efforts have slowed in the search for four youths who went missing January 19 in Point Finney.

In a mystery that's shaken this sleepy town northwest of Tacoma, residents are beginning to lose hope that the children will be found.

"It's just so tragic," says Claire Schuman, a lifelong resident of the former lumber town. "Nobody feels safe right now."

Mike Marlboro agrees. "My wife and I won't even let our daughter walk to the store up the road anymore." Marlboro, whose family has lived in Point Finney for four generations, owns a house less than five miles from where the minors were last spotted.

"The things they say about those woods, I just won't risk it."

Anna Riley (12), Jack Dodson (14), and brothers Russ (11) and Blake (12) Torrey of Point Finney have been missing for 34 days. The youths were last seen together around 3:00 p.m. on January 19 behind Keller-Finney Middle School in Point Finney. First reported missing by Joy Riley, Anna Riley's grandmother, authorities issued a missing children alert the same day. Using a shoe determined to belong to Russ Torrey, police canines tracked the boy's scent to the southern tip of the Kitsap Woodlands Reserve before the trail went cold.

"I've been working for this department my entire eighteen-year career, and I've never seen anything like it," says Sergeant James Meckel of the Pierce County Sheriff's Department. "Normally we'd see some evidence, some indication of abduction or foul play. But we haven't even recovered a footprint. Not a trace of them anywhere beyond that shoe."

Search teams are gearing up for their 35th day of searching, this time scouring the area of the region known as the Center Thicket, widening their coverage beyond the perimeter. "There's not much in there," says Sergeant Meckel. "No one's lived in those woods for a while, and it's hard to contain a search area that wild."

Asked whether they'll be able to continue searching if the snow that's called for on Tuesday falls, Sergeant Meckel is reluctant to give specifics.

"We'll search as long as we can. We're already tight on resources, and we'll be hard pressed to put any more people at risk sending them into the woods in that kind of weather."

The three families and the Pierce County Sheriff's Department are offering an undisclosed reward for any information on the whereabouts of the missing children.

3

Summer 2013

THE SIDE OF THE HIGHWAY is a blur of greens and grays. I start fiddling with the focus on Linda, pointing her lens out the window and seeing the passing landscape from her perspective.

Mr. Jakes probably shouldn't have loaned his precious camera to me. I'm sure it crosses some ethical boundary or another. Except that Mr. Jakes doesn't have the emotional capacity to cross any sort of boundary.

"So what, does this make me your protégé or something?" I'd asked him as I held the camera the wrong way as usual. He looked like he might faint as he watched my fingers edge closer to the lens.

"No. You're absolutely not my protégé. You're not good enough to be anyone's protégé."

"Awesome. So . . . I guess I'll just sell your precious Linda on Craigslist or something." I started swinging it around by its strap.

"Don't you dare. Don't even joke about that." He leaned toward the camera, hands flinching.

"The point is—the idea I have—is that you'll take Linda—temporarily, and I mean that—and get better. And when I make it to my third mojito on my next night out with my friends, and we're all lamenting how we've exhausted every last hope of ever making a difference in a fraction of the lives we're supposedly helping to mold, I can tell them that I loaned one promising student a camera and a knapsack packed with bundles of photography lessons, and maybe, just maybe, that'll buy me a few more years of this miserable teaching existence."

I blinked and considered Mr. Jakes's prematurely graying hair and sloped shoulders. He wasn't the first teacher I'd ever heard speak bluntly about his apathy toward teaching. But he was the first one whose act I didn't fully believe.

"You drink mojitos?" I said.

He sighed genuine exasperation. "I called you promising."

"I caught that."

"So don't blow it," he said. "And treat Linda like the queen she is. She and I have been through some things together."

As I started to walk out of his classroom he said, "And re-enroll in my class when you come back. You know absolutely nothing about photography yet."

I just nodded.

"I'm not a psychologist," he said.

"Right, I gathered that," I said.

"I enjoy photography. That's why I teach photography."

"Yes," I said. "I'm tracking." He shifted in his chair behind his desk of faux wood, looking as uncomfortable in this spontaneous heart-to-heart as I felt.

"So I'm going to say this quickly, and after that, I'm not going to say another word. And frankly, I'd prefer it if you didn't say anything after I say this, because that's only going to make it that much more awkward for us both."

"I'm getting the impression I should have left about two minutes ago," I said.

"You need this," he said, and I knew what he meant immediately, so I couldn't have said anything in response even if he'd allowed me to. *"You need this in order to get past whatever you keep trying and failing to capture in a picture. It's why you're no good at it. Not yet. You need to start thinking about the story you're going to create for yourself. Think of it as your folklore. You have the ability to write your own legend, starting with whatever you see behind that lens. So you'd be stupid to give up that opportunity. Don't be stupid, Penny."*

"Penny?"

Now I turn the camera lens to April, the events of yesterday already growing stale, the sheen of photo paper adorning the walls only a trace memory. April's peachy skin is here now, bright against the blurring green-gray backdrop of the passing landscape. She eyes the phone I've abandoned in her Jeep Grand Cherokee's cup holder.

"Oh, right. You're on I-5 for, like, eight thousand miles," I say.

"Sarcasm is a shortcut for saying what you really want to say," she says, and I know from the way she says it that she recently read that somewhere.

"Sarcasm is my native tongue," I say. "English is my second language."

This at least gets a smile out of her, so I know she'll lay off long enough for us to maybe enjoy a playlist I've put together, one full of the Pixies and Clap Your Hands Say Yeah and Grouplove and enough Flaming Lips to make her say her head will explode if she hears one more screeching voice crackle in that way that gives me goose bumps.

We make it exactly three songs in before April declares her veto right.

"But we're five miles north of Tacoma!"

"But Point Finney's south of that, then west, then north, and no, Penny, I can't make it through one more song. No," she says, eyes laser-focused on the road.

My phone vibrates, and my mom's face invades the screen.

April never bothered to send the address of wherever she's dragging you off to, her text says.

I type **Worried she's bringing me back to you?** and launch it back to her before I can reconsider. I shove my phone deep into my pocket.

"You're not going to believe the trees around this place," April says. "The woods border practically the entire peninsula around there and then some." It's her way of dangling something sparkly in front of me as a distraction. Which is why it pisses me off even more when it works.

"What kind of natural light does it have?" I ask before I feel ready.

"Perfect for photography," she says.

The sign says POINT FINNEY 5 MILES, but I'm way more interested in the sign that follows: REST STOP 1 MILE.

"I have to go."

"Can't you hold it? We're practically there." April has been going over the architectural details specific to the Carver House, a home built in 1844 by none other than the Carver family, a little known threesome of two parents and a child who fell in love with the woods and built a house there, a house that became known by their name because the address would mean nothing to anyone who asked. If the Carvers were ever hoping to have neighbors, it sounds like they would've been disappointed.

April's rambling on about original cedar flooring and a nonoriginal wood-burning stove she'd like to have removed. And from what she's seen in the photographs of the kitchen, it'll likely have an original Stewart, otherwise known as an older-than-dirt, unusable contraption masquerading as an oven. It's only now I realize that she hasn't ever seen the house in person. And now it's hers.

But right now, I don't care much about that, and I couldn't possibly care less about the architecture of this house. I'm having this feeling like I'm rising to the top of a deep pool and I've forgotten how to breathe on land, which is the same feeling I stopped getting when I was taking the little white pills the doctor gave me after the shit hit the fan back in Phoenix. I thought maybe I was through feeling this way. And then, suddenly, April was talking about nineteenth-century furnishings and I remembered that time Rae pronounced century like "cent-tree," and for some reason that was the most hysterical thing either of us had ever heard, and we laughed so hard tears cut a path through the powder on my cheeks, and now I can't feel my hands and I think I might throw up, and April's going on and on about inspections and resale potential.

Which is how I know she would never understand. She believes I could take even the slightest interest in a fucking house when I know Rae will never mispronounce another word again. Because of me.

I just shake my head—no, I can't hold it. I'm sure April thinks I'm sulking because she sighs and pulls off at the next opportunity.

"Just hurry, okay?" she says. "I want to get there before dark. Apparently it's hard to find even in the daytime."

A wave of nausea threatens to crush me, and I keep myself from barrel-rolling out of the jeep, but only barely. Once the cool, damp air hits my face, I feel the claustrophobia from the car begin to dissipate. A pretty terrible smell takes its place.

The rest stop is one of the grungier I've seen. Not one of those sparkly new stops with vending machines on the outside and folded maps courtesy of the state tourism office.

Fat black flies hover low around the cement wall shielding the door to the ladies' room, which is conveniently locked.

"Hey, Penny!"

I come back around the corner to find April holding her phone far above her head.

"I can't get any reception out here, and I need to let the agent know we're on our way so she can meet us at the house.

I'm going to try moving toward the road. Just wait for me in the car when you're done. I'll let your dad know we're almost there, too. Any messages for him?"

"Gosh, not a single one," I say.

Her lips pinch over her teeth, but she turns without a word and heads for the road.

I consider telling her that the reception was pretty spotty on the highway, too, but the thought of a few minutes alone in the jeep with some of my own music and not much else is too good to pass up, so I nod before moving on to the other side of the rest stop.

The men's room door was clearly locked at some point, but it appears to have been jimmied open by force. The door's bolt is hanging by a screw, and the frame is gashed deeply by what might have been a crowbar. I'm starting to hear that warning voice in my head, the same one that tells you to lace your keys through your fingers like metal claws when you walk to your car at night. I turn back to the gravel parking lot, the two-lane highway just beyond. Not a person in sight, not a single car besides our jeep. It's strange to go from the company of so many cars on a highway to sudden isolation on the side of the road. The forest around the rest area encroaches on the restroom as though resentful of its intrusion, and when I nudge the bathroom door open and cringe against its groan, I see that I'm not altogether wrong.

Vines have begun to twist through the tiny openings where the walls meet the ceiling. I think those spaces are meant to create some ventilation in the bathroom, but they're doing a horrible job. It doesn't just smell like waste. It smells like *old* waste. I clench my jaw to keep from heaving.

Welcome back, nausea.

A clouded mirror above a bone-dry sink distorts my reflection, bulging my forehead and midsection. Someone's scrawled in blue letters across the glass "Tami B Sucks Great Dick," to which someone responded below in red "I heard you couldn't even get it up!," to which someone else wrote "That's not what your girlfriend said!!"

I instinctively think of poor Amanda Zeigler, Str8 Up Slut.

On the wall beside the mirror, a flyer just starting to yellow with age clings to the wall for dear life, the masking tape holding it to the slick tiles nearly giving up.

Bold letters in all caps across the top read HAVE YOU SEEN ME?

Beneath an overly photocopied picture of a face so grainy no one could possibly answer that question, a girl's shoulders slope under the loose straps of a light sundress. The starkest of descriptions reads:

Brianna Jade Sandoval

Age 12

4'6" 89 lbs.

Help us find Brianna, last seen on July 13 at Her Lady of
Grace Home for Children. Call tips in to Pierce County
Sheriff's Dept: 555-273-TIPS.

I shake my head, wondering who looks for a girl nobody
wanted in the first place. I bury the voice that asks me why I
didn't go looking for Rae that night.

Now that I'm standing in here, I realize I actually do have
to go. Two stalls stand behind me, one tiny and one larger
for disabled users. The bigger one doesn't have a door, so
I reluctantly turn to the tiny stall. Not that I think anyone's
going to come in, but the thought of some guy charging
through the door after five hours in a car with nothing but
the company of a Big Gulp and catching me with my pants
around my ankles mortifies me enough to close myself into
the only remaining stall.

"Don't look," I tell myself. "Leave your body." But as I
prepare to hover over the seat and get this over with immediately, a snapping from overhead breaks my already failing
meditation.

When I look up, I see that the sound didn't come from

overhead, but traveled through the ventilation hole where a vine is hugging the edge. Another snapping, this time closer, and I can tell it's the sound of a twig breaking. Footsteps from outside. Someone is walking around the rest stop.

"April?"

Nothing.

"Guess I was smart to close the door," I mumble.

I finish quickly and try to wash my hands, but my suspicions about the sink were right. Bone-dry because there probably hasn't been running water in this place for a year. I say a silent thank-you to myself for remembering to slip hand sanitizer in my bag and sail out of the bathroom and into the thick wooded air, pulling in a deep breath to try to erase the memory of the stench from inside the men's room.

But when I emerge, I'm surprised to still see only April's jeep in the gravel parking lot. No car to go with the footsteps I heard a second ago.

I peer over my shoulder, then scold myself immediately for being so jumpy. Too many slasher movies. It was just a squirrel for all I know. All that cement just amplified the sound.

But just as I turn back toward the car, I hear a girl's voice.

"Don't leave."

The voice isn't close, but it's clear enough. Almost as if

the sound traveled along the branches, pinging off the leaves and needles.

My heart is thrumming enough to make my chest ache.

Probably just some hiker yelling to someone on a path up the way.

After another minute of examining the sea of green and brown in front of me, I've pretty much convinced myself that's true when I hear her again.

"Don't leave me here!"

I whip around, because this time the voice sounds much closer.

"Hello?"

Nothing.

I strain my eyes to detect any movement underneath the shadow of the dense tree canopy overhead. But I can't even see leaves moving. I can't hear birds. The air is stiff with silence.

"Is someone out there?"

Still nothing.

"Look, this isn't funny. Do you need help or not?"

I might have sounded pretty tough saying that last bit if my voice hadn't cracked under the strain of my breathing, which seems to have gotten more shallow in the last few seconds.

The wall of vegetation gnarled around itself is blocking visibility into the woods. There might actually be a hiking path behind there, and someone really is in trouble. Maybe she fell and twisted her ankle or something. But a quick scan of the grounds surrounding the bathroom reveals no path. Still, that doesn't always keep people from stumbling around in the woods looking for a nature fix. Or a nice secluded place to get high.

Then, almost too faint to hear, "Please."

I look back toward the jeep. Still no sign of April.

I take a few steps toward the wall of foliage.

"This is so stupid."

I pull in a deep breath and fill my lungs, which slows my breathing sufficiently to do what I do next. Mom always said I got Dad's sense of social responsibility, which never seemed to make her as proud as I think it should have.

And maybe just to spite the memory of her in this moment, I take a few more steps.

I'm officially in the woods. I look back toward the jeep and, after dodging a few low-hanging branches, I can hardly see the parking area at all. I pull my phone from my pocket. One bar.

"Awesome. So basically if I find this chick, I'm going to be no help to her."

I will April to come back around the corner to keep me from what I'm about to do.

"Five minutes," I say. "Spend five minutes looking. If you

don't find her, get back to the jeep and wait for April."

I look around and examine the tree trunks, all the same shade of deep brown, like mirror images of one original tree. I look up at their leaves, identical in their clustered greens. These woods are unlike any I've seen in Seattle. Under the right circumstances—and with maybe even a sliver of natural light—it could make a beautiful photo. Maybe April was right about that.

I fish around in my pocket and pull out my tube of That's So Cherry lipstick. With a heavy sigh as I grieve for its loss, I draw a jagged red *X* across the bark of the tree closest to me, marking the edge of the wooded area nearest to the parking lot.

It seemed like the voice came from somewhere off to the left, so I pick my way through the squishy ground, where, thankfully, a bed of pine needles has blanketed most of it, keeping my boots from sinking.

"Hey, are you out there?" I yell. "Call out if you can hear me, okay?"

Nothing. I'm more convinced with every step that it was just someone's idea of a joke.

Still, I've already sacrificed a brand new tube of lipstick, so I mark another *X* on the tree beside me and delve a little deeper into the woods. I check my phone again. No bars this time.

I've traveled a little farther before I notice that I can see my breath between the cracks of gray light that have managed to slip through the canopy. But that's about all I can see. I pull my flannel closer around my body and mark another cherry *X* on the tree beside me.

I scan the ground for safe footing, but I can barely see my boots. I'd turn back the way I came, but now I can't seem to figure out which way that was. There's a tree trunk close to my right side, and one immediately behind me, and another to my left.

But didn't I just come from the left?

The dank trunks feel like they're encroaching, and I pick my way faster through the forest until I finally spot a beam of light ahead, clouded from the sky and dim with dusk, but enough to see that a small clearing lies ahead.

I emerge into a bare spot of land maybe ten feet across, the only empty space before the trees crowd the ground once again. I turn around immediately and peer through the dark tunnel I just came from, feeling oddly paranoid that something might have followed me out. But when I turn, I see nothing but darkness. And even though I know it's useless, I check my phone anyway. Still no signal.

And now I'm way farther from the parking lot than I ever meant to be.

"Hey, are you there or not?" I yell, more pissed than frightened by this point. Not only am I going to have to make my way back through Ye Olde Freaky Woods once this is over, April's probably going to get back to the car before me, and when she can't find me, the inevitable panic will ensue, quickly followed by a lecture from her I'm already resenting.

"Great, thanks for wasting my time!" I holler.

"You're it."

I whirl around. The voice is close, but I can't tell where it's coming from. And this time it sounds younger, almost childlike.

A twig snaps somewhere behind me. I spin to find the source of the noise, but all I see is dense darkness under heavy foliage in every direction.

My hands are trembling, and I want desperately to believe it's from the cold. But when my phone slips from my clammy palm to the forest floor, I can't fool myself anymore.

"Shit." Of course it would land in the one place that pine needles aren't covering the ground. I crouch to rescue it from the mud and begin to wipe the face. But as I stand up, I see the faintest flicker of movement deep in the thatched trees to my left.

"Hello?"

All at once, my lungs start to ache. Like something thick is filing them up, caking the walls of my chest.

I try to take a deep breath, but panic flutters through me when I can only manage a shallow inhale.

I push my palm to my sternum and try to rub some life back into my lungs. Because that's exactly it—it feels like something in my chest is . . . dying.

Arms outstretched to stave off stray branches, I launch back into the dense trees from the direction I'm pretty sure I came. I stumble twice, and the second time lands me on my hands and knees, sharp needles piercing my palms.

As I start to rise, I feel the closeness of the tree trunks once again pressing on me. A low-hanging branch drags its way across my shoulder and catches my flannel, yanking me back with enough force to make me bite my tongue. The forest in front of me is darker than ever, and I'm starting to get dizzy from lack of oxygen.

Full panic is at the corner of my brain when just ahead and to the right, I catch sight of a bright red *X* slashed across the wet bark of a nearby tree, capturing maybe the only snatch of light the woods have to offer.

I lunge forward and hold on to the tree for stability, the dizziness claiming my eyesight momentarily. But as I cling to the bark, its coldness welcomes the ache back into my bones, and the thickness in my chest begins to spread to my limbs.

Then I feel the unmistakable sensation of four fingers and a thumb lace through my own hand on the tree trunk.

I try to scream, but the erosion in my lungs stifles the sound. I push away from the tree so hard I fall backward into another trunk. I peer into the darkness, but I can no longer see anything, the meager light that illuminated my red *X* only seconds before now completely extinguished.

"Who's there?" I try to shout, but my chest is about to collapse.

Sit here and find out or get the fuck back to the car!

I push myself from the tree to a stumbling run. I'm practically on top of the next tree before I see it, dismiss it, and move to the next, going mostly by touch now while I search for another red *X*. I try three more trees before I find the one I'm looking for. A few more steps, and I find the last one.

I take off the rest of the way like I'm on fire, breaking through the thick foliage with so much force, I'm halfway to the cement enclosure by the bathroom wall before I notice that I'm sobbing.

I stop, pull in a lungful of air, my throat burning, and cough out a rasping exhale. Only then do I dare to look behind me, backing all the way toward the jeep, my shaking hands searching out the door handle. I breathe again, and each time I do, it gets a little easier, the pressure on my chest mercifully lifting.

The orange light illuminating the restroom hums at the effort, flickers a few times, threatens to go out, buzzes back to its half-life. I find the door handle and hear it clack against something plastic and look down to find my phone practically cemented to my hand. I must have gripped the life out of it while I was running. I don't even remember holding it.

All I remember is . . . a hand holding mine. *Grabbing* mine.

I yank the jeep's door open and lock it behind me as soon as I'm inside.

"It was a joke. Someone playing a joke. They were messing with me. That's all."

I say it maybe a thousand times more. I believe it a little more each time. But I can't keep my hands from shaking, and finally I have to start the car with the keys April left in the ignition and hold my fingers against the vents, hoping the heat will melt the chill, and maybe exhaustion will take care of the rest of the trembling before she gets back.

I hear footsteps on the gravel outside and my breath catches.

April's face is pressed against the window, one finger pointing to the side of the door.

"I heard the car start and came back," she says.

Of course she did. She probably thought I'd try to make a break for it while she was gone. She should know that I don't exactly have anywhere else to go.

"I got cold," I say, which is about five percent truth.

"Got the Realtor. No luck with your dad," she says, holding her phone up. I say nothing.

"You look pale," she says, eyeing me. "Are you sweating?"

"Carsick," I say.

She stares at me for another minute, and I discretely move my hand to cover the smudge of dirt marring the knee of my jeans.

Believe me. Just believe me and get us the hell out of here.

"Do you need to take a second?"

"No!"

Her eyes travel toward the woods, and I follow her gaze reluctantly.

"I mean, I just want to get there. I'm tired of being on the road," I say, fumbling to find a frequency for my voice that she'll hear.

"Amen to that," April says, shifting gears and checking her side mirror as she backs out and turns us around, rolling us too slowly out of the parking lot while I keep my eyes locked to my own side mirror. The deep green of the woods is all I see, and I close my eyes hard against whatever just happened, convincing myself it was just a joke, it was just my imagination, it was just my mutinous brain trying its hardest to crack under the pressure. Soon, all I hear is the dueling sounds of highway traffic and April's voice as she resumes her monologue of big plans for the house.

"Oh, well that's just wonderful," April says, the change in her tone launching me from fresh comfort.

"How is it that I've been driving for this long and still can't ever remember to check the gas gauge?"

I lean over and see that the needle is well past empty. My hands start shaking all over again at the thought of stopping the car this close to whatever just happened.

"I'm sure a few more miles won't make a difference," I say, doing a bad job of keeping my voice from quivering.

"Relax, you'll be out of your cage soon enough," April says. "Besides, we're meeting the agent in town now. That'll buy us a little time. And there's a gas station at this next exit." She's pulling off the road before I can think of a reason not to—a reason that wouldn't force me to explain what couldn't have just happened.

The gas station is surrounded by cement. Not a tree in sight, which makes me feel only a little better.

Even past the closed door, I can hear music playing through the speakers at the station. It sounds tinny and hollow, a melody that runs like an undertow through the mind. You don't know it's there, but it grabs you every couple of seconds if you stop to consider it. I don't know how the attendant doesn't want to run screaming through the place every day just to block the sound of that bland, festering tune.

I survey the pumps under the awning. We're the only car parked in this giant station, but we're not the only ones here. A kid sits hunched by the door of the market, sitting so still his khaki coat practically camouflages him to the wall he leans against. If not for the way his knees knock together to the rhythm of that insidious melody, I might not have seen him at all. He's dirty and he looks tired, but his eyes are wide and he's staring at me.

I pull out my phone, determined to banish the outside via a wall of my own sound.

When I illuminate my screen, it's not on the home menu. The camera app is open.

Did I open that while I was holding the phone?

Confusion slips away along with my breath when I scroll to the last picture taken. Because it's of the woods. And a face is staring at me from the tangle of trees, not more than five feet away from where I stood in the clearing.

To someone else, it would be a tree, the face just a distorted twisting of bark and moss. But the whites of the drooping eyes and the yawning mouth are unmistakable, the arms by the sides of a sinewy body in muddy rags, limbs unnaturally long and curled around the neighboring tree.

And those white, gaping eyes are looking directly at me.

4

FEAR HAS AGAIN REDUCED ME to a basic set of senses. The transition took place somewhere between the gas station and the house, and I don't so much welcome the feeling back as simply acknowledge it when it arrives, this way of existing that coats me against hard questions. Only instead of hearing each minute sound, instead of seeing each trickle of light that passes through the dense foliage, instead of feeling the dampness of the house's interior, I notice the smell.

It must be evident from my face, because April says, "It just needs a little airing out."

"Uh huh," I say as I see many, many things that could serve as the source of the mildew.

There's the moth-eaten mauve sofa directly in front of

us, the crumpled yellow bedsheet in the corner that even *looks* damp, the gray wool coat hanging on the hook by the front door, not to mention the entire house appears to be made of wood that's been soaked in a hundred years' worth of rain, from the floors to the trim to the banister leading to the second floor. The wallpaper is doing a poor job of covering whatever horror lies behind it, puckering and bubbling every two feet across every wall.

"Penny, look!" April lunges for the gray coat by the door and spreads it to reveal, well, a coat. "Do you think it could be vintage?" she lifts her eyebrows at me, like maybe she's hit on a language we can share.

"Please don't try it on," I say.

"Hmm, maybe not." She frowns. "Actually, it's kind of small." I can tell by the boxy shoulders and the way the buttons are on the right side that it's a boy's coat. As April's face continues to fall, I think she's arriving at the same conclusion.

"Oh." April frowns deeper. Her thumb uncovers an Old Navy label beneath the collar.

"I'm pretty sure you would have caught something if you'd put it on, anyway," I say, not comforting her and not really meaning to, either.

"Maybe." She considers this, then hands me the coat anyway. "But oh, Penny, look at this place. It's even more incredible than I'd pictured!"

I stare at her with the same wonder with which she gazes at the home surrounding us. I think for a moment that we've somehow managed to stand side by side in two different houses.

"What? You don't think it's beautiful?"

"No."

"Well, don't hold back," she says. I know I've hurt her feelings, though I can't imagine how she would have expected me to feel about this place that means such different things to her than it does to me. She sees the realization of a long-sought fantasy finally fulfilled, the claiming of some real estate ambition she's fostered from her career's infancy.

I see the bottom of a deep, deep hole.

The hem of the coat dances against my leg, and I watch as an impossible draft moves the fabric's corner against my dirt-smudged knee. I reach down to pull it away, and my hand slips into the pocket instead, my fingers scooping up a small plastic button and a dulled pencil stub. I drop them back into the pocket and look again at the Old Navy tag my thumb covers like April's did a second ago. I scoot my thumb over and find the name Dodson written in black marker.

April lifts the coat from my hand and sniffs it in three

places. "Not the source of the smell. The coat stays," she declares, replacing the jacket on the hook by the door with misplaced decisiveness. It's almost imperceptible, but I can tell that some of the rapture at her find from a second ago seems to fade.

"I thought you said this place was built in 1850."

"Around then," she says, her smile returning.

"But that coat's obviously newer, unless the Carvers shopped at an Old Navy on the Oregon Trail. And I'm no expert on design, but that funkadelic wallpaper . . ."

"Well, the record shows one or two owners after the Carver family, in addition to the banks, but there's not a lot of information on title transfers."

"And that's real estate speak for . . . ?"

"It means I have basically no idea when those families sold or how much they sold it for," she says. "Part of the charm of short sales and foreclosures."

"I see."

"So, where's your camera?"

"In the jeep with the rest of my life," I say. Two months suddenly feels like life without parole.

"Excellent. Because you have an important job." April is fast becoming an expert at ignoring half of the words I say. I get the sense my dad prepped her.

"Great. I was just wondering when you'd finally put me to work."

"Your job," she says, again ignoring the sarcasm, "is to document the before and after."

"That sounds a little existential."

"Come on, you know! Capturing the house before all of our renovations, then after."

I trace my finger absently along the banister beside me, which instantly gives me a splinter.

"Um, I think this place needs a little more than a new coat of paint. Seriously, April, the smell."

"Well it's been vacant for years," she says, but I can tell from the way she shoves the words out that it's getting harder for her to ignore my negativity.

"But who even knows if it's safe to stay here?"

"The plumbing and electricity are old, but preliminary reports say they're sound. We'll have to see what the inspections say, but it's fine for now."

And this. *This* is the moment I realize April is far too good at pretending like she's not full of shit. Is it possible she's actually this clueless? I reflect back on the dinner conversation with Dad, the moments after April's grand announcement about her first historical find, on Dad's skepticism, on Rob's half hearted congratulations. I am horrified to realize

I have zero understanding of how April does her job. If she even knows *how* to do her job. She bought a house sight unseen from a Realtor who could barely make time to meet us long enough to turn over the keys.

And Dad let his wife drag me off to a possibly condemned structure to camp out for the summer.

"It didn't feel like a clue when the agent insisted on meeting you in town instead of at the house?" I ask, no longer capable of disguising my incredulity. "You weren't, I don't know, maybe ten percent afraid that she knew the whole thing might flood the minute we flushed a toilet? Wait, does this place even have indoor plumbing?"

"And that's where we stop. I mean it, Penny. It's home for the next two months. Start calling it that."

The finality she can so easily assert, the sheer stubbornness that is her "bonding" with me, is the first evidence I've seen of the April that Rob warned me about. The woman of chocolate cake legend.

My heart warms at the thought of Rob, a feeling I never would have been able to predict three months ago. Being the new kid in school three quarters of the way through my junior year should have done me in, but driving to campus five days a week with Rob had me wondering every morning if maybe I would be able to survive it. Stranger things had happened. I now had a quasibrother, one who made me forget enough of the bad stuff that I actually felt like I could pour the little white pills down the sink. Then once Dad (using words that sounded more like April's) convinced me to pick up photography again, suddenly I had something to fill the space carved out of me.

The camera I have, but I miss Rob already.

I sneak a peek at my phone and see that I only have one bar. Life without parole—in solitary.

"You can talk to me that way, but Linda doesn't take kindly to scoldings," I say to April.

She looks at me like I've given her something new and exotic to worry about, which brings me a hint of joy.

Outside by the jeep, the trees sway in the breeze, and I look up at the sky in search of something, the moon maybe.

I remember Rae doing that, except she wasn't looking for the moon. It was one of the first times we hung out together, and she was looking up at the sun as it nudged the clouds out of the way.

"You're not supposed to do that," I'd said. "I think you can go blind or something."

"That doesn't seem fair. It's the closest we'll ever get to a star, and we can't even enjoy it."

I reach behind my ear and trace the cluster of stars we

each had inked there so we could be closer to them than the sun would ever allow us to get. I wonder how many times Rae thought back on that day when we each sat in a ripped vinyl chair and lied about being eighteen. Mine came out better than hers. She resented me for that.

"The sun seems shy," I'd said another time.

"That sun . . . what a pussy," she'd said. Rae could dismantle a serious thought in five words, a quality that should have been maddening but brought me relief more often than anything. It felt nice to have the weight of those types of thoughts lifted occasionally.

And then I remember the heaviness that would settle in later, the holes she left after taking away so much of what I wanted to feel for myself. The confusion at how so much empty space could weigh me down.

I open the cab of April's jeep and grab my camera case from where it toppled to the floor. As I climb out and close the door, I search the area, suddenly aware that my surroundings have shifted, though I don't fully understand until I hold still for a moment. That's what's changed—everything has gone still.

The breeze has stopped blowing, the groans and creeks of the deep forest have quieted. Even the leaves on the branches have stopped trembling. I exhale and see my breath form in front of my face.

April appears in the doorway of the house.

"Find it?"

"Hmmm?"

The breeze returns, carrying the cloud of my breath with it, and the leaves resume their dance without missing a step. The events at the rest stop are too fresh, and I feel my entire body seize up at the memory of that twisted face that couldn't have been anything other than a tree. Except . . .

"Your camera."

I hold up the case, forgetting for a moment that I was holding it. I scan the forest once again before following April back into the house, seeing nothing more than shades of green and brown through the approaching night.

"This looks to be the master bedroom," April says when we're back inside, nodding to a room situated to the right of the stairs. "It has the smallest bathroom I've ever seen in there, but it's a bathroom. There's one more next to the kitchen. Oh, you have to see the kitchen," she says.

She leads me by my wrist into what I first assume is a closet, until I see a large basin sink and what looks like a green and white table with burners attached to the top and cupboards stacked next to it.

"It's a Stewart. This has to be worth thousands on its own!" she says.

"Does it work?"

April shrugs. "I haven't checked yet. Look, the interior of the oven is blue. How adorable is this?"

I have stopped listening to her and am looking out the tiny door leading to the back of the house—what would be a backyard except that the trees have taken ownership of it. I can hardly see past the dark that their canopy creates. A rusted latch that used to brace the door from the inside is bent and warped, hanging on by a single loose bolt.

"Want me to get a picture of that?" I ask, nodding to the door.

April follows my gaze, grimacing. "That's pretty common in abandoned houses," she says. "Probably just squatters. We'll get a new bolt."

"Oh, just squatters. No biggie," I say, then remember her moratorium on negativity.

"I say we start with the kitchen," she says, and just because she says that, I turn on my heel and climb the staircase instead. I think I'm done with April's ideas about where we should start and what we should do and where we should live and what I should call home.

"Penny, come on," she calls after me.

But not today.

Because April wasn't there when I lost who I was entirely

behind the equipment shed, Rae's fist finding the softest part of Melissa Corey's face while I watched. And she wasn't there that night when I told Rae I couldn't be friends with her anymore, that it scared me how much she could color all the shades of gray in my mind before I even had a chance to try. How she could compel me to be someone I thought I wanted to be until I finally understood I didn't want to be that somebody anymore.

And April wasn't there when Rae's mom showed up and screamed and collapsed in the dirt in front of the cops even though she hadn't noticed that Rae hadn't come home the night before.

And April definitely hasn't been there each and every time Rae has talked to me since, telling me all the reasons why I will never be able to erase the letters I wrote to her, the ones that I was never going to send. The ones she was never supposed to see, but did.

I know now it was her in the woods today. What April doesn't understand—*won't* understand—is that Rae isn't quite done with me yet.

5

THE SMELL IS WORSE UPSTAIRS. It's equal parts mildew and long-ago cooking odors, but not foods that leave the sort of aromatic life in the air that tells you the house was once occupied by people. It's old food of the left and forgotten kind, tucked into discrete places I know I'll likely find during April's remodeling.

And there's something else. A sour odor overlaying it all. Acrid, like a campfire hastily snuffed out, but not before it could do a little damage.

And when I examine the frame of the hallway at the top of the stairs leading to a long row of doors, I see more evidence to support that smell. Charred pieces of wood spot the frame, crumbling under my finger when I touch the burnt places. I flip the switch and blink against the light that flickers to life.

What did April say? Some plumbing and electrical issues, but still livable? I don't recall her mentioning anything about fire damage. I don't know much about home ownership— okay, I know nothing—but shouldn't that be something that's at least casually thrown into the conversation before you buy a house? *Oh, by the way, there was a fire here, so that might have whittled some of the structural components down to toothpicks. Still want the house?*

Charred remains of yellow-and-green-flowered wallpaper cling to the walls of the hallway, the plaster behind it a progression of dark rust to yellow. I raise Linda to my eye and make the wall my first picture. As though I've flipped a switch, her flash sparks and I hear rain begin to tap the roof. The wind exhales, and the branches on the trees grumble against the disturbance.

The hallway exposes six doors, three on each side, before coming to an abrupt end. I start with the first door to my right.

The window to this room is open, raindrops dotting the outside of the yellowed fabric hanging limply from the rod above. I cross the room and pull closed the ancient window that will no doubt need to be replaced. Even closed, the draft that creeps in around the sides puffs the curtain around my head, tenting me in a mildew cloak.

This room is pretty sparse, with an ornately carved bed frame resting without its mattress in one corner and a mismatched dresser hunched beside it, the bottom drawer jutting like an underbite. A pop of turquoise color peeks out from the corner of the opened drawer, all the way to the back. I recognize it immediately after walking a little closer. Reaching in, I pull out a plastic My Little Pony, complete with pink mane and matching tail, a smattering of lollipops adorning its left flank. I used to babysit a girl who had one. I remember telling her that they weren't new, that they were just resurrected from somewhere in the 1980s. I remember seeing that same pony sit in the backyard sun for days on end after that, like it was being punished for my revelation. I'd dashed this girl's fantasy about her pretty teal pony, and now it would bake in the unforgiving Arizona sun because of me.

I pluck the pony from the drawer and tuck one leg into my back pocket. I have no idea why it's here, but I'll be damned if I banish one more plastic pony to the subexistence of neglect.

Before I leave the room, I raise my lens and zero in on the spotted curtains of the window and the bed empty of its mattress. I notice a trail of dust and a dried smear of mud on the wall by the window, most likely the product of rain getting in from the open window. Except that it should be speckled like the curtain instead of smeared.

The room across the hall is practically a carbon copy of the previous one. Instead of a wooden frame, this room contains a bed made of ornate but rusted wrought iron. Still no mattress. There's not even a dresser in this room, just a folding meal tray with faded pea green marbling that looks like something you'd find at a yard sale after someone's grandma dies. This window is open too, and harder to shut against the now pouring rain.

The room beside that one is also missing a window covering, but at least this one has a mattress. And while the rain is making a sizable puddle beneath the window, the wind hasn't quite blown any moisture to the bed. I think this might be where I sleep tonight, and I place the pony on the bed.

The room across the hall and the one beside it are duplicates of each other: twin rooms of rosebud wallpaper, all pinks and purples and oozing femininity. But old femininity. Like doilies that have been sitting underneath potted plants on side tables for too long, the dirt forming a brown ring. Charred ends of wallpaper strips stop and start, with gaping holes exposing custard-yellow glue that failed to do its job long ago. These rooms are the first since the hallway in which I've seen a recurrence of the fire damage.

I walk to the corner of the room at the back of the hall— the second of the pink rooms—and examine the heap of moldy bed linens piled and abandoned, their once pink hue looking peachy now.

I pinch a corner of the sheets and lift, leaping back when a brown spider the size of my palm skitters out of its hiding place and through a massive hole in the back of the closet.

"So that's what I get to think about before I go to bed tonight," I say. "Where that thing's crawling while we're sleeping."

I take a picture of the bed sheets and a picture of the closet hole. When I lower the lens, a smudge on the window catches my attention.

Crossing the room, I see that it's less of a smudge and more of a print. An upside down hand print. I hold my own up to it and cover it easily, my fingers reaching over an inch beyond the print on the window, though it makes my wrist ache to get it angled just right.

Upon taking my hand away, I notice I've left my own print, which should have obscured the first. Instead, they're overlaid.

Then I finally see the problem. Disbelieving, I raise the window and let in some of the rain, reaching for the smaller print and rubbing it with my thumb. My suspicion is confirmed when it smears easily. The print is on the outside.

I close the window fast, the chill from outside snaking its way up my arm.

I picture myself as the owner of this little hand, bending my wrist to make an upside down print from where I'm standing. Given that the torque of my wrist is still struggling to right itself, I can't figure how it could happen.

The final room is perhaps the biggest train wreck of them all, the place where previous renovation attempts came to die. It's as though every ounce of furniture missing from the other rooms has migrated here. Five dusty, yellowed mattresses form a kind of fort across the room, lining a sheltered pathway from the window to the closet door, which stands firmly shut thanks to one fallen blue-striped mattress with satin piping. I have to climb over three dressers, all emptied of their drawers, a lamp with no shade, and heaps of papers and blankets and damp bedsheets to reach the window, which is, thankfully, easy to shut against the downpour outside.

Robbed of its sound, the room feels somehow embarrassed now, like that sudden hush that falls at a party, and only one person is still talking loudly about what she found in her dad's sock drawer. A few of the papers piled around the mattress fort still titter under the remaining draft, but the rest of the room waits for me to make a move.

I snap a picture of the barricaded closet door and push away the thought that I'll find an even bigger spider than the one setting up camp in the room across the hall.

While the hallway and the twin pink rooms exhibited some evidence of fire damage, this room displays none of that aside from the strong acrid odor. It's worse here than in the rest of the rooms by far. I search for the source—sure something in this room is charred to a crisp—but I can't see even a square foot of flooring in the midst of all the rubble.

It might be the clutter that kept me from noticing the wall to my right until now. The only wall that isn't painted a sort of overcast gray color in this room. Instead, it's covered over sloppily with the same floral wallpaper from the hallway, though it runs out halfway down the wall about a third of the way across. The remainder is covered in the pink wallpaper from the twin rooms. The tops and bottoms run up short or too long over the molding against the floor. It looks like it was hung in a matter of minutes.

I move a few scattered drawers belonging to the empty dressers and clear a path to the wall before pulling the loose end where the yellow and green meets the pink. Loose wallpaper is kind of like a hangnail. You can't not pull it.

I tear until a triangle the size of my hand has curled away, exposing blue paint beneath the floral design. I pull the paper into my fist and yank as hard as I can, relishing the destruction I'm responsible for—an old, familiar feeling. A feeling that precedes April and my dad's disinterest and my mom's abandonment. A feeling that precedes that night in the desert. And now I remember what it's like to feel in control of something, and I have to choke back a sob it feels so good.

After setting Linda in one of the abandoned drawers, I push stacks of damp papers and end tables and heavy quilts from the wall, clearing a space for the chaos I'm suddenly desperate to unleash.

I dig at a new corner of the wallpaper, but I can't get a hold of the end. I scratch until my fingers start to burn, but the paper won't budge. I frantically search the room for something to aid me and spot a stick lying by the window. It must have blown in from one of the branches outside.

I chisel at the corner of the wallpaper until it comes up, and I tear a new sheet from the wall, this one almost a foot long. More blue wall exposes itself. I tear again. Another two feet fall to the floor in tendrils of discarded design. I dig and tear at the paper until I'm kicking through shreds like a hamster in its cage and sweating from the effort. But it's better than what I was feeling before.

I look at the wall I've marred. Swipes of newly exposed plaster peek through the shreds like shy creatures. And upon closer examination, it appears as though that's not too far from the truth.

Faint against the blue are fine strokes of lighter colors. Thin lines, drawn with a frenzied hand depicting a forest. I spot the tops of evergreen trees and paths painted into a mural of some kind, with tiny flowers and squirrels and birds dotting the scene.

I scrape another corner of the paper from the wall and tear carefully so as not to leave any of it behind. The wallpaper separates from the plaster with a sigh and lifts away to reveal a head of hair so red, it's purple. I pull a little more, and there, staring at me from six inches away is a set of bright green eyes painted into a young face of permanent contemplation.

"What are you doing?"

I spin to find April in the doorway, her worry searching for a place to land in the frenzy of the room and her unstable stepdaughter.

"Home improvements," I say, gulping for the air I hadn't realized I was missing.

After her search of my face, she finally notices the wall I've begun to strip.

"Some kind of mural?" she asks, as if I might have the answer.

"The wallpaper's hideous. Basically everything's hideous. Oh, and the house has fire damage," I share, leaving no bit of bad news out. I wasn't quite done unloading my immense emotional baggage in here, and frankly, her interruption bothers me a lot.

April takes a breath that puffs her small chest and lets it out in three, two, one. She looks down at the floor and back up at me.

"I won't do this, Penny. This sniping every other minute. I swear to God it's like being married to my ex all over again. I've been trying. For three months, every day, I've been trying. And I know I shouldn't say this, and I'm probably going to regret it, but I'm not really in the mood to filter myself right now. I'm the *only* one who's really been trying. So you can keep doing what you're doing and make the next two months miserable for us both. Or you can consider—just consider—the possibility that I wanted you here with me."

April walks away, leaving the air heavier than before. That quiet fills the room again, only this time not even the papers are chattering about how embarrassing that must have been. For her. For me.

I take one last look at the green eyes in the wall, convinced they witnessed and judged that entire interaction. And even though I found this mural with its pastoral trails and earnest face with shocking red hair and whatever else the wallpaper hides, it feels strangely against me. Like it wasn't ready to be found and hurled out of hiding into the wreckage of this room and my life.

"Sorry, kid," I tell the wall. "Looks like we're all in it together now."

As I leave the room, I hear the paper flutter in my wake.

6

APRIL AND I STARE INTO our respective coffees in Ripp's Caffeinator. Her hand is frozen, pen limp in the crook of her fingers between scribbles and stops, never taking her eyes from the steaming mug in front of her. I assume she's waiting for it to tell her what else to add to her list of renovation items to be purchased at Scoot's General once they open.

"Duct tape," she says. "Everything can be fixed with duct tape."

I stare at my own latte, its foam pool undecorated, a departure from so many Seattle coffee houses. Not that I need a reminder that we're in another world now that we're in Point Finney.

"And I need to ask if they know who can install a garbage

disposal," she says. "Buyers might be charmed by the oven, but they won't be charmed by having to scrape everything into the trash, especially if this becomes the bed-and-breakfast I think it will. All those rooms on the top floor. It's practically screaming to be a B and B. Except for the bathroom situation . . ."

"Mhmm."

"Oh, that reminds me. Hand soap. I forgot to pack any."

I cover my eyes with my palm, which is warm from cupping my mug of coffee.

"Penny."

I mentally replay the list of items she's put forth, unable to fully block her out. Duct tape. Garbage disposal. Hand soap. Penny.

"Penny?" she says.

"What?"

"Do you have a headache?"

I open my eyes. Jagged worry lines groove her forehead.

"I'm fine."

She gives me a look that speaks an entire novella about all the ways I'm not fine, which makes it a little easier to dislike her. She has no place deciding that. Except I can't help thinking about what she said last night, about how she's the only one trying.

About how she's right.

"I mean, yeah. Headache. I have one," I say.

She nods. "Tylenol. I'll add that to the list. Oh, window cleaner," she says. "I can't tell if the windows are really that old, or if they're just neglected. That whole house is neglected," she tsks. I think of the awkward little handprint on the window upstairs.

April's purse chimes from beside her on the table, and she pulls her phone out, her face beaming in a way my mom's never has.

"Your dad says hi. He misses us."

I nod, unable to say the same. I try to remember the last time I missed him. I could describe every last detail of his appearance to anyone who asked. The way he smells like aftershave and spearmint, which should be gross but somehow just smells clean. The way he seems to growl instead of laugh, even when he knows something is really funny.

But it's been more years than I can count since I've felt the pull of him.

I stop looking at April's phone with all its ambiguity and pull my eyes back to the list in her hand. Ink on paper is so much easier to decipher.

"Add a new door bolt to the list," I say, remembering the jimmied lock and the probable squatters.

The caffeine begins to do its job, and I pace the floor of Ripp's, the soft wood bending and straining in places where weather and time have warped it.

The wall is lined with vintage signs ranging from the early 1900s to the mid-sixties, from the looks of the fashion and women's hairstyles. Box frames interspersed between signs feature newspaper clippings, all mentioning something significant involving the building that eventually became Ripp's.

A clipping on the far wall boasts the headline SMALL BUSINESS OWNER PROVES THE LITTLE GUY CAN WIN. The picture under the headline captures A stocky guy in his forties standing behind the counter. I recognize him across the café, his crew cut making him look more like a drill sergeant than a local proprietor. The paper is folded to fit the frame at the corner, but one half of the headline to an adjacent story reads ANOTHER LOCAL TEEN FOUND IN NOR—

"They wanted to open one of those god-awful chains," says a voice over my shoulder. His breath smells like cinnamon.

I turn to find the man from the picture, though his face has sagged a little over the years, his eyes a little puffier, his cheeks more hollowed.

"I can't really take much credit," he continues. "It was the townspeople who signed the petitions, picketed, all that. I just kept serving 'em coffee."

His laugh is startling—too loud for this quiet space, but impossible not to love.

"It's good," I say, nodding to my mug, which is still sitting across from an engrossed April. Her list has grown to three times its prior size.

I point to the only framed piece of art that isn't a vintage sign or newspaper clipping. It's a black-and-white, shaded drawing of a cloud passing over the faintest outline of a sun. The sun still wins out in the picture, somehow, despite the overbearing cloud and the picture's lack of color.

"That's beautiful," I say, nodding to the drawing.

"Oh that," he says, his face going pink. "That there is the scribbling of an untrained artist. Don't look too closely. I only framed it because my sister used to gush about her talented brother."

I just smile. There's nothing really to say in response to such fierce modesty.

"Just passing through, or can I count on seeing you two more often?" he asks, expertly changing the subject.

"A little of both," I tell him. "Here for the summer. Or at least the first part."

Apparently hearing her cue, April looks up from her list. "I'm fixing up one of your originals. I think it was one of the first houses ever built in Point Finney, actually. Maybe before it was even Point Finney!"

"Oh yeah? Up on First Street? One of those old Victorians?" the owner asks.

"No," April laughs. "Not quite in my price point. The Carver House, that beautiful old farmhouse in the North Woods."

The man stops smiling. His skin burns red and splotchy for a moment before losing its color altogether. "Are you now?"

I look at April, and she looks at the man, who looks at her with the same expression that girl had before I smacked her friend's face in the girls' bathroom. Like he knows there will be pain, but he's powerless to stop it.

"Indeed we are," April says, watching the man's face closely. "We're actually just waiting for the general store to open so we can pick up some supplies."

"Uh huh," the man says, his hands looking for a place to go. They start with his pockets, then fiddle with his apron. They finally settle on the chair in front of him.

"Any idea when they open?" April keeps trying, but I think she's doing more than that. She's leaning on him, trying to see what he'll say if she pushes hard enough. It's that stubbornness again. But the whole interaction is getting a little too uncomfortable for me.

"Nope. Not a clue," he says, a lie that only seems to inflame April.

"Really. You have no idea when the business across the street from you opens. That's . . . shocking," she says, boring a hole through him.

"I'm Penny," I say, extending my hand. He stares at it for a second like he's trying to figure out what a hand is, then puts his in mine, though he doesn't grasp it. He just lets it sit in my palm.

"Ripp," he says, which I should have guessed but didn't want to assume.

"That's April," I say, and April sits up a little straighter.

"Your . . . sister?" Ripp asks.

"Stepmom," April says before I can come up with a better response.

"So, you've sort of cornered the market on small town hospitality." April leans in harder. Ripp's hand, still in mine, suddenly squeezes, and I have to pull mine away before April can see that it's starting to hurt.

"Yes, ma'am," he says, holding April's gaze, ready to challenge her now that he's apparently gotten over his momentary shock. I officially want to leave as soon as possible. This guy looks like he's about to . . . actually, I can't figure out what he's about to do. Scream or call the cops or grab an ax from the back room and chop us to pieces. In any case, I want to leave.

"I think they're open," I say after catching the slightest movement in my periphery. The blinds to the general store just parted.

April lifts her coffee to her mouth and, in three gulps, drains the giant mug of its contents. She sets our cups slowly on the counter, her eyes on Ripp the whole time. Ripp watches her with the same intensity, and I wait until we get outside to say anything.

"What the hell, April?"

"What? You're blaming me? That guy was clearly off his nut. And language."

"Yeah, but why did you have to push him?"

"I wanted to see what he'd do."

"I'm pretty sure of what he'll do *now*," I say. "I hope there's another place to get coffee around here because I think you've managed to have us banned from the only café in Point Finney."

Scoot's General is one of those places with a bell above the door. Not an electronic bell that simulates ringing, but an actual brass bell that tinkles when the door hits it.

"Help you find something?"

I can't tell where the voice is coming from, but if I didn't know better, I'd say from the bottom of a hole. He sounds far away, his question still echoing from wherever it originated.

"Yes, many somethings," April replies, also looking for the source of the voice. It all feels a little Great and Powerful Oz-ish.

"Oh, and coffee filters," April says to me, inspiration clearly striking in the midst of our café encounter. She scrawls that on her list, too.

"Sorry, we don't carry that," the voice echoes back, though it sounds like maybe it's getting closer now. "Ripp's across the street. He'll probably sell you a stack if you ask."

"Not likely," I mutter.

"Scoot's. Ripp's. Wonder if they're related or something," April mutters.

"Brothers. Well, brothers-in-law," the voice says, and I finally see where it's coming from. A hole, in fact, in the floor. A basement just inside a doorway leading to a back room.

"Well, what'd'ya know?" I say.

"I know that they were brothers-in-law," the voice repeats, teasing, and now I finally see the person attached to it.

He's not particularly tall, but definitely taller than me. His hair is that kind of red that looks brown in most lights. Only he's not standing in most lights. He's standing in the gray haze streaming through the window beside him, and somehow that makes it look burnt. He's older than me, but not by all that much.

Green eyes. Deep, like the evergreens that are so close to the buildings in this town, they act like they want to be walls.

I've seen a version of this person before. A younger version, depicted in paint strokes on a wall behind ugly paper. If not him, then someone who looks a hell of a lot like him.

He takes the list from April, who is compulsively wiping droplets from her fleece like they're lint.

"My dad was Scoot. Ripp's my uncle. He sort of looks after me ever since my parents died. And now you know a strangely personal thing about me."

That and your younger doppelganger is painted on the wall in our new house.

As though he hears my thoughts, his hand gropes the back of his neck, and he seems to remember suddenly that he emerged from the basement with something, and focuses intently on that—a case of beer under one arm.

April takes the list back from him. "I'll just start wandering," she says, apparently finding the limits of local hospitality.

"I'm here against my will," I say as soon as April's out of earshot. I have no idea why I say it, or why it feels like I can say it to him. But he just confessed to me, and besides, it feels like we've already met, and it feels like I haven't talked for months. Which is, in some ways, true.

He looks at me like I might have just emerged from a hole

too. Like he's not exactly sure what he's looking at. I'm positive I am the most awkward human being to stumble into Scoot's.

I look around for April and spot her head bobbing purposefully in the back of the store, examining the various electrical and packing tapes.

"Okay, so I guess I'll go with paper towels," I say.

"What?"

"Since you don't have coffee filters," I say.

"Oh, right. Because paper towels are a good substitute for filters?"

Now it's my turn to wonder about him. He's making fun of me. I know that much. But not in a superior way. Not like he's trying to embarrass me. Like maybe he's trying to get me to talk back.

So I do. Because I can't seem to stop now that I've started.

"Because it's next on the list. We're fixing up this house. . . . " I approach with caution. "It's, uh, a little neglected."

I want to say what it really is: an inch away from collapsing. But now I'm wondering if this was his old house. He clearly has some connection to it. And he'll probably find out from his uncle where we're staying, and this is already off to a very strange start.

Somehow I followed the boy with the green eyes and burnt hair to a claustrophobic aisle stuffed with all kinds of paper products: toilet paper, paper towels, Kleenex, paper plates, napkins. I don't even remember getting here, but here we are, and here he is, handing me a package of paper towels and looking at me with those incredible evergreen eyes.

"I'm Miller. Dodson."

The way he breaks it up, it almost sounds like two first names. Like I could call him either. But the last one is familiar, and then I remember that I've seen it written in black marker on the tag of a musty coat hanging in our house.

He waits. I know because he hasn't let go of the paper towels.

"Penny. Um, Warren," I answer, my own last name escaping me for far too long.

"Penny, I don't know you really well. I mean, I know that you just moved here, and that you're living in a house nearby or you wouldn't be shopping here. And I know that your friend over there already hates me."

"Stepmom," I say.

He smiles at me for the first time, and a single dimple creases the corner of his lip.

"But I think you should let me hang out with you some night," Miller says.

"Why?" I ask, my throat feeling suddenly constricted.

He releases the paper towels and walks to a refrigerator case lining an entire wall of his family's store. He pulls out the largest bottle of water they sell and hands it to me without answering my question. "If your new place is anywhere around here, your tap isn't going to taste very good."

"Oh, well, it's not near anywhere. It's out in the middle of the woods. There's no one living for, like, a thousand-mile radius around that place."

But you already know that, I guess.

I trail off for so many reasons, but mostly because now this Miller guy with the burnt red hair is staring at me. Hard. Like he can hear everything I'm thinking.

"Eggs," April says, her arms full of spray bottles and roles of silver tape and pads of pink Post-it notes and a bucket with a mop and a broom tucked under one arm and a bucket of paint and supplies tucked under the other.

She looks at Miller, then at me, then back at Miller. "And toilet paper," she says firmly, like she's scolding one of us. Maybe both of us.

I break from Miller's stern gaze first, then grab a package of two dozen rolls of toilet paper, feeling embarrassed and pissed for being embarrassed over nothing.

"Don't have eggs," Miller says, flipping a switch and showing April the tiny dimple in the corner of his mouth he showed me just a minute ago. "But there's a grocery store called Maggie's just a quarter mile up the road. Might even find your coffee filters there."

"Guess that's something we're going to have to get used to, Penny. No more life in the big city." I barely hear her. I just set the toilet paper down beside the register, give the guy with the burnt red hair I've inexplicably managed to offend an awkward wave good-bye, and walk straight out the door, the tiny bell singing me farewell before I'm standing in the early morning mist. I scroll through my phone and pull up Rob's number.

"Are you on your way back yet?" he asks.

"Fifty-eight more days, but I'm not counting or anything," I say.

He waits because he knows there's more. He's the only person in my life who waits.

"She should just leave me here."

He waits.

"Like, after the house is ready to sell. She should just pack up and leave me."

"That's what you want, huh? For her to leave you there."

"Why not? It's not like I fit anywhere else."

"I think Dad would probably wonder after a few days. He says hi, by the way."

"I'll bet."

"Seriously. He told me to tell you the next time we talked."

Because he can only afford the time to call one of his kids. This is what I don't say. It's not Rob's fault.

He's quiet for so long, I start to wonder if the call dropped. Then he says, "She's not going to punish you just because you don't know how else to punish yourself."

Now it's my turn to wait.

"Look, I'm going to tell you something, but it's going to be the only time I tell you because it has to do with my dad, and I don't like to talk about him because he's a dick. But I guess you need to hear it, so just listen and don't say anything, okay?"

I don't say anything.

"I know you're going through things. I'm not even going to pretend I understand. But . . . just try not to make my mom do the dirty work, okay? I already did that to her once. After my dad left. She always says it's because they married so young, but I thought it was because of me. I didn't understand that he just didn't want to be an eighteen-year-old dad. Anyway, Mom's the one who didn't quit on me, even though I'm sure she wanted to a few times when I got older and she got tired of doing it all on her own. It's not her fault we can't figure out how to be mad at ourselves."

The jingle behind me tells me that April is done with her shopping and ready to get on with the housework.

"Call me again," Rob tells me.

"When?"

But he hangs up, and I consider the invitation an open one.

7

I CAN HEAR RAE SCUFFING her heels behind the equipment shed, and I know this is my last chance to walk away. I could pretend I got the place confused. I thought we were meeting by the track or the parking lot. I thought it was tomorrow. I thought it was yesterday. But I'm here, and my feet are moving me down the path, and I can hear my own false comfort falling from my lips, landing at the feet of Melissa Corey.

I won't walk away. Girls who are weak walk away and then make up lies later on.

"I didn't say anything, though. I barely even know her."

"Just . . . talk to her," I say, knowing it won't do any good.

"But why would I—?"

"Just tell her, and I'm sure she'll calm down. I'm just trying to be

a good friend." It's as though someone else is forming the words on my tongue.

"Wait, are you mad at me too? Do you actually think—I just sit next to her in chemistry! Can't you just tell her I didn't do it?"

When we round the corner, I see Rae. She's wearing her sympathetic face.

"I didn't say anything about you. I swear to God. I mean, I don't even know you—"

Rae looks at her pityingly. "I know. Which is why it's just so hard for me to understand. Why would you go talking shit about someone you don't even know?"

Melissa Corey shakes her head swiftly, brown curls slapping her round face as punishment. "I don't know who told you I did, but they're lying."

"Oooh," Rae says, and now I know it's begun.

"What?" Melissa Corey is on the brink of panic. Her skinny legs poke out of denim shorts too long to be worn by anyone who would really be guilty of talking shit.

"See, now we really have a problem," Rae continues.

Now we're both looking at Rae.

She leaves Melissa Corey and walks to my side. "Because Penny's the one who heard you say it."

Melissa Corey is pale and sweaty. Her hands feel cold and heavy by her sides. I don't know how I know, but I do, and my own fingers are tingling like they might go numb in a second.

Melissa looks at my shoes. "What . . . what did you hear me say?"

But she already knows the answer to that question. And this is when we all know that Rae holds the only important truth between the three of us. No matter what happens now, it will be Rae's words that feed our ravenous actions. Melissa Corey probably knew that the minute she agreed to walk with me behind the equipment shed.

And I knew it even before that.

So when Rae looks at me, silently feeding me the heinous crime Melissa Corey never committed, I eat every last bite of what she offers before taking one, two, three steps away from a trembling girl in long shorts and prove to Rae I'm a true friend.

Thirty minutes later, in the bathroom Rae shares with her mom and her mom's boyfriend, I look for what's out of place and find nothing. The pieces of my face are all there. Until they rearrange and scatter, refusing to show me something recognizable. And when I push my head into the sink and come up for air only after I think my lungs might burst, the face I see isn't mine at all. It's Rae's.

She reaches a bright red fingernail to the glass and taps a steady rhythm to a tune I vaguely recognize.

My sheets are soaked with sweat when I wake up in the middle bedroom of the Carver House, though it takes me a minute to remember that. Two nights in someone else's house isn't enough time to establish a feeling of comfort upon waking, and it's been a while since I felt permanent anywhere.

So when I finally remember I woke up for a reason, I search out the clicking. The needles of a nearby tree branch drag across the windowpane, and I follow their shadows' movement on the wall across the room, the silver light of the moon brightening the scene a little too much for this late at night. I vow that tomorrow I will beg April to get a shade for the window and maybe—just possibly—get a decent night's sleep in these insanely loud woods.

But as I follow the branch's dance across my window, I notice that it's moving with more force behind it than a mere gust of nighttime breeze could provide.

I go to the window and search the ground below in time to see a hand relinquish control of the branch that was tickling my windowpane—a hand attached to an arm leading up to a set of large purple curls pinned to Vargas Girl perfection.

Rae backs into the woods and out of sight.

"No," I tell her. But I know she's still there, just outside the light of the moon, and she'll stay there until I come out to meet her.

"You don't get to dictate what I do anymore," I tell her. But I say it softer this time. And I'm already sliding my jeans on, and my boots over my jeans, and my fleece over everything.

"You're dead," I say through gnashed teeth.

"Promises, promises," Rae sings from somewhere in the dark.

"I'm serious," I tell the dark.

"That's the problem," she says from the shadows. "I can't quite trust what you say anymore, you know?"

I could pretend she's not there, but I'm half asleep and too tired to pretend. And it's not like she's going to let me ignore her anyway. The nights are when she's at her best.

I hit every creaking step on the way downstairs, but still manage to slip past April's room on the bottom floor without hearing her wake. I grope my way into the kitchen, squinting through darkness until I make out the tiny square window cut into the back door, its new bolt already in place.

Grabbing a flashlight April must have brought with our meager kitchen supplies, I unlatch the door, catch it before it slams shut behind me, and immediately wrap my arms around me to brace against the night chill that has blanketed the woods. I stare at the tree responsible for tapping me awake and can't find Rae anywhere near it, not that I'm surprised. She wants me to come to her, and so far, she's getting her way.

So I aim the flashlight and walk.

At the base of the tree, I see grooves in the damp ground where shoes might have stood. They look a little small to be Rae's, but it's hard to see anything, even with the yellow glow of the ancient flashlight. It flickers for a second, as though sensing my disdain with its performance, then sputters back to life.

"Seriously, we couldn't have put a real flashlight on that massive supply list?"

I cast the beam across the trees in front of me, deeper into the woods. I bury the twitch in my stomach that warns me against walking farther out. There's nothing out there but Rae, and she's followed me all the way to this tiny wooded town. I won't let her chase me back to Seattle. Or Phoenix. Or wherever I'm deposited next when even April has exhausted her supply of hope for me.

"I know you're here," I say softly. I mean to sound commanding, but I end up sounding tired.

"This is stupid, Rae. It's the middle of the night, and I've had enough. Whatever you want, you win, okay? I'm done."

The bulb in the flashlight fades, blinks back to life, then wastes away, a quiet death. I toss it into the grass by the kitchen door.

Wind slides between the branches of the trees, and the trunk closest to me groans under the weight of what it's holding. I hear a pop in front of me and look up in time to see a branch pull back and snap forward, catching the quickest flash of iridescent skin under the meager light of nighttime.

I stomp forward, no longer caring how much noise I

might make. The trees catch every inch of my clothes and whatever skin I've left bare in my haste to come outside and rid myself of Rae, and dampness soaks the skin I haven't covered. I look up but already know it's not raining. It's the perpetual moisture that hangs low in the air in these woods. And when I notice that I'm panting, I stop moving, finding only now that I've been practically sprinting between trees, my eyes on constant alert for some sign of her. I stand still long enough to pull in three deep breaths and swat away the branches that feel closer than they did a minute ago.

When the sound of my breathing ceases, a different sound takes its place—a steady squeak singsonging its way across the forest floor and climbing into my ears. A flicker of light catches my eye, and I venture more slowly this time toward the movement, which I soon see is attached to ropes in a clearing.

The ropes hold a flat plank of wood, dulled gray and dangling from a nearby tree branch on the outskirts of a brief expanse of open space. The nighttime breeze carries it back and forth, eking out a new creak with each rhythmic movement.

In the makeshift swing sits Rae, cradling a bottle of vodka in her lap.

"You look cold. *I'm* not cold," she says, uncapping the bottle.

"That's because you don't feel," I say, standing uneasily beside her. The moon is nearly full, and this is the first time I've seen it this clearly since we arrived in Point Finney.

She offers me the bottle, and I see myself refusing but feel my fingers grasp the neck before I sit on the hard ground. I'm freezing and want to feel something burn me. The bottle should be cold but it's warm from her grip.

"I don't know how to make you leave me alone," I say after mentally rejecting a hundred other confessions first.

"Then you don't really want me to," she says and takes the bottle back.

"I know that's what you always thought," I say. Moonlight reflects off her diamond labret. "But I'm done letting you make my decisions for me."

"Oh, I know. I read all about it. Face it, Penny. I'm with you for the long haul. Don't worry, though. I'm entertaining company."

"So at the rest stop? Was that your idea of entertainment? It wasn't funny. I thought you were someone who needed help."

"Well, aren't you the patron saint of the Pacific Northwest? And who says that was me, anyway?" Rae takes another drink, ponders the taste for a second before swallowing without a flinch. "And if we're talking about people who need help . . ."

"I'm not here to do any of this with you," I say, nodding to the bottle and alluding to everything else. "I'm just here to tell you this is the last time we're going to talk."

I start to get up, but she beats me to it.

"That's quite the declaration. So much to live up to." Rae eases the bottle into my hands. "Sounds like your evil stepmom is starting to get through when your real parents couldn't be bothered. I'm sure that'll last."

I open my mouth to tell her all the ways she's wrong, but all that comes out is a tiny puff of white air.

"Has it ever occurred to you that I'm only here when you come looking for me?" Rae asks.

She looks up at the moon I was just looking at, which makes me feel oddly jealous, like that's not her moon to enjoy, and turns in the opposite direction of the house. Ducking under the branch of a nearby tree, she looks it over, offers it a tiny smile and a pat on its bark.

"I like these woods," she says softly. "It's like they want you here, you know?"

Then she disappears into the deep part of the woods, and as I search for her vanishing form, I blink back the suspicion that she's still watching me from the darkest shadow she can find. The longer I stare into the murky depths, the harder it becomes to convince myself I'm not seeing those same white eyes that I saw at the rest stop gazing back at me.

I uncap the bottle she gave me (which looks awfully similar to the one I remember stealing from the kitchen and burying in the Rubbermaid before leaving Phoenix) and pull in another swallow. I feel the drink land in my stomach, on top of the anger I try and fail to tamp down. I consider what might happen if I drink the whole bottle. I picture Melissa Corey's face smooth from confused pain to vague recognition when she looks at me. I picture the letters I wrote to Rae, all the horrible things she was never meant to read but should have already known. I picture Rae in the desert, walking back to me where I slept, telling me to just leave her alone and she'll do the same. It's okay. Sometimes friendships simply don't last. Sometimes you just part ways amicably. I picture my parents parting ways amicably.

I picture it all melting in a bubbling puddle, evaporating under the wind of these woods, growing over with moss.

I lie down in the needles beside the swing and listen to its ropes creak under the breeze, then I tilt the bottle back and swallow until things look foggy and I've forgotten what cold feels like on my skin.

I close my eyes for a moment. For maybe more than a moment.

And when I open them, I see two small feet pass over me.

They pass over me again, then again, in time with the creak of the swing. They're bare but muddy, limp on the ends of dangling legs clothed in frayed denim.

They pass over me again. A torn white T-shirt drapes over a set of sharp shoulder blades. A dark baseball cap sits beside a boy on the swing.

I ease onto my elbows, and his dangling feet narrowly miss my face. But before I have a chance to react, he leaps off the swing and sets off running, hat in hand, his bare feet springing against the blanket of pine needles that grows thicker the farther he runs. In an instant, he's disappeared into the woods, the same way Rae traveled.

"Hey," I mumble, but my mouth is coated and dry and I can't focus my vision. I hear distant laughter, a kid giggling, and know I must sound as wrecked as I feel.

I struggle to steady myself on my feet, my bones aching from the dampness now plastering my thin fleece to me. I consider brushing the needles from my legs, but my body feels like it somehow filled itself with slowly drying cement, and I'm struggling to keep upright.

Which is probably what I get for falling asleep on the ground in the middle of the woods after—I examine the bottle by my feet—too much vodka.

"She did it to me again." I make sure to say it aloud. I need constant reminding of how easy it is for me to fall back under Rae's spell. And how easy it is for me to revisit those same old habits while I figure out how to fill the spaces she scooped out of me.

The walk from the woods back to the house feels like it takes a year. The trees crowd me, their branches seeming to lower into my path at every turn, their needles lifting and pulling the fabric of my clothes. I slip through the kitchen door and drop the bottle of vodka in one of the boxes before dragging myself upstairs to a bed I know won't feel like my own for the duration of the summer.

8

MAGGIE'S GROCERY IS THE SIZE of a large post office. And, in fact, it does mail letters and packages, so long as you have cash to pay for it, or so the handwritten sign in the corner by the dairy refrigerator says. There's a lady behind the foggy Plexiglas eyeing me over the top of her paperback, and I do my best to look as suspicious as possible just to piss her off.

What am I going to steal? A stick of butter?

My head is throbbing and my stomach is rolling and my bones and joints and everything else padding them pulse under my skin like pipes straining under water. I never drank before Rae, and I've never seen anyone do it like she did it—like she was trying to get back at someone. My drinking always felt like more of a response to a question no one actually asked.

I never threw a single punch before I met Rae, either, in case we're counting all the things I never used to do.

April meets me at the back of the store bearing a new treasure.

"They have wooden baskets," she says, holding one up just in case I don't understand what a basket is. "Not to buy. I mean, this is what you shop with. No big metal carts. How cute is that?"

More charm.

"Don't forget coffee filters," I say. April's face falls a little at the reference to the whole Ripp's interaction, and I remember the silent promise I made to try a little harder. After she came home from meeting the Realtor and the engineer who never showed up, she looked more disheartened than I've seen her look since we rolled into this crazy little town that only sells eggs in one store. And I was too caught up in the strangeness of my own afternoon to be of much support, something I'm still not quite sure how to offer her.

But I know I should try, so I follow up with, "Maybe you should ask if you could buy one of those baskets. You could put bath towels in them or something. I don't know. Aren't people who run bed-and-breakfasts always putting bath towels in baskets?"

Her face brightens a little under the flickering neon light above the dairy case. "Brilliant! Penny, you act like you're not into design, but you might just have a knack for it, you know. It's that photographer's eye of yours."

I fail to suppress the shudder that skitters over my shoulders at the thought of my phone's camera and what it showed me the other day.

April's eagle eye catches it and gives me a questioning look. I tilt my head toward the dairy case.

"Freezing over here," I say, and she nods in a different direction.

"I'll get the perishables last. Let's head for the bread now. Here." She hands me my very own basket for shopping.

Four full wooden baskets and one and a half hours later, we've circled Maggie's Grocery five times, weaving in and out of every aisle with more focus than a police K9. April had to be sure we didn't leave a single jar of locally made blackberry preserves unturned.

At the register (a single register, mind you, with one very slow cashier named Roberta), we get more than a few stares, our load clearly bordering on maximum capacity, like it's a crime to buy too many bottles of local honey adorned with five thousand ribbons and a cartoon bee.

When it's finally our turn to ring up, Roberta is mostly as pleasant as she's been to all the people before us, though not without a touch of suspicion, a characteristic I'm beginning to equate with this entire town.

"Doing a little stocking up?" she asks April without looking up from her scanner.

"Something like that," April says, her own wariness after the Ripp's ordeal keeping her tone polite but more distant than I know she'd prefer it to be. "We're fixing up one of the old homes, and we're not exactly close to any stores."

"Baskets," I mutter to April, and she stops digging for the wallet in her purse and looks up.

"Oh, right! Yes! I was wondering, I know it's a stupid question, but do you, well, see, we're thinking of staging this house as a bed-and-breakfast for people looking for a remote getaway, and this house could use as much help as we can get. And your little baskets are so . . ."

"Charming," I finish for her, and she nods.

If she was hoping Roberta would complete her thought for her, April might be waiting a little longer. Because all she can do is stare at April. She's stopped scanning, and a quarter of our food waits patiently on the conveyer belt, which is more than I can say for the line backing up behind us.

"Anyway, I was wondering if we could purchase a few of these—"

"Where'd you say you folks were staying?" Roberta asks. I'm beginning to get that Groundhog Day feeling. My head starts pounding a little bit harder.

April's apparently getting it too, because I can practically feel her tense up next to me. The air gets that static feeling, like an open flame could spark and set the whole place on fire.

"Actually, I don't believe I did say," says April, hackles up.

I shove our food a little farther up the conveyer belt because the guy in line behind me is starting to breathe a little too heavily for my comfort. I inch closer to April.

Roberta begins slowly scanning again, her eyes unmoving from April's. Maybe it's that silent confrontation that sets April down the same path I thought she regretted from yesterday.

Not that I'm one to criticize the wrong path.

"We're fixing up the Carver House. The one in the Kitsap Woodlands. I'm guessing you've heard of it. Seems like everyone around here has."

Roberta slams our loaf of bread onto the scanner and lets it lie there. She looks furious with it, like it somehow betrayed her. But instead of looking at April like I expect her to—actually, I expect her to throw the bread at April—she turns an apologetic gaze to the breathing man behind me.

Then she does turn her ire to April after a long moment. "Maybe you should just go on," she says.

April and I both stand there, our groceries in limbo, the air popping with static electricity all around our heads.

"I'll go," says April so quietly I almost can't hear her, and I'm a foot away, "as soon as we have our groceries. Now, if you'll kindly finish and tell me how much I owe you."

"I said you should—"

"Just let her buy her damn groceries, Roberta," the guy behind me says, and now I swear the entire line is holding their breath.

I turn to look at the guy I tried to get away from a second ago. He's tall and big, and for a split second, I think I'm looking right at my dad. Even the man's tan jacket resurrects an old autumn memory I never realized I'd stored away. I'm suddenly at the Woodland Park Zoo, and my mom is at the counter buying us all crappy zoo tacos, and my dad and I are sitting at a sticky table playing that game where you try to slap the person's hands before they pull them away. And I'm winning, as always. My dad never once let me lose to him.

But this guy's jacket has a Riley's Autoparts patch sewn

onto the front, and he looks like the world has swallowed him up, spit him back out, and left him to live a mangled existence right here in Maggie's Grocery.

"George, I don't have to—"

"Just give 'em their food and let 'em get the hell out," he says, the least comforting defense of two people who have done nothing wrong that I've ever heard.

"Look, I don't know what your problem is, but—" I start to say, but April puts her hand across my chest like she's trying to brace me against a fast stop. It's clear nobody in this store is going to finish a sentence today.

April turns her attention back to Roberta. "Our total, please. And three of these charming wooden baskets," she says, holding one up and smiling the world's fakest smile.

Roberta looks once more at the guy—George—behind us before roughly swiping the rest of our groceries and dumping them straight back into the wooden baskets we brought them up in.

"You can find your way out, I'm sure," Roberta says to April after we pay. "And I trust you can find your way to another grocery store in the future."

"Well, that's an awful lot of trust to place in a stranger," April says, then turns to the rest of the line, finding George first and then every set of eyes after his. "I'm taking it that's not something you folks like to do. Trust strangers. If you all change your mind, I'll be more than happy to invite you into our home. We'll be here for most of the summer, and you're welcome to come by if you'd like."

"April, what the hell?" I whisper, not nearly as forgiving as she is at least pretending to be.

"Language," she says through gritted teeth, and I know I'm smearing up some sort of illusion she's trying to create.

"I think you've made your point," says Roberta. "Now if that's all, the door's behind you."

April turns toward the exit and pushes her way out, but I stay for a minute longer. I'm not looking at Roberta, who has now busied herself with the business of ringing. I'm looking at the man in the tan jacket. George.

And I'm only looking at him because he won't stop looking at me. I can't tell if he wants to hug me or throw me out the window. His face is red splotched, broken blood vessels dancing across his bulbous nose and puffed cheeks. He's entirely bald on the top, the ring around the back of his head overgrown and gray. A matching mustache adorns his upper lip, pushing his mouth down on his face.

I wait until he turns back to Roberta, who is desperately trying to engage him in conversation, before I join April outside. She's struggling to push the groceries into the back of her jeep.

"There you are. I was going to send SWAT in there if you didn't come out in five more seconds," she says, winded at her effort.

"Sorry," I say, and I can't tell what I'm apologizing for, but April answers like she knows.

"I'm not," she says. "I'm thrilled. If these people are a little afraid of a ghost story, that's just better for business, which means that's better for resale. If they want to come and check it out, all the better."

"Wait, what?" I ask, but she waves me off.

"You know. Old towns, old houses. People are so superstitious. Even the Realtor told me some nutty story about the Carvers just sort of disappearing. I mean, come on. Everyone disappeared back then. It's not like the mid-nineteenth century is known for its immaculate record-keeping."

But I'm not satisfied by her answer, and I think she knows it because she says, "Look, the scariest part of this house is the roof. I'm having a hell of a time lining up meetings with anyone in this town. If I keep making scenes at coffee shops and grocery stores, I'm never going to get it fixed up by the end of July."

At least that much I understand, and for maybe the first

time ever, April sounds rational about the house. Maybe not totally competent, but rational at least.

But as we drive off, I'm still pushing away the memory of George and his sagging face. I have enough faces haunting me these days. I hardly need to add one more to the roster.

9

Dear Rae,

It feels like I'm cheating on you.

You'd make fun of me if I ever said anything like that to your face. "This is why people think we're going out," you'd say.

But I know you'd know exactly what I mean, and you'd agree. Because if you knew all the stuff I'd been doing without you lately, you'd be pissed, and you'd say something awful like I'm totally selfish or that I'm afraid to share anything good with you because I'm incapable of being a real friend. Like that time I went to see 20 Minute Loop

*play in Tempe, and I went alone because I didn't feel like
listening to you trash all the other underage kids who snuck
in just like we would have done but who for some reason
don't get to share the same sort of cool you think you possess
over all of them. And I had such an awesome time and
forgot you weren't there, and I was talking about it in front
of you later and you called me a poser and stopped talking to
me for a week.*

*I think the thing you'd be most upset about is the
photography classes. It's not like I think I'm some sort of
incredible artist or anything. I've only been going for a
few weeks, but I already know that this is what I'm going
to do forever. We get to borrow these fancy cameras for two
days and basically do whatever we want. We can make the
pictures say all these incredible things, with just one image,
just one click. I get to say everything I want to say without
writing a word. I could stop speaking for the rest of my life.*

*And I don't want you to know anything about it. I don't
want to share how this feels with you. I think that means
something huge. Only now, instead of trying to write what
I think it means in a letter I'll never give you, I'm looking
everywhere for an image that captures it. I'm seeing words*

*in shapes and colors and light. And I'm seeing you so
differently.*

*I heard Melissa Corey is transferring to Truman. I heard she
has to take a little white pill every night just to go to sleep.*

Penny

I don't know if Rae read the letters in order. It wouldn't
have mattered to her, I know that, but I wonder anyway. If
she had read them in order, I consider how that might have
blunted the blow. And like always, I wonder if I really care.

I look to Linda, waiting patiently for me to see her next to
my notepad. I run my finger over the dust that's already begun
to accumulate on top of her even though it's only been a few
days since I used her last. Her lens cap covers her Cyclops eye.

"Show me something new," I tell her. "Something other
than this."

My phone buzzes on the bed beside me.

"Hi, Mom."

"Jesus, where are you, the bottom of a well?"

This is the first thing she has to say to me. A criticism of
the cell reception.

"I'm doing great, Mom. Thanks."

I stand and begin to pace the room, my usual exercise for this category of phone calls. I push aside the instant regret I feel these days whenever I pick up her call.

"Oh, here it comes. Penny's pity party. Everyone's invited," she says. Teasing never really sounds good on her.

"The cell reception is spotty here. Actually, so is the Internet. We don't have cable or anything. It's kind of remote," I say, finding the blandest tone in my repertoire. Anything that doesn't sound self-pitying.

"That explains why you haven't responded to my e-mails," she says, and I suddenly remember her last argument with Dad. *There she is, Passive Aggressive Natalie.*

"I'd ask if this is a bad time for you, but you're the one who called me, so . . ." I try to get her back to a neutral topic.

"I'm at that place with the weird chicken tikka masala."

Which explains the Bollywood soundtrack in the background.

"The place where we went last Christmas?" I ask. I know where this is going, but I'm not in a hurry to indulge it.

"Do you remember that hysterical couple who sat next to us? The ones who kept offering to share their food?" she asks. She's really going to make me be the one to say it first, even though I've earned hearing it from her. She'll never be the first one to tell me that she misses me. That maybe she was a little hasty in sending me away like she did.

Today I just don't feel like letting her off the hook.

"You're lonely," I say, more of an accusation.

"There, you got your shot in. Feel better?" she asks, her tone dimpling under offense she has no right feeling. She wasn't the one who was thrown away. She wasn't the one who was expendable.

So indeed I do feel a little better.

"How's the house?" Mom asks, trying something new.

"It's a dump," I say. "April calls it charming." And immediately, I regret saying it.

Mom snorts. "Well, she has a thing for older projects."

She can find the smallest opening to zing my dad. She must feel like she scores a bonus point when she can trash his second wife, too.

"It's just hard to meet people while school's out," I say, diverting the topic. I have no desire to meet anyone, really. This is the kind of conversation I fall into when I talk to my mom: someone else's. It's like I temporarily occupy some other kid's body and say what I think disgruntled teenage girls say to the mothers who don't understand them.

"A fresh start is what you need," Mom says, playing her own role in the fake conversation. "Some solitude will do you good."

An image of Rae's face glowing under the moon from the other night invades my memory. Mom doesn't want to know who I'm keeping company with, not that she ever really wanted to be bothered with that.

"Well, mission accomplished," I say. "I'm officially a shut-in."

"Would you like some balloons?"

"What?"

"For your pity party. You might need some balloons," she says.

I suddenly feel tired. I lean against the wall of the middle room and slide down, puffing dust around me as I land.

"You're right, Mom." I give up. It's just easier to get this part over with.

"I find it impossible to believe I raised a daughter who could be this much of a victim. You have no idea how hard it is for me to hear you beating yourself up like this."

There's so much I don't understand about her logic, how this has become about *her*.

"I'm sure it's very hard on you," I say.

"I know what that tone means, and I don't care," she says, then away from the phone, "Can I get the check please?" before returning to me. "I didn't do everything right with

you. I think that much is obvious. But I did not raise a victim.
That's for girls with weak mothers."

"This has been great, Mom. Really. But I have to go."

"Wear a rain jacket," she says. "June doesn't mean it's summer yet." Then she hangs up.

I throw my phone across the room, and it lands with a
muted thud on the floor.

I can hear April struggling to move something downstairs.
Maybe that behemoth of an antique sofa. I hear it scrape
against the wood floors below, then she grunts, sighs, tries
again. More scraping.

I know I should go down there and offer to help her. I
can't offer anything to her without it coming out reluctant
at best, downright hateful at worst. And that's the strang-
est part. When I hold my brain still for a moment, when I
demand that it give me one reason for despising her, it can
only conjure the most trivial proof. I wish I could say the
same about my own parents.

I'm so caught up in thoughts of Mom and Dad and April
that I almost don't notice the humming.

Only after it stops do I feel something missing. So when
it starts up again—down the hall somewhere—I'm immediately aware of its presence.

The melody is one I can't quite place, but that isn't what's so jarring. It's the high, resonant sound of the voice that bothers me. Because I know it isn't April's voice. It clearly belongs to a little kid.

I follow the sound, first into the hallway, then to the pink room in the corner, the dirtier twin with the spider occupying the closet. The singing is growing louder, and not just because I'm getting closer. The little voice is pushing on the melody, insisting it be heard.

But as I approach the doorway and the room comes into view, the singing suddenly stops, and all I find are the same dirt smears on the floor that haven't been wiped away yet.

No, that's not entirely true. There's something new on the floor, something that wasn't there earlier. A pony. The same turquoise pony I rescued from the adjacent room our first day here. The one I'm positive I left in what I'm now calling my room, even though it feels like anyone's but mine. And now the abandoned pony is once again adrift among old furniture, lying in the middle of the floor, a tiny yellow brush with a broken handle tangled in its matted hair.

"Who's there?"

It's such a stupid question. I know there's no one here. I can see the entire room. Even the door to the closet stands open, but the memory of that insistent singing is still bouncing between my ears. And something about that pony is unnerving me. I retrace the memory of sliding my fingers over the synthetic hair. There was no yellow brush the last time I held it.

I weave quickly through all the rooms. Nothing else is any more out of place than it was before. I double back to the pink room, then cross the hall to the room with the mural on the wall. The boy's green eyes still stare above the shredded wallpaper at something I can't locate. April's stripped away the rest of the wallpaper, and now I see all of the boy, with his crisp white T-shirt and loose jeans.

"Hey, if someone's in here, it's called trespassing."

I talk a very big game. I'm not sure what I'd do if some little kid came out, hands in the air, ready to surrender.

I scan the room's cluttered corners from the doorway. I trace the piles of furniture for any sign of additional disturbance but find nothing.

I return to the boy on the wall, his face fixed in contemplation; whatever the painter of the mural was thinking at the time, perhaps. But something about his eyes seems different now. Before, they had a dreamy quality to them. Maybe it was in the way the brow was painted, with a tiny crease above. That childlike wonder so many artists like to capture, even if it was a little out of place on a kid who looks like he's only a few years younger than me. But maybe I was just imagining that look because I don't see it now. Instead, I see a smooth surface, a definitive stare. A gaze of purpose.

I follow the painting's line of sight to the little mattress fort that forms a tunnel to the entrance of the closet. The opening of the fort faces the window on the far wall, which I only now notice is open.

Hadn't I closed that the other day to keep the rain out?

I stare at the mattresses, waiting for some sort of movement to give away a hiding child. But there's no indication that anything exists beyond the dirty fabric and busted springs.

I turn to leave, but a sound from behind me pulls me back. It's like someone clearing their throat, but not quite. A gravelly, phlegmy sound, but nothing that forms a word.

Until it does.

"Play."

A laugh burbles out, at first childlike, but then it recedes into the deep, throaty laugh of someone too old to have a voice that young. Then a gasp, and the voice struggles against itself. It tries to form another word and fails, only managing to gurgle another sound that transitions with disturbing speed from that same childlike giggle to something old.

A sharp pain sears through my index finger, and I turn to find that the door frame I've been gripping has shoved a splinter deep under my nail.

I glance toward the boy on the wall for answers, but something else has shifted in the mural. Something I'm positive I would have noticed before. From a branch on one of the trees deep in the distance hangs a tiny rope swing, a plank of wood for a seat.

The gurgling sound from the mattress fort has stopped, and once again, the room is drenched in murky silence.

"Penny, I need to run out to meet—"

April stops midway down the hall when she sees my face. Then she rushes the rest of the way to join me in the doorway.

"What?"

"There's someone . . ." I start to say, but all I can do is point to the mattress fort. I drop my hand when I see my finger trembling in midair.

April points to where I just indicated, her face puckering, a request for details I can't provide.

She takes one step into the room, but before she can go any farther, I'm overcome with some bizarre, protective urge and barrel past her, knocking the first mattress in my path over with fists I didn't notice forming. I release a battle cry from somewhere deep in my gut, one that only reaches my ears after I've thrown the second mattress down to reveal absolutely nothing.

"Jesus, Penny!" April is across the room now, standing clear of the demolition I've initiated in my animal state. She's clutching her cardigan around her, a flimsy shield against my mania.

I topple the rest of the mattresses for good measure, but I can already see that it's utterly pointless. There's no one there.

"Stop! Just stop!" April shouts, even though there's nothing to shout over. The chaos has passed.

"I heard a voice," I say, desperate not to show her how terrified I was a second ago. I'm not sure what I expected to find, but it wasn't a little kid. That I know for sure. And Rae's never sounded like that.

"Well, the window's open," she says, thrusting an arm toward the fluttering curtain. "You must have heard someone outside."

"Who? Nobody lives here, remember? The agent told you that right before you signed your life away for this heap."

April starts to say something, but then her eyes roll to the ceiling, and I can see the record in her head turn over.

"The Realtor. Dammit, I'm going to be late. She still hasn't given me the full inspection report, and I told her I'd meet her in town in . . ." She looks for the watch that's missing from her wrist. "Well, I'm not going to make it in time," she says. Then she remembers my mini-breakdown. "Are you going to be okay if I leave you alone for a few hours?"

I don't answer her. I'm still looking at the mess of mattresses at my feet, the rubble where someone should have been hiding. I continue to scan the room for anything I might have missed.

"Penny?"

April's in front of me now, ducking to find my eyes, but I barely see her. All I see is the boy's face on the wall behind her, his forehead a smooth surface, unworried. And something else. A tiny, almost indistinguishable upturn at the corner of his mouth.

"I'm fine," I say, an automatic response.

"Three hours max," April says on her way out the door, then calling from the bottom of the stairs, "Maybe try priming the walls in that room? Could be a good way to release some of that pent-up energy, huh? But leave the mural. It's so beautiful!"

As soon as I hear the front door shut, I pick my way through the wreckage of the room toward the mural, heading straight for the swing hanging from the most distant tree of the little painted forest. I get up close, my face two feet from the boy's face, his eyes fixed on the remains of the mattress fort. I run my finger over the swing's wood plank, and it smears under my print. I pull back and rub the wet paint between my fingers.

I turn with some reluctance to the destroyed tunnel

leading to the closet and kick one of the fallen mattresses. Now that I'm up close, I see something I couldn't have seen from my perspective in the doorway: a handprint, maybe two-thirds the size of my own, outlined in mud, smeared by falling mattresses.

I bend down to touch it. It's still wet.

From this angle, I see something else, in what I thought was an empty closet. Far in a shadowy corner, the edge of a bright red box no larger than a pack of gum is visible. Ornate yellow letters spell out THE WASHINGTONIAN, EST. 1889. I slide it open to reveal two wooden matchsticks.

Setting the matchbox down, I turn back to the boy on the wall, but his little smirk is as cryptic as before, the changes on the mural fraying the twine holding my nerves together. When I peer closer at his palms, I see something else has changed as well.

The boy's hands, still empty, are no longer identical. One of his palms is now smudged brown.

I hate this painting more and more as each hour passes.

A clicking sound in the room next door pulls me out of my trance, and I return to my temporary quarters. I find Linda lying on the floor, lens to the ceiling.

I consider and discard a thousand possibilities about how she could have wound up here.

Picking her up, I check for damage and find none. Her lens cap dangles from its string.

Then I think back to the last thing I told her. *Show me something new.*

I turn the menu dial to view the register of digital images and see the last two pictures captured are of the ceiling. Then I advance to the previous frame.

I see my own heels, standing in the doorway of the room next door. A long strand of dark hair obscures one side of the picture almost entirely, but there I am and there the mattress fort is.

And there somebody was, taking a picture of all of it from right behind me.

10

THE WEIGHT OF LINDA'S STRAP feels good against the back of my neck, and I close my eyes and count to five, the meditative practice recommended by Mr. Jakes, who freely admitted it was hippy crap but insisted we do it anyway.

But after the other day, I'd say Linda has seen stranger things than meditation.

I brush away the chill that's crept to the surface of my skin probably a hundred times since then. No amount of renovation has been able to fully clear my mind of its questions. April and I primed all the walls in that room after she got back, but the wall with the mural stays. Much like the rest of this house that's inches away from being condemned, April thinks it's charming.

"Charming like marionette puppets are charming," I'd said in response to her assessment. "Like clowns, or those antique dolls with teeth that look real from a distance."

Now, alone while April focuses on all the wrong things and tries to find a repairman who works on ancient ovens (her earlier sense of reason apparently taking a backseat to adorable kitchens), I raise Linda, then slowly open my eyes, my first vision reborn inside the lens.

It's out of focus, a too-tight close-up on a moss-covered tree stump. I click to capture the image, another lesson from Mr. Jakes, who thinks the first shot is the genesis of photographic magic. And while I'm still not sure I believe him, he was always so passionate about his process that I can't imagine doing it any differently.

Now that I've got my first shot, I'm free to fiddle. I pull the focus out and scan my periphery, never taking my eye from behind the viewfinder. I capture a tree, horizontal when it should be upright, its roots exposed and curled into loose coils. I follow my ear and chase a squirrel up a tree, capturing at least three good shots of a rodent in flight. I imagine that series on a vertical display, framed, titled "Heads or Tails." I'm not that great with titles, or photography for that matter, but I click away and try not to think too hard about how this feels exactly the way it used to.

Before tattoos of stars or Melissa Corey or letters written to no one or bonfires in the desert.

I follow another sound, this time to a monstrous tree with needles bunched in knobs all over the branches like spiny tentacles. Spindling arms sway in the ever-present breeze of the woods, and as I stand underneath the tree, I hear better the sound that drew me, though I have no idea what it is I'm hearing. It's crackling, almost as though tiny popcorn kernels are bursting in every crevice of the tree. Now that I'm standing underneath, it feels less like a tree and more like some sort of needled umbrella, the clear kind that hugs maybe a little too closely to the person holding it.

"Bugs." Miller approaches, his burnt red hair looking violet under the tree canopy. "They should be dead by June, but stuff never seems to die out here."

I snap a picture of him without even thinking about it, ducking from under the tree's claustrophobic enclosure.

"Would you think I was weird if I told you it sounded like the trees were chattering?" I say.

"I would probably think you were weird even if you didn't tell me that," he says.

"Thanks," I say.

"You *should* thank me," he says. "Boring people are boring."

"Profound," I say. I notice he's carrying a paper bag and ask, "So what brings you to our creepy little house in the woods?"

"*Your* creepy little house," he says, and I get that same feeling I got from him in the store, right before April came over. Like I crossed some imaginary line.

"I mean the house where we're staying while my stepmom fixes it up to sell it to someone later. Why are you here?" I find a smooth oblong rock beside my foot and pick it up, thinking how it would make a great photo sitting there in the bowl of my palm, but feeling too self-conscious now to take a picture.

He reaches into the bag and pulls out a box containing a Pulverizer Max Strength In-Sink Disposal. "April ordered it the other day. I know the supplier, and he was able to rush deliver it."

"Pays to be connected, huh?"

"Oh yeah, I know all the important people. Plumbers, electricians, general contractors. And from what I know about this house, she's going to need all of them."

"Yeah, well, you might try telling her that. Right now, she seems to be more focused on authentic decor, whatever that means," I say, not wanting to be rude, but wishing I could have just a few more minutes alone to take some pictures in peace. I didn't realize how much that house was getting to me, and even though the woods don't exactly feel inviting, it beats breathing in the stale air of someone else's abandoned problem.

He lifts his chin toward Linda, which I've only half-dropped out of my sightline. "You want to aim that thing somewhere else? Cameras make me nervous."

"Worried you're not photogenic?"

"Point and click feels, I don't know, too fast. You should have to take your time with a picture. Painting's kind of more my thing," he says.

"You know, some might call *that* weird," I say, and it totally sounds like I'm trying to flirt, which just makes me want to be alone even more. I can't remember the last time I even thought about a guy in that way.

You mean aside from the other day in Scoot's?

"And I'd take it as a compliment," he says pointedly, and I let the camera fall around my neck. Even though I know he's referring to my last comment, I can't escape the feeling that he somehow divined my internal dialogue instead.

Miller takes a seat on the fallen tree with its coiled roots, and I fight the urge to ask him not to. It's not my tree, and these aren't my woods. But now that their images reside in my camera, I feel responsible for them. So I sit with Miller, maybe to take some of the ownership. Or maybe to snuff out the feeling that any of this should have an emotional response beyond me just wanting to be alone right now.

"So, what's new? I mean, besides the need to fight the skull-crushing boredom of living like a hermit out in the woods?" he says.

"I'm here against my will, remember?"

"That's right. I forgot. Kidnapped by your evil stepmother."

I pull in a deep breath, then look at him. "It's your garden-variety troubled teen sabbatical," I say, hoping this closes the topic.

Miller flips the Pulverizer box in the air, then turns it between his hands, examining it from every angle.

"You don't seem too troubled," he says, his thumb tracing the *P* on the box over and over. "I've seen troubled, and you don't seem like that."

"Okay, no offense, but whether or not I'm boring or screwed up or whatever else you think I am, I'm not really interested in changing your mind. I just want to take some pictures and get a decent night's sleep in this place and get the next two months over with so I can go back to Seattle and resume my other screwed up existence."

"Whoa, okay," Miller holds his hands in surrender,

standing up from the tree I was so protective of a second ago. Now I wish he'd sit back down.

"I'm sorry," he says. "Look, I got this sense that maybe you wanted to talk the other day. Maybe I was wrong. Maybe I don't know how to tell anymore." He laughs, but there's no humor in it. "I'm nineteen and I run a business. I'm not supposed to be running a business. I'm supposed to be, I don't know, irresponsible or something." He looks at me. "Right?"

I shrug. I thought he just worked at his dad's shop. I didn't think he actually owned it. Then I remember what he said about how his uncle looks after him now that his folks have passed away.

Suddenly, Miller seems a little more screwed up than me.

"You're so asking the wrong person about normal," I say. "I think normal people can have a basic conversation without biting the other person's head off." It's my version of an apology. I'm clearly as good at saying sorry as my mom is.

He lifts the Pulverizer. "I'm going to install this for your stepmom so she'll like me. Then I'm going to go back to the store until we close up for the night. Why don't I come back around eight? I mean, if you're interested in that whole relearning how to talk thing."

I eye the Pulverizer box while I consider everything he just said. Then I look at Linda in my hands. Miller's face is still the last image showing on the screen. The digital version of him looks past me into the woods.

It would be nice to be around someone who doesn't know everything about the last four years, who doesn't look at me and see what I could have done differently.

"Eight o'clock," I say before I can understand what I'm saying.

He backs away, turns, and heads for the house, a smile buried behind a distant gaze.

As he leaves, I raise Linda to my eye, point, and click.

In a warm car under a busted street lamp with a guy I barely know.

Wet clothes plastered to my body under a jacket that isn't mine because I was too stubborn to bring one, even though I knew it would probably rain. But because it was the last thing Mom said to me on the phone, I left my jacket on the hook.

This is probably one of those scenarios I should be avoiding. The kind I used to find myself in whenever I hung out with Rae. Guys we didn't know, guys Rae invited into the car to get to know better. One for her, one for me. And I was done with that long before she knew it.

Rain hammers the roof and windshield, assaulting Miller's car with random fury.

"How can you not drive in the rain and live here?" I ask, sipping the rich coffee from a Ripp's to-go cup.

"I said I don't *like* to. I can, but you don't know the roads here like I do," he says. "The ones leading into the woods are the worst. I have four-wheel-drive, and it's barely enough. I think the real question is why *you're* afraid of getting wet. Aren't you from Seattle originally?"

"I don't *like* to stand under a downpour without a jacket. That's different than being afraid."

"Well, you have a jacket now," he says.

"You can have it back."

"It's cool. I was getting too hot anyway."

"You don't say," I mutter.

"What's that?"

"Nothing, it's just . . . I don't want to give you the wrong idea. When I said I'm going through some stuff, I wasn't lying."

I had planned on telling him that the minute he drove up to the Carver House, but it never quite felt like the right time to say it, and the nicer he is, the stranger this all feels.

"I didn't think you were lying," he says. Now he's squirming, and I've made him feel awkward, and this is exactly why I shouldn't have agreed to go anywhere with him, especially not to his weird uncle's coffee shop, which he clearly had no idea would be the beginning of this exceedingly uncomfortable night, with his uncle giving me the evil eye the whole time until we finally had to take our coffee and sit in Miller's car behind Scoot's.

"It's just that I'm—"

"You're screwed up. Yeah, I get it," he says. "Penny, my parents both died before I turned sixteen, and my grandparents died right after I turned eighteen. What do you think that does to a person?"

There is no possible answer that could fill the gaping space Miller's confession just left.

"So just get it over with and tell me so we can move on to something else."

I try not to feel wounded, but my face must give away some of my struggle because Miller follows, a little more gently, with "Relearning how to talk. Remember?"

The pines outside the window bend and bow against the wind, stoically enduring the abuse. I wonder if they even feel it anymore.

I try to remember anyone ever making me an offer like that. Anyone ever telling me they'd just listen. They'd just let me say it. All of it. Someone who hasn't heard the back story third-hand, who didn't know me before I came to Phoenix, who didn't know me after Melissa Corey. Who didn't need to see me as something just so they could make sense of the next something I became.

Rob made the offer once, but I shut him down flat.

I try to remember the last time I opened my mouth to say anything that meant anything. Suddenly, my jaw feels rusted shut, a hinge unpracticed and lazy.

"Rae." Just hearing her name on my lips is enough to make me want to get out in the rain and walk home.

But saying her name. Not saying her name. Either way, she's with me every day. The hinge loosens a little in the silence that follows—as Miller listens—and I try a little more.

"She was my best friend. Basically my only friend after I moved to Phoenix."

Miller doesn't say anything, so I keep going. I've already come this far.

"It was cool hanging out with her at first. She was like me, but not at all like me, you know? She was the version of me I wanted to be. I mean, I guess I thought I did. But then . . ."

I lose my way, and for some reason, the only thing that brings me back is the sound of Miller sipping his coffee two feet away.

"Then she wasn't what I wanted to be like anymore."

If Miller is following, he doesn't say a word. And maybe

right now, he doesn't think I'm horrible. Maybe right now, he thinks this is all pretty ridiculous. But the rain is starting to let up, and if I'm going to tell him all of it, at least I know I could probably walk the road home and find my way back to the Carver House if he tells me to get out of the car.

"This girl got beat up."

My heart cracks against the impact. A confession I have never, not once, owned out loud.

"I let it happen," I say after the cracked pieces have fallen to the floor of the car, the destruction nearly complete. "This girl, she didn't do anything . . . but Rae hit her like she did. And I let her. Afterward . . ."

Miller says nothing, and I force myself to keep going.

"I knew I was done after that. I couldn't tell if I hated Rae or me more."

I try to swallow the knot in my throat, but it refuses to budge.

"I wrote some things she wasn't supposed to see. Nobody was supposed to see. But I should have known that she would find the notepad because Rae was always going through my stuff. She had this thing about secrets. How they were worse than lies."

I take a sip of my own coffee, but not because I want it. Because I just need a second more before the final confession. I'm not Catholic, but I wonder if this is how it feels behind that little curtain. And if it is, I wonder how Catholics repair their hearts each time. If they have a special glue that mends things by the time they pull the curtain and step out.

"She confronted me, and it was awful. And she got super high because of it, and I didn't stop her when she went off on her own for a walk. I just let her go."

My face is wet. I think at first it's because I never dried the rain off it, but my throat hurts, and now I know I've been practically screaming my story at Miller, who has let me scream and sob my horrible story of my horrible self, and he hasn't said a word in response, which is how I know that everything Rae said to me that night was true.

"Some girl she didn't even know found her."

Miller lets me cry. He lets me shiver under his jacket and wipe my face on the sleeve. He doesn't touch my shoulder or clear his throat or offer me those empty words of recycled sincerity I got from everyone else after it happened. He doesn't even sip his coffee anymore. He just sits there next to me while I empty my soul. I didn't think I had any tears left to sacrifice to this pain, but they must have been there all along, tricking me into believing they'd run dry. And maybe it's because he doesn't know what to say to someone who doesn't really deserve to be crying these types of tears at all. Because it's not like I'm some poor victim. I could have stopped every single thing that happened. I could have led Melissa Corey away from the equipment shed. I could have ripped those pages from my notepad and shredded them to fine strips.

I could have stayed with Rae that night instead of letting her wander into the desert by herself.

When I finally wipe the last of my unearned tears away, I notice that it's stopped raining completely. That's when Miller finally says something.

"So who's in Phoenix?"

I turn to face him now. "What?"

"You're from here, but you moved to Phoenix, and now you're back here. So that means either your whole family moved back so you could get away from what happened, or someone decided you needed to be . . ."

There's a sharp edge to his voice, and even though I'm trying to stay away from anything that can cut me after Rae, something about the way he says it makes me think he might know what it feels like to be—

"Returned," I say. "My mom. She brought me back. Like a sweater with a snag in it."

"Yeah," he says.

We sit in his car for an hour and a half and do absolutely nothing but sip our coffees. The trees dance so hard, they make their own music under all that creaking.

We don't say another word the whole drive back, and the sound of the car door closing behind me echoes in my ears until sleep takes me several hours later.

11

THE BOY FROM THE PAINTING calls to me by name, invading my sleep with uninvited familiarity. At the end of my first exhale, I'm in the room at the end of the hall, standing before the mural. I spot the swing in the corner on the tree, the muddy hand of the boy before me, and I know I don't want to be here.

But the boy doesn't care. The paint that holds him to the wall cracks and crumbles to fine dust, leaving snowy peaks of debris atop the discarded wallpaper below. He's sitting in the grass painted below his brushstroked feet, legs crossed over each other, kneecaps jutting to each end of the room.

"How are you talking to me?" I ask him, my pajamas too thin to block the night air passing through the open window I can't believe April or I didn't shut.

"I have to show you something."

"I want to sleep," I tell the boy.

"Maybe you are sleeping. Do you know the difference anymore?" he asks me, challenging. He's younger than me, but authoritative. Dominant. His emerald eyes bury me under their weight.

"Well, what does the difference feel like to you?" I ask him.

He looks toward the open window, silent for a moment before muttering, "It all feels like I'm walking through mud."

I look at his hand again, and as though he sees me noticing, he curls it into a fist, concealing the evidence he already left behind.

I continue to stand there, growing less aware of the chill creeping beneath my pajamas and more aware of the blades of painted grass on the wall that bend and sway impossibly under the breeze sliding through the open window.

"I have to show you," he insists, and something about his eyes, wide and familiar, make me walk toward the wall, my legs like lead, my own eyes lazily searching the wall for what he wants to show me.

The brushstrokes bend backward and swirl in opposing directions, reconstituting to create an entirely new picture, one that I can see because I'm a part of it now, witnessing the moving painting beside the boy who recedes to a corner just out of sight. But he's there, watching. Showing me.

We're in a house I've never seen before.

"It's time, Doris."

A small woman nods in response, hardly hearing the tall man behind her, but flinching at his touch when he approaches. She's clutching a wool coat, wringing the scratchy thing in her hands.

"He'll need a jacket. There was a cold snap."

"It's time to go," the man says again, a response they both seem to think is inadequate, their bodies sloped away from each other.

The man walks out the door without another word, and I hear the car start somewhere outside.

She turns, her eyes searching even though there's a small boy not more than eight years old right in front of her. A boy with burnt red hair. Then she crouches, but she doesn't reach out to the boy.

"Uncle Dom is on his way over. Don't open the door for anyone else, okay? Mommy needs to go lie down for a while."

"Why can't we go with Dad?" the boy asks.

"Only Uncle Dom, okay, sweetie? Mommy just needs to lie down."

She shuffles to the bedroom, her feet never quite leaving the floor.

Her bedroom door hangs on its hinge, refusing to close all the way, and I follow as the little boy slips down to the basement as soon as the bedsprings from her bedroom sigh.

In the basement, the boy slides a box aside marked "Jack, 1993–1995" and another marked "Taxes" until he finds the one he's looking for. From the box marked "Xmas," he pulls Matchbox cars and University of Washington pennants, a plastic bronze trophy of a pitcher on the mound twisted in perpetual freeze. He shoves those and the actual Christmas decorations aside in favor of the real prize—a Huskies hat that he slides over his head, folding the bill until it fits.

Upstairs, a knock at the door. The boy piles the trophy and the cars and the pennants back into the box, then pushes the other boxes back into place, the only evidence of his presence a tiny drag mark in the dust on the floor. He runs up the stairs two at a time and opens the door to a man I recognize from a framed newspaper clipping, the smell of coffee now strong in my nose.

"What's this?" the man asks, flicking the bill of the boy's hat.

The boy takes it off quickly, hiding his face from his uncle, but not fast enough.

The man stays in the doorway for a second, and the boy twists the hat in his hand before shoving it into a bookcase and closing the front door behind his uncle, who eyes the bookcase now too.

"She's asleep," the boy tells him, even though the man never asked.

He walks past the boy and knocks softly on the open bedroom door anyway. He waits for a muffled answer, then goes inside and closes the door behind him.

"I know," I hear the boy's uncle say. "Shhh, I know. You have to be strong. You have one son in there who can't understand—"

"How could he understand? I can't even understand! We're monsters, Dominic."

"If you really feel that way, then it's not too late."

"No, Dom. No. I'm not having this conversation again. I can't."

"I could leave right now. I could get to Burt in enough time."

"Don't you see? It's already too late. Once we made the decision . . . there's no turning back from that."

"*The price for that decision was too high. The Doris I know would never have paid it. Why didn't you let me keep trying? He needed help, not—*"

"*You didn't live with him, Dominic. You didn't see what we saw. And the Doris you knew? She died a long time ago. Now let me sleep this day away. Please, just let me sleep it away.*"

The boy's mother doesn't move from bed all day. She doesn't turn over. She doesn't shift. She lies in her room and stares at the far wall, visible from the hallway by the crack in the door the boy's uncle left when he finally succumbed to her wish to be left alone. Her face reflects on the vanity mirror.

The boy's uncle walks from the living room to the kitchen, then back to the living room, then back to the kitchen. He paces all day. The boy stays in his room, absently moving his toy cars from surface to surface, lining them up, lifting his head of embers at each crack and click from somewhere in the house.

By the time the day bleeds into night, the boy puts himself to bed. He scratches at his arms nervously until little trickles of blood smear his skin and crust underneath his fingernails. He stares at the ceiling, moonlight turning his face a sickly green.

A key finally rattles the lock.

"*Doris,*" the boy's uncle says.

Bedsprings creak to life.

"*Doris!*" he says louder, but his voice shakes.

The bedroom door at the end of the hall opens, and the little boy leaves his bed too, hovering inside his own doorway. The woman leans against the boy's uncle as the front door opens and her husband comes in, looking past her. Past them all.

A stooped figure enters behind the husband, a head bowed, a form so caked in earth it looks more like a root than a person. The only clue that it's human lies in the whites of two wide eyes.

The woman goes limp against the boy's uncle. Her hand flies to her mouth, her words hiding behind it.

"My baby." The woman pulls out of the uncle's support and folds herself around the muddied thing. She breathes words muffled under dirt-clotted hair. She strokes the cheeks of a face barely visible, clutches a body that stiffens against her, kisses hands that release small piles of soil on the floor before uncurling.

The small boy in the bedroom doorway looks at his own empty hands and digs the dried blood from underneath his fingernails, eyes traveling back to the figure in his mother's arms with reluctance.

Then he looks at his uncle, but his uncle is staring at the filthy figure in front of him too.

And though the uncle opens his mouth to say something first, the little boy robs him of his words, blurting a confession that saps the room of its last remaining sound.

"That's not him."

Sleep launches me from unconsciousness like a ball from its cannon. But even though I'm not in the dream anymore, I still feel somehow like I'm flying, the bed under my legs a million miles away.

I find the floor, still not trusting my feet, but with each step, the house around me feels a tiny bit more real. I make my way to the room at the end of the hall and stand before the boy in the mural, painted face locked in far-off wonder, just as it was the last time I saw it. The last time I saw it while I was awake, that is.

It should make me feel better, but it doesn't. Whatever happened while I was sleeping wasn't a dream. Not like any dream I've ever had. I look down at my hands and there, just visible under the moon's invading light, is the thinnest layer of dried paint tracing the ridges of my fingerprints. I examine one of my fingernails a little closer and dig a tiny clump of dried paint from underneath it.

I look at the boy in the painting.

"What the hell did you just show me?"

I dare him to lure me back in so I can tell him to go to hell this time, but a sound from the middle bedroom draws me back.

"Jesus, no wonder I can't sleep in this place."

I'm not even back in the room before I conclude that it's tapping.

I've heard the sound enough. More than enough.

"I'm not going outside," I tell Rae. I'm tired of her. I'm just plain tired. After her last visit to me the other night. After that weirdness with the mattresses. After my epic confession of my overall horribleness to Miller. After this bizarre mural I've already vowed to paint over first thing in the morning, even if it takes five gallons of primer and ruins all of April's "charm."

Tap. Taptaptap.

"Go *away!*" I tell Rae, thinking my voice must be pretty loud, loud enough to wake April, but no longer caring. She can hear me lose my last marble if she wants to.

Taptaptaptaptap.

"Would you just leave me—" I stop, because I see something I shouldn't when I reach the room and look to the window. Impossibly, I see the briefest outline of a hand leaving the pane. But the smudge where it was is unmistakable. A handprint, smaller than mine, in the lower corner, right where I found one in the room across the hall on our first day in the Carver House.

I sneak to the window, expecting to see the same branch tickling the glass I saw the other night. Needing to see the same purple curls on the other end of that branch. But what I see when I look out the window is not Rae. It's the shadowed figure of a little girl, long dark hair obscuring her face.

She wears a white summer dress, her bare feet and hands and arms and legs making me cold just knowing they're exposed in the chilly night air.

I open the window and consider calling out to her. But once I've pushed the window open, I can't think of what I should say.

She doesn't give me an opportunity. Instead, she turns on her bare heel and darts into the woods behind her.

"Hey!" I yell without thinking.

I pull my jeans over my nightshirt and grab the nearest sweater, locating my boots by the back kitchen door where I left them after Miller dropped me off.

I slam the door behind me and stumble outside, finding myself once again at the base of the tree below my bedroom window. I peer into the darkness in the direction I saw the girl go and have just about convinced myself she was never there when I see the slim impression of two feet, sunken deep into the mud by the tree. Sunken as though a heavy weight had pushed the girl, rooted her to that spot.

"Hey, are you out there?" I call. I take a few steps into the woods.

A twig snaps in response. I take another step forward.

"It's okay," I say, hoping I'm not terrifying this kid more than she might already be.

After the longest silence yet, a scream slices the air. I back into one of the trunks and feel the cool bark catch the balance I've lost. My heart knocks against my ribs.

I scan the darkness before me, my eye seeking out the movement of each swaying branch. The night breeze reaches beneath my sweater.

"I'm here!" I call stupidly. Is that supposed to make her feel better? I try to make my brain rest on a reason for the little girl being out in the woods, and though I can conjure several possibilities, all of which are horrifying, I push myself from the tree and launch into the forest, using my hands as guides, the needles snagging whatever clothing they can reach.

I will April to hear what's going on, but I don't dare go back into the house to get her and risk losing this poor girl.

I train my ears and wait for another clue as to the direction she might have gone. Another breeze finds its way through my clothes.

"Call out if you can hear me!" I yell to the girl—and maybe a little to April—then watch my breath form in front of my face. I silently beg the moon to cut through the tree line and give me at least a glimpse of the path in front of me.

I stop for a moment to find my bearings, wondering for the first time how I might find my way back, if in fact I do find this girl. And suddenly, the memory of the rest stop floods over me.

"It was just Rae that time," I remind myself. My voice sounds so assured, so certain, I almost believe it.

"Can you hear me?" I try again.

And then I hear breathing.

The short puffs, the gulps in between that try to dampen a throat dried by panting. I hold so still, I think my pulse might reverberate through my feet and vibrate the forest floor. I scan the darkness, and my vision—finally beginning to adapt to the inky night—traces the outline of a small structure that looks from this distance like a large wooden shed.

The trees around me groan, and though I know it's not possible, they feel closer to me now, their cold bark suddenly visible in my periphery.

Then, from the side of one of the dark edges of the structure, I see silver clouds of air, formed at the ends of the smallest set of lips.

"Hey, it's okay! I'm not going to hurt you!" I call. But before I can take another step forward, the breath dissipates, the mouth retreats, and I hear a door creak on a set of rusted hinges and slam shut.

"Hey!" I call, plowing forward and finding a chipped green door on its splintered frame. I look down and see the vaguest impressions of two small feet left in the mud.

"If you disappeared tonight, do you think anyone would notice?"

I whirl around, my hand slamming against the knob of the splintering green door. Rae's breath is still warm against my ear. Now she stands several paces away, giggling in a way that's far too immature for her.

Another memory attacks, this one the grotesque laughter coming from beneath the mattresses in the room at the end of the hall.

"Where is she?" I demand, brushing off the memory and taking a step toward Rae.

"You know when I stopped wondering if anyone would miss me if I left?" she asks. "After my mom disappeared for three days. She drove to Flagstaff with some guy she barely knew so they could see the snow fall under the moonlight. She told me all about it when she got back, how it looked like fairies dropping little soapsuds from the highest treetops. I was eleven years old. I didn't think she was ever coming back. I ate cereal nine meals in a row."

I want to tell her she told me that story years ago. I want to tell her I'm not even sure I believe her. I watched her lie about so many things to so many other people just so they would see her as damaged. But right now, all I can think about is that girl.

"Where is she, Rae?"

"My mom? Taos. At least at last check. I think she had me cremated just so she could have an excuse to scatter my ashes in a place she'd always wanted to go."

"The girl!" I yell at her.

"I don't know, and I don't really give a shit," Rae says, suddenly serious.

I turn back to the shed and try the door, which resists my attempt so strongly I wonder how it could be rusted shut if I just heard it open a second ago.

I walk around the perimeter searching for any sign of the girl, but all I find when I come back is Rae.

"Did you hear the one about the coyote?" she says, her eyes smiling but her mouth turned to a solemn frown.

"It's been you this whole time," I accuse, not fully believing it. But she's standing right here, and the memory of the little girl is already growing cloudy in my mind.

"They said all they found was my shoe. Gross, right? The shit people come up with. You know it was that chick with the tacky dolphin tattoo that found me. Screaming her head off like she was the one who had something to be afraid of."

I look once more over Rae's shoulder. The woods only get deeper after that, and I know I won't be able to see a thing in there. Not with that thick tree cover. I pull my sweater closer to my body and hunch my shoulders against the latest chill to find its way under my clothes.

"They talk about how serial killers lack empathy, but teenagers, I think they're the real sociopaths," Rae says.

This is when I give up. I take step after step back toward the house, the trees crossing their branches the way I cross my arms over my stomach. I must have cut a different path through the woods when I was chasing the imaginary girl. This path feels thicker, the trees reluctant to let me through.

"I saw what you did to that poor girl's face, by the way," Rae says from behind me. "In the girls' room. Respectable."

I stop walking and almost turn. But this is what she wants, and I will not say another word to her.

"I mean it, Penny. Really, really commendable. She was probably already on her way to rhinoplasty anyway, but you sped things along for her, I'm guessing."

I start walking again, and her steps are just out of sync with mine, an inconsistent rhythm that grates on my nerves enough to make me clamp my hands over my ears and tug.

"But it doesn't really make up for it. You know that, right?"

The air feels thicker around me. I suddenly think I

know how the ground feels with all those pine needles choking up the surface, blocking the air above.

"See, here's the thing. When I couldn't feel my hands. When I couldn't hear anything but the blood pushing through my veins, crowding out all the rest of the noise from the bonfire off in the distance. When I thought my head was going to lift off of my neck and my heart pressed against the inside of my chest and wouldn't back away. When I heard you laughing at someone's stupid joke because you thought you were so fucking right and I was so fucking wrong, and you'd won, and good for you for being the person more deserving of a life outside of me. When all that happened, you were exactly where you told me you were going to be from now on. *Without* me. And I was exactly where you wanted to leave me. Alone."

I can see the silver outline of the Carver House's rooftop searching above the tree line, but I can't feel my feet on the ground. I can barely feel the icy chill beneath my sweater anymore, either. All I can hear is Rae's voice.

"So I don't know why you're so unhappy, Penny. You got everything you asked for in those letters. You got every single thing you wanted."

She spins me by my shoulder to face her, with her iridescent skin and her perfectly pinned curls. "So why am I still here?" she asks me.

My face is wet with the same undeserved tears from Miller's car. The same tears I thought I was done crying. The same tears I don't want to cry anymore.

"Go home, Penny," she says, then walks backward into the shadows of the woods, the place she lives now.

"And Penny," she says just before I've broken free of the trees. I can't see her anymore. I can only hear her voice. "These kids, they aren't playing around, you know. They have something to say. But you know what my dear old mom always used to say: Not all voices deserve to be heard."

12

I FEEL LIKE A TRUCK hit me this morning. Worse than a hangover. After I got back to bed last night, it took me another three hours to fall asleep. When I finally nodded off, I could see the first shoots of sunlight peeking through the clouds. That couldn't have been more than three minutes ago. But that doesn't seem to matter to April.

"Ugh, you and Rob could compete for the prize of most hours slept in daylight."

I drag the pillow over my head. It can't possibly be that late. It's not my fault she's probably been pacing the floors since dawn.

"Seriously, Penny, I need your skills."

I lift a corner of the pillow and bring her into focus with

some difficulty. She's got her hands up in mirrored Ls, miming what I guess is supposed to resemble me holding Linda. "Click click," she says, confirming my suspicion.

"April, I need to tell you something," I say, lack of sleep and caffeine clouding my judgment. The effects of last night have not yet worn off, and I'm still struggling to make sense of any of it.

"Something weird happened. I think . . . I think I saw someone in the woods."

April shakes her head. "Impossible. We're off the beaten path, remember? No one for miles. That's the pitch I'm working on anyway. But 'off the beaten path' sounds a little, I don't know, like camping. Maybe something more like 'rustic hideaway.'"

I put a palm to my temple and press hard. "No, I mean . . . okay, have you noticed anything about this place . . . I don't know . . . odd, or . . . ?"

"Jesus, Penny, not this again. I swear to God, it's like you're just looking for excuses to sabotage this whole thing for me!"

This wakes me up. I guess I shouldn't be surprised at April's irritation, but I am. Because this is more than irritation. This is a full-on accusation.

"Is this a bad time?" I ask.

She closes her eyes. "I'm sorry. And yes. Sort of," she says.

I do nothing to mask my dissatisfaction with her answer.

"It's just that I finally got a plumber to call me back, and if I don't meet him at his shop in thirty minutes, who knows if I'll ever get that toilet in my room to stop running. It's kept me up for the past four nights straight."

Now that I look a little closer at April, I see the faintest trace of dark crescent moons peering out under a heavy spattering of concealer.

"Since when do you go to see a plumber? Are you bringing the toilet to him or something?" I ask. I refrain from asking whatever happened with the Realtor. I'm going to take it on faith that the roof and the floor below aren't milliseconds from collapsing, even though faith has an extra-short expiration with me these days.

She holds her hands up in a move that reminds me of Rob so much I feel a sudden twinge of loneliness. "I know. Honestly, I'm really starting to feel like I'm getting the runaround. It's getting old. And apparently, not a single contractor from Tacoma or anywhere else will touch the work. Something about a city ordinance Point Finney passed ages ago to keep work local. Anyway, I was wondering if you maybe wanted to come into town with me. Bring the ole camera, snap some pictures."

I drop my head back down on the pillow. The prospect of

getting out of bed hardly even seems like a possibility at this point. And the thought of another trip into town doesn't exactly tempt me. In three seconds, I conjure an image of an encore of the scene in Maggie's Grocery. But then I look at April, her eyes still managing to sparkle despite the heavy shadow cast over the rest of her face, and I remember that she's the one who's actually trying, even if that optimism is starting to show signs of cracking. So I let my feet drop to the floor and get dressed as fast as I can, convincing April with some difficulty to let me at least brush my teeth before we hit the road.

"I haven't been able to get an electrician to call me back," April says as her old jeep searches out every single hole and struggles to recover traction on the dirt road leading into town.

"Guess they don't need the work," I say, watching the smear of green and brown pass through Linda's lens. "Your tires might, though."

"What were you asking me before?" April says, ignoring the comment about her car. It wasn't a dig. I sincerely think we might slide off the road at any second.

I set Linda back in my lap. "Nothing. It's not important."

April seems to want to ask me more, but we arrive at our destination quicker than I think either of us was expecting, which is odd considering she's the one driving.

"Wait, I thought we were going into town."

"Well, I'm going into town, but I thought maybe you could start with some photographs here?"

I look between Ripp's and Scoot's, knowing after our last visit that Scoot's won't open for another half hour and Ripp's is the only place I could possibly hang out while I wait.

"Come on, Penny," April says, pleading like she's the teenager in the car. "It would be so great to add some environmental details to the sales materials. Anyone investing in a bed-and-breakfast is going to want to know there's an adorable general store and coffee shop nearby."

"Yeah, except the coffee shop owner—"

"Is just a little eccentric," she finishes. "Besides, he liked you just fine. It was me who obviously rubbed him the wrong way."

"Thanks for that, by the way," I say, not caring now if she knows how annoyed I am. "This is a total bait-and-switch, and you know it."

"I know," April says. "I know, I am truly an awful person. And I owe you big. But if you don't get out of the car now, I'm going to be late, and that toilet will run into perpetuity, and I think I might tear my hair out if I have to hear it flushing on its own for one more night."

I'm already getting out of the car just so I can hear anything but the sound of her pleading.

"Whatever you want for dinner tonight!" she hollers as she backs out of the dirt parking lot and drives away. "Your choice!"

And in a flash of dust and rubber, she's gone, and I'm standing in front of Ripp's holding Linda, wondering if Miller would think I'm a stalker if I tapped on the door and begged him to let me in early. And considering he hasn't texted or stopped by since I unloaded on him the other night, that possibility has just become a mini reality.

Taking the opportunity to reconnect with civilization now that I have a decent cell signal, I text Rob.

Your mom's officially losing it.

I wait for a response but get none, not that I'd expect him to know how to respond to that, and eventually, my desperate need for coffee wins out. I enter Ripp's as quietly as I can, considering for a moment that maybe Ripp won't be there today. Maybe some random barista who's never met me or April will take my order instead.

But as I survey the utterly empty coffee shop, the door slamming shut despite my best effort to catch it, I know I'm not going to get my wish. There he is, his compact body leaning on the counter, frowning as I take another step inside.

"Um, morning," I say, since one of us has to and he's clearly not making the first move.

He apparently doesn't think he needs to make the second move, either. Instead, he disappears behind one of the steaming latte machines, and the whir of the milk steamer fills the dense silence of his otherwise pleasant little shop.

I continue to walk around the café, knowing I'll eventually make my way to the counter, knowing he'll have to pour me a cup of coffee and take my money, knowing I'll have to look him in the eye and ask him without actually asking him if he could please not hate me so much. It's strange, but years of standing by Rae's side in order to be feared didn't leave me with the coat of armor I was hoping for. Instead, it just left me feeling like I was looking down at myself from somewhere on the moon. I've had enough of sensing the wariness of other people.

Right now, I like the sound of the milk steamer, and I like the warmth of his shop, and I'd prefer to look at the newspaper clippings and think about anything other than the dream or whatever it was I had last night, or the little girl I still can't get out of my head, or the way Rae left me with the vaguest of warnings after the heftiest of verbal beatings.

I return to the same framed newspaper clipping I landed on the first time I ventured in here with April. Ripp looking proud in his apron, confident in the love and support of his town. I think about the way the clerk Roberta formed an invisible bubble around her customer, George.

The frame is crooked on the wall, but that isn't what gets my attention first. Just as before, my eye travels to the headline that's cut off at the bottom, the one announcing ANOTHER LOCAL TEEN FOUND IN NOR—. It's not too hard to fill in the blank: North Woods. That's what they call the woods where the Carver House is.

I brush the hairs down on my arms as I think about what Rae said: *"They have something to say. . . ."* Isn't that what she said? But because it was Rae, it could have meant everything and nothing at the same time. Sometimes she just says shit.

I lift my finger to straighten the frame.

"You're the latte, right?"

Startled, I pull my finger away too fast, hooking it on the frame and bringing the entire thing down to the wood floor with a crash of glass and plywood.

"I'm so sorry," I groan. "I'm a total klutz."

"Nah," he grumbles, that richness from the first time he spoke to me in his voice again. "That nail's been loose for a while now."

He runs to the back and returns with a broom and dust pan. He hands me the pan and I hold it while he sweeps the shards, careful not to spray any of the stray dust and coffee grounds on me. I look up at the table where he's left me a latte I didn't even have to ask for.

"I'm glad you came back in," he says. "Been hoping you might. I feel like I ought to apologize."

I don't say anything because I agree.

"It's a small town, you know? Guess I'm not too used to seeing outsiders. Forgot how to behave and all that."

I lift the newspaper clipping gingerly from the remaining shards, unfolding it to shake out the splinters of glass. While Ripp is busy sweeping, I see that indeed the rest of the headline reads North Woods. The story's dated July 2004, and there's a row of four pictures beneath it, each clearly a school headshot of a kid. And though I want to read what the story describes, I can't tear my eyes away from one of the images, the boy in the middle, the one with burnt red hair and dark green eyes. The boy from the wall. The one I'd been assuming this whole time must be Miller.

The caption beneath it reads JACK DODSON, 14.

Ripp takes the paper from my hand and folds it without a word, tucking it into the pocket of his apron before I can register what I've just seen.

"Coffee's gonna get cold," Ripp says, pointing to the mug on the table without looking at me.

"Do you know what time Scoot's opens today?" I ask, but

he's ducked behind the counter again, busying himself with something I can't see.

"Not open today," he says.

"Seriously? I thought general stores were open, like, all the time."

"Even owners of general stores get sick."

"Miller's sick?"

He steps into sight again, but remains behind the counter. "And contagious," he says pointedly.

I duck under the not-so-subtle implication that I'm some kind of bad influence he's trying to keep from his nephew and decide to take a page from April's book. It seems Ripp's forgotten how to "behave and all that" again.

"Who were those kids?" I ask.

He doesn't say anything, so I know I've touched on something, though I couldn't begin to say what.

"One of them, the one named Jack? He looks exactly like Miller," I say this part a little softer. If I'm right—if that kid is somehow related to Miller, which he clearly is if he shares the same last name—then that would make him somehow related to Ripp, too. And if he went missing in the woods with those other kids, then chances are there's some sort of traumatic story that accompanies it.

So when Ripp comes around the corner to face me without the counter or anything but the coffee he gave me to separate us, I'm a little surprised. Surprised and intimidated.

"What do you want to know?" he asks. "Just get it all out now. This'll be the first and the last conversation I have about any of it. Damn reporters took it out of me and the rest of the families years ago. I got no more stomach for it, so ask all you want now, and don't ask ever again. Clear?"

I search his eyes for the malevolence he is trying to level me with, but all I find is poorly concealed pain. His eyes shift between mine, searching for something in me as well, but good luck finding it, buddy. I can't even find it myself.

"Who was he?"

"Jack. My sister's oldest son."

"Oldest?"

Ripp closes his eyes, and when he opens them, his pupils have all but disappeared they're so small.

"Jack was the oldest. Then Danny. Then Miller."

"And Jack went missing?"

"With three others, yes. In the North Woods."

"Near where I'm living?" I ask before I consider what it'll mean if he tells me I'm right.

But he says nothing. Instead, he crosses his hands over his chest and takes a deep breath.

"Near the Carver House?" I try again. Again, he doesn't

answer, and I think it might be time to slam this latte and get the hell out of here, but he surprises me and nods instead.

"Was he . . . were they okay? The kids who . . . got lost?"

His pupils shrink a little more. "They came back. It was a miracle, and it was a long time ago. All the kids went their own ways. Miller stayed."

And though he continues to stand where he is, eyes trained more steadily on mine now, I know that the conversation is over. I take one more sip of my latte and pull out my wallet to pay him.

He shakes his head. "It's part of the apology," he says, and I accept it even though I know it's also so he can get me out the door faster.

As I push the door open to leave, he offers me one last statement. "Miller's already been through enough."

He doesn't say more, just walks back behind the counter to wipe the equipment he's been wiping all morning.

And though he's given me answers to questions I never asked, I feel more adrift than ever. And April isn't coming to get me anytime soon.

13

It took surprisingly little for me to abscond with April's car tonight. After another night of sandwiches (we're burning through our Maggie's Grocery rations at breakneck speed) and a rundown of the disappointing meeting with the plumber (who will definitely not be fixing the toilet or any other pipe "anywhere near those godforsaken woods"), I think she was still feeling guilty enough about this morning to let me meet up with Miller. She also had an ulterior motive.

"See if he knows anybody," she said before I could shut the door. "I got the cold shoulder at the hardware store today. I can't even change a doorknob! And I've bought up all the paint supplies from Scoot's, and—" She'd stopped there to gather herself before starting again. "Seriously, Penny. If we don't get someone to take a look at the basics, we're never going to get this project done by August. We need to get some people out here."

Translation: I just sank a ton of money into a house I'm never going to be able to sell. Now I'm the proud new owner of a dilapidated wreck in the middle of the woods.

But while I was in a hurry to leave the Carver House, I'm not sure I'm in much more comfortable company now. It's hard to say what I thought Miller's house might look like. He looks vaguely like a medieval woodsman—or at least what I imagine a nineteen-year-old medieval woodsman might look like—so I suppose I thought he'd live in a wood cabin forged by his own hands. The Carver House is the only other house I've been in since we got to Point Finney, so maybe I figured all the houses looked like that.

But not Miller's house. Miller lives in a trailer.

"I own it," he says.

My face goes hot, and before I can catch myself, I say, "I'm sorry."

Now we both look sorry. Me for thinking it, then saying it, then looking embarrassed for saying it. Miller for guessing what I was thinking, then saying what he thought I was thinking, then for bringing the silence to a fresh state of awkwardness.

"My pop left it to my grandparents when he died," he says, cracking the silence with another try. "And when my grandparents died, they left it to me. So now I don't have rent to pay. It's clean, and it's mine. Which I already said, so now I'm just starting to sound crazy."

The worst part is that I wasn't thinking it was ugly. I wasn't thinking anything other than the place looked lonely. There's only space for one person to live here. I can see from one end of the trailer to the other right from the front door. A little twin bed at the back, neatly covered with a plaid comforter. A tiny shower stall next to a toilet and miniature sink jutting from the wall of the bathroom. A recliner by a small television, a kitchenette with exactly one cupboard and a coffeemaker below it. Everything made for one.

But there's no way to tell him all that now, so I take the coffee he offers me and lean against the kitchen counter so I don't claim the only chair.

From that angle, I see something I didn't expect: a tower of canvases organized on a sturdy wooden scaffolding in the one space not taken up by the efficiently arranged furniture attached to the walls and floor. The edges of the tightly pulled white canvases reveal tiny hints about what exists on their faces—smatterings and smears of navy blue and gray, red and buttery yellow.

"Oh my God, are these all yours?"

Miller's face locks up for a second behind his coffee mug, and I worry that I've embarrassed him again, but it doesn't look like embarrassment. It's that same warning that tells me I've crossed the line, the one I can't see.

But the tightness melts away behind a ripple of steam from his mug, and soon I'm looking at a more familiar expression on Miller—bemusement.

"Yeah, not exactly a fancy studio, but it works for me, I guess."

"Seriously, Miller, there must be fifty paintings here."

The largest canvases reside at the bottom of the tower. They're maybe four feet square, and I crouch to see what's exposed. The edges that peek out display a midnight blue sky with a crescent moon adorning its upper corner. Something in the way the brushstrokes move along the canvases makes my stomach flip, but I can't see enough of the paintings to guess why.

"Sixty-four," he says. "I'm not the fastest, I've just been doing it for a while. I'm not trained, though. Don't look too closely."

I smile a little at the ferocious modesty he's clearly inherited from his uncle.

I peer through the gaps between shelves to catch glimpses

of a familiar scene in almost every canvas. The top of a night sky, the silver outlines of evergreens interrupting the midnight haze. A landscape dotted by the living things of the forest.

When my stomach twitches again, I realize why.

"Miller, this is . . ." I start to say, trying to slide one canvas from its resting place.

"Let me. It's a little tricky," Miller says, taking the edge of the canvas from my fingers and positioning his whole body against the shelf tower, pressing his hands against the canvases below it and pulling down, slowly easing the shelves off the wooden frames so as not to mar the paintings above. I try to turn away from the sight of his bicep tensing against the sleeve of his T-shirt.

Actually, I don't try that hard. That is, until Miller notices me noticing.

He falters slightly when the entire tower starts to lean toward me. He shifts his weight, and I'm no longer focused on Miller and instead am frantically searching for the best place to stand if it comes crashing down. But there's no place to go, so I back myself into the recliner, looking absurdly like I'm taking a rest while Miller overcorrects and pushes in the other direction, leans against it from the opposite side, and finally steadies the stack to a precarious but still-standing tower.

"Well, that was dramati—"

Before I can finish, the smallest canvas all the way at the top topples to the floor between us, making me yelp.

". . . dramatic," I say.

Miller scoops up the tiny six-by-six-inch painting, and when I look at the thin carpeting at his feet, I see tiny tufts of purple and blue, white and green sticking up from the floor. Miller is frowning at the canvas in his hands, a child that's maybe disappointed him.

It could just as easily be a mirror he's staring into. Or a framed newspaper article in his uncle's café. Even the frowns of these identical faces sag along the same arc. If not for the age difference, he and Jack could have been twins.

"Is it ruined?" I ask, my voice an interruption. I hate myself for ever trying to get a closer look. I just had to see.

"Nah." He frowns, and I know neither of us is convinced. "That's the beauty of paint. No matter how it turns out, you can always paint over it, start again."

We stand in silence for a moment before he seems to snap out of it and asks, "So what brings you to my humble abode?"

"I heard you were contagious," I say, recovering a little more slowly. "I like to live on the edge."

His face flashes red, mocking his hair. "Oh. Yeah. See, here's the thing. I don't get a day off unless I'm—"

"Sick," I say.

He shrugs. "Sometimes I just can't take it, you know? It's not like running that store is what I signed up for.

Ripp's gravelly voice crowds my ear. *"Miller stayed."*

"I can't remember the last time I hung out with anyone, really. I mean, until the other night . . ."

I duck under the memory of my immortal meltdown and try instead to piece together the scraps of his life, what he's shared, what his uncle has revealed, even if reluctantly. I set aside mortification and think back to the other night, how he sat with me while I told him all about awful me, and he sat there and listened and drove me home when it was all over. I think about how I texted him tonight, how he responded right away with a simple yet effective, "You should come over."

I wonder how much of his soul he's been waiting to empty.

"I think you should let me hang out with you some night."

I thought he'd said it for my sake, that he felt sorry for me. But maybe I had it all wrong. Maybe he's just as alone as I am.

Now Miller leans against the kitchenette counter, and I curl my legs under me on the recliner, leaning toward him.

"I heard a rumor, and I need your help," I say.

"Rumors. That's something I don't miss about high school," he says, rubbing his chin, then moving to the back of his neck.

"It's about the house," I start cautiously. With the paint of Jack still drying like blood on the carpet, I don't want to press on any fresh wounds.

"Can you be a little more specific?"

I strive for patience. Now more than ever, I know he knows what house I'm talking about.

"The Carver House. The one my stepmom is fixing up. The one we're living in." I take a sip of coffee, which is already cold. Then I go for broke. "Your old house."

Miller's head scoots back on his neck, and confusion gives way to understanding in the time it takes for him to slowly blink. "Right. The wall." His eyes shift without permission to his scaffolding. "That was just a place I went to paint after my parents died . . . that was never my house."

He might as well be talking to me from another galaxy he's so far away.

"My uncle, he's the one who always encouraged us to do the creative stuff, even though Jack never really got into it. And my pop wasn't big on all that. After my folks were gone, my uncle thought it'd be good if I put all of my feelings into painting. Coping or whatever."

Miller's been through enough. That's what Ripp warned me about, and here I am dredging up all the traumatic memories of how his brother went missing in the woods, how he's had to paint him onto sixty-four different canvases ever since just to cope.

I watch the green of Miller's eyes drain a little of their piney color. It looks as though an entire lifetime passes behind them.

"He just didn't want me 'coping' in that house, I guess."

After a moment, the saturation of green returns, and he finds me, shrugging off that lifetime with some effort. But not before I see the faintest glimpse of a small boy lining cars along the furniture in his room, the habit of quiet pretending that lonely kids fall into.

"It's old. The house, I mean, if that's what you're asking. That usually means old and neglected. Or so my buddies tell me."

"Right," I say. "Your contractor buddies. Remind me to ask you about that later." Sorry April, but plumbing is far down on my list of priorities at the moment.

"What about the woods?" I press on.

He turns away, this time looking directly at the tower of canvases.

"Look," he says. "My uncle called me this morning."

"So you know we're old pals now," I say, humiliated at the image of his uncle warning him against me.

"He's just being protective," Miller says, and I nod like I know what that's like.

"I'm not trying to pry," I say. "I wouldn't be asking if I didn't have a reason."

This seems to get Miller's attention because he shifts to a different position against the kitchenette, his hand flinching at his side.

"It's just, I mean, you've been out there," I say.

"So?"

"Have you ever gotten the feeling . . . ?"

I genuinely have no idea how to finish that thought. And if I was hoping that Miller would do it for me, I was dead wrong. He's not looking at me like I'm crazy. That might be preferable. He's looking at me like he's *daring* me to finish, like he could wait all day for me to get there on my own.

"It's just that sometimes I look at the painting, your painting, and I would swear . . ."

His eyes narrow, and I can practically feel a pickax inside of me, like he's trying desperately to unearth what I'm trying to say, but he won't dare finish the thought himself. I can't seem to finish a single thought, either. Saying it in its entirety might make it true.

"And nobody will come out and work on the house," I say, pressing on but having difficulty hiding my frustration with him. It's like he's trying to make this harder.

"Let me ask you something," he says, and now he looks

more serious than I've seen him look all night. More serious than he's ever looked, actually. "If you could go back to that night with Rae and change what happened, you would, right?"

I suddenly feel like I've been punched in the gut. When I told him all about Rae, I sort of thought that might be the end of it. Isn't there this mutual understanding that's supposed to bridge the expanse between people who have shared a confession? They're supposed to leave it there, in that time and place, to fossilize with the rest of the conversation. I don't know why he's bringing it up again, but I get the sense he was waiting for the right time to resurrect it.

"I didn't think we were talking about me," I say.

"I don't remember agreeing to talk about me, either," he shoots back, and I bristle under his rightness. But he doesn't spend any time gloating.

"If you could change things, you would, wouldn't you?" he persists.

"What the hell, Miller?"

"It's a simple question," he says, his confrontational tone anything but simple.

"What happened to Jack and his friends? How's that for a simple question?" If he wants to rummage through our respective pasts for weapons, I can rummage with the best of them. I'm renovating a house, goddammit. I practically have a doctorate in rummaging.

When his face darkens, I know I've struck a chord. But then his tone shifts, and he's trying to make his way back to Bemused Miller. He doesn't make it all the way there, though.

"What's with all the intrigue?" he says, shimmying his hands in midair, palms out.

"I don't follow," I say, getting the distinct impression I'm being made fun of, and this time, it's far from charming.

"Sorry, it just sounds like you're kind of bored or something."

Miller has no idea how wrong he is. I'd welcome boredom. I'd kiss boredom on the mouth. I'd let boredom get to second base. So fuck Miller and all his sarcasm that burning red hair can't make up for.

"Forget it. I've got to go." I start to leave, but he puts his hand around my forearm. Not tightly, just enough to keep me still.

"Sorry. I'm sorry, okay? I guess I didn't realize what sort of conversation we were having. I wasn't . . . I wasn't ready to talk about Jack is all."

His forehead wrinkles, so I should believe him when he says he's sorry. But there's something about the look in his eyes—something searching—that makes me doubt it. His apology goes about as far as his uncle's did this morning.

"But it was okay to bring up *my* past? Forget it," I say, turning back around.

I start to open the door, but I stop when he says, "It's not in your head."

I turn back, and he's looking at his feet again. The hand that was just holding my arm is searching for a place to land.

I wait for him to tell me more, and when he doesn't, I turn to leave again.

"Penny, wait. I know you don't believe me, but I'm not this much of a jerk. I'm just a little messed up right now, and maybe you telling me all that stuff the other night, and knowing you live out in those woods, maybe it's just bringing up a lot of old crap."

"Miller, I'm—"

"I know. You're in the middle of your own shit, too. I'm not trying to make it worse. Just . . . tell me, okay? Tell me the truth. If you had a chance to right a wrong, something truly awful. Just paint over it and start fresh. You'd do it, wouldn't you?"

I take a step toward him, and he stays where he is, but he looks like he's ready to back up if I get any closer.

"I would do a million things differently. I would've torn up the letters so Rae could never read them. I'd have never written them in the first place. I'd have stopped being her friend months before that. Years before that. I would've erased the first conversation we ever had, and I would have gone on being the freak nobody talked to, but at least I would've been a freak who never ruined some girl's life for no reason or woke up in the desert with my sort-of best friend dead or hated myself so much for all of it months after I should've gotten over it. So yes. If I could erase it all, I would. But here's the thing about 'would.' It's the most useless word in the entire dictionary because it has no place in any point in time. It's a stand-in for an imaginary space between what *might* happen and what *actually* happens."

"If you believed it was hopeless, you wouldn't still be thinking about all the ways it might have been different," he says. He bites his bottom lip, and I can tell he's looking for a specific response by the way his eyes scan mine. Right. Left. Right. Left. Like the register on a typewriter.

But I have no answers for him, and if he knows anything about me now, it should be that.

I leave without a word, mostly convinced that I'd be fine if I never set eyes on Miller again.

14

Jack beckons me from the painting.

I don't want to go, but I'm in the room at the end of the hall before I can count the paces it takes me to reach it. His hand is still wet with the mud that shouldn't be there, only now I see it dripping to the ground, a phantom breeze bending the blades of grass at his feet in a confused dance.

"Have you figured out how to sleep yet?" he asks me.

"You won't let me," I tell him, my disdain buried somewhere under my exhaustion. If he were to give me a little more time, he'd see the fruits of that tilled soil of anger. But for now, he'll only see the creases under my eyes grow deeper.

"Are you sure it's me not letting you?" he asks, a wiser question than his years should allow him to ask. And he seems to know it. He seems to relish it.

"I don't want to see any more," I tell him.

"So why are you here?"

I shudder at the familiarity of his question. It seems even this kid knows I'm destined to be haunted for the rest of my half-waking life.

The trees in the painting creak and moan against the wind, snickering all the while. Dried paint swirls around me in a fine dust, and I'm back in the house he showed me the last time.

"He'll come home," the man says to his wife, flashlights weighing both of their hands down at their sides.

"He's not right," the woman named Doris says. Her voice is hoarse, like she's been talking for an entire century into an empty world. "He's never been right, Burt. Not since he came back."

"He's your son, for God's sake. I won't hear it," Burt says to her, his grip tightening around the flashlight.

Doris looks as though she has fought this fight, that she is tired from this fight, that with enough time the weight of it could crush her.

But just when it appears she might give in, she raises her head and levels her husband with a stare that says she may be sinking, but she's not going down alone.

"When I said those same words to you six months ago—when I

said to you, 'He's your son'—you said the same thing. 'I won't hear it.' When will you hear it, Burt? When will you hear it?!"

The man turns so fast I think he's going to burn a hole in the floor, and he slams the basement door and stomps down the stairs.

Doris follows him and slaps her hand hard on the door. "When will you hear it?! When will you hear it?!"

She walks past me and I feel the chill of her wake. I look for Jack, but he has again receded to the background of his own painting. He might as well be one of the anonymous trees from the scene Miller housed him in.

A young Miller stands once again in the frame of his open bedroom door. He must have been there the whole time, but nobody noticed. He grips the back of his neck, a gesture of an older man, and tugs a little, his hands too small to have much of an impact.

He ventures toward his mother's room, hanging tentatively in a different doorway now. He watches as she sets the flashlight on the bed and paces, her hands on her hips, then on her cheeks, then through her thinning hair.

"Mom," he says so softly that I think maybe I imagined it. The woman continues to pace.

"I heard Jack leave," he says, his voice only a shade louder this time. But it's enough to make the woman stop her pacing. She doesn't *face him in the doorway. She looks at nothing and waits for him to continue.*

"He was staring again. Out the window, then at the wall. It was for really long this time."

The woman shakes her head slowly, a force field against the sound of her son's voice, one that tells her what she already knows but can't hear.

"I don't want him to come back," the boy says, this time loud enough for the woman to turn to him.

"Don't say that," she says. "Don't you ever say that."

"It's true though," the boy pushes on. But I can hear his voice shaking, and I want to pull him out of the doorway, out from under the frantic gaze of his mother, out of this house altogether. But I can't do anything but watch.

"I don't want him to. You've seen it too. I know you have. When his mouth does that . . . I'm scared. Please don't let him come back again."

He pleads, but his mother won't stop shaking her head, and now she's squeezing her eyes shut, taking on the denial for her husband and herself against this small child.

"Make Pop lock the door this time. Please!" he begs now, and he's trembling so hard I can almost feel floorboards rattle beneath us.

"Shut your mouth!" she hisses and charges toward the boy, who takes two steps back as he watches her hand raise above her head like it's on a hinge.

I wake up flinching, the image of the woman's swinging arm outlined in silver moonlight, a handprint on my waking memory.

I weave my fingers into a basket and rest my aching head in them, searching for something else to think about than that horrible, tortured hand attached to a wretched, tortured woman.

And though I search for a happier thought, I come up short and think instead of another tortured soul.

Miller. And what he said to me just before I left his trailer tonight.

He isn't wrong. If he was, I'd be sleeping like a baby right now, snug in the warmth of my rightness. Instead, I'm pushing around the scattered rubble of my mind, living in a half-conscious state of waking nightmare, lying on top of the covers, even though the June gloom chill of outside has made its way inside, the house grumbling under the insistent breeze that won't leave until July, when the Pacific Northwest finally gets to enjoy what the rest of the country calls summer.

"If you believed it was hopeless, you wouldn't still be thinking about all the ways it might have been different."

He said it like it was a good thing to dwell on the very event everyone else in my life seems to wish would just fade to dark. Instead, the grit of desert sand lingers on my skin, making its way underneath to scratch me into madness. I can still feel the grime of it on my hands.

And as I trace the lines of my palms with my fingers, I do indeed feel some of the grit, but when I look down, all I see is a fine white residue. And from under my fingernail this time, I pluck out a chip of evergreen paint.

"Sorry, but no amount of paint could cover this mess," I say to the imaginary Miller sitting on the edge of my bed, who's looking at me like I still don't understand anything. And most of me thinks he's probably right.

Then the thought of Miller sitting on the side of the bed I'm lying in—with my T-shirt and underwear and nothing else—flushes my face with heat, and I'm right back to wondering how I could have misjudged him so much.

I roll over to face a new direction, which is why at first I think the thump behind me came from the bed frame hitting the wall. But as I lie still for another moment, I hear it again, a soft but distinct thud on the wall I share with the room next door.

I sit up in bed as quietly as I can on the squeaky bedsprings, kneeling as I lean toward the wall, pressing my ear to the cold plaster with its cracks tracing thin veins across the surface.

Another thud, this one inches from my face. And harder.

I consider going downstairs to get April, but her room is so far away, and this sound is so close, and it's probably nothing. Maybe she left the window open while she was cleaning in there today.

Before I can blink, I'm standing in the doorway of the room with the painting of Jack staring at the closet across the way. I squeeze my hands together, my fingers still searching out the film of dried paint.

"You're not dreaming," I tell myself. I say it a few more times to make the point.

I squint through the silver light at the mural and think about the sixty-four smaller versions of it stacked up neatly in Miller's trailer and consider how the one I handled while I was there could have left its mark on me. But I don't fully trust this story I tell myself, either.

Then I picture Miller coming out here by himself for days, weeks, months after his parents died, pushing his brush across the wall, carving the hollows of his brother's cheeks, tracing the events of a childhood he could never let go, until his uncle brought him home.

I can barely see to the other side of the room in this dark, even with the light trickling in through the window, its moth-eaten white curtains indeed billowing behind an open sash.

"Get a grip, Penny," I scold myself, moving across the room on wilting legs. I pull the window closed and slide the lock into place before turning to the mural, my mind resolute to eliminate all possibility of absurdity. The smeared swing still hangs from the farthest tree in the distance, but other than that, I see no difference in the painting from earlier.

"What the hell happened to you?" I ask Jack. I still can't bring myself to call him by name. Not aloud. Maybe I know that naming him will make his disappearance a trauma I might have to bear as well.

He stares defiantly at the closet now robbed of its mattress tunnel. The closet door stands ajar, just as I left it before, the damp handprint mopped and almost forgotten. The picture on Linda's digital card will take a little while longer to banish from my mind, deleted or not.

As I turn back to the mural to bid the boy goodnight, I catch sight of an infinitesimal change that nearly escapes my notice. I wish it had escaped my notice. I wish I hadn't looked back at the mural. Because now I see the tiny frame of a brown structure, so mired in the thick of the trees at the densest part of the painting, I can only make out the outline of the structure by squinting. Even then, the brown of its sides blends almost completely with the trunks and tangles of tree branches that seem to be embracing it. But there's no mistaking the shed—the one that wasn't part of the mural before. I'm nearly positive.

I look at Jack's face, my own face close enough to the wall to feel his breath if he had any to breathe. And from this angle, I would swear that his eyes have shifted just the slightest bit, now not focused on the closet across the room but on the window behind me.

I feel warmth on the back of my neck, and though impossible, I swear I feel the tiniest breeze part my hair. Breeze from a window I just shut.

Turning as quickly as I dare, I peer at the window, its curtains dancing in front of the panes. The brightest beams of silver moon flood the space in front of it—*was the moon this bright before?*—and I close my eyes against the glare for just a second. When I open them, I'm staring at the curtains once more, though they hang board straight against the now dark night sky, the moon obscured by a passing cloud.

But as I let my eyes fall to the floor beneath the hem of the curtains, I see the outlines of two sets of small shoes, one on each side of the closed fabric.

Rounded black shoes, clumps of mud oozing from the soles, puddling on the floor. I put my hand against the wall behind me because I can't stop myself from backing up. But I can't back up any farther than that, and suddenly my heart is a rabid animal in my chest, and my legs are going to give out.

The clouds relinquish their hold on the moon once more, and to my horror, I can see more now, the silhouettes of two little boys, neither more than five feet tall, standing stock straight behind their respective curtains, staring at the same closet the boy in the mural stares at.

Until one turns to stare at me, and the other follows.

The curtains billow under their impossible breeze once more, and this time I can see the boys fully. Their enormous, drooping eyes, the bottom lids pulling skin down to the middle of their faces. Their arms and legs bent and knotted at painful angles. Their fingers long and pointed, splintering to jagged ends.

Their jaws lowering, dropping, pulling, their mouths emitting not a single sound.

My legs finally give way to the fear, and I drop to the floor, my voice lost in this cluttered room.

Then, as quickly as they appeared, with the frantic gulp of one breath, they've vanished, the clouds once again taking the moon captive.

I regain movement quicker than I thought I'd be able

to, and I dash to the window, ripping the curtains back with enough force to pull the rod off the wall's hooks, one rusted finial coming away and clattering to the floor.

I check and recheck the window. It's closed. Of course it's closed. I hear a door open downstairs. April's bedroom door. I hear her feet padding up the stairs.

As I turn to meet her in the hall, I look across to the twin room directly in front of me. There, standing in front of the open window are the boys, their shoes glistening with the same mud.

"Penny? Is that you?" I can hear April at the end of the hall, but I can't answer her. All I can do is stare at the boys, their mouths agape, their eyes as white as the moon.

"Penny?"

Before she can reach the doorway, the taller of the two boys clasps his long, crooked fingers around the frame and crouches on the sill, pulling one leg over and then the other. The second boy follows, his back hunched with the unnatural angle his wrong joints have to move against. And with one look back at me, his bottom jaw dusting the backs of his hands, he jumps from the window.

April is beside me now, staring at the same open window. She moves in front of me, tired eyes on top of dark crescents. In this light, she looks like she's been punched on either side of her face.

"Penny, what?" She puts her hand on my shoulder, shakes me a little. But I can't begin to tell her. It's not possible to put into words what I couldn't have just seen.

Except I wasn't the only one to see it.

I push past April and run back to the room with the mural. Jack is there, just as he should be.

I get up close, searching for the little shack. It's still there, too, held in seclusion by its protective trees. But Jack's eyes are focused once again on the closet behind me.

"Penny!" April is shouting now, and I turn to face her, horrified at what I might see next. But it's just April, staring at me expectantly.

"What did you hear?" I ask. I plead, actually.

"What do you mean?"

"Did you hear them too? Did you hear them knocking on the wall?"

Now April is the one looking horrified. She swallows, but that does nothing to coat her still raspy throat.

"You're scaring me, so I'm going to need you to slow down a bit," she says, approaching me cautiously.

I laugh, a move that takes both of us by surprise. "Of

course you didn't hear them. It's impossible to hear what's not there," I say.

"Come here," she says, holding an arm out to me.

I look back at the mural. I look at the closet, its door open, its walls and floor blank and clear but for the tiny matchbox still tucked into the darkness. I look back to April, her arm still out. I don't even know what she wants. To shake me again, to tell me to snap out of it, that it's been far too many months and it's time to get a firm grip on what life looks like after you make horrible decisions. To pull me out of this room so she can get some sleep.

I walk toward her anyway, and her arm encircles my shoulders and pulls me into the hallway, out of the room with the mural, out of sight of the doorway where I couldn't have seen two boys crawl out the window moments earlier. And then she puts her other arm around me and puts a hand behind my head, and I try to remember the last time I've felt anyone hold me the way she's holding me.

Like they know how bad it really is.

"I thought it was real," I tell her, my words muffled in her fleece robe.

"I know," she says softly.

"I'm not sure I can even tell anymore," I say, startled at my own confession.

"I know," she says again.

"What's happening to me?" I ask her. I don't even try to guess at what her answer might be.

She's quiet for a long time before she says, "You're griev-ing." And though I know I should believe her, something in the way she says it—like a guess rather than a statement—makes me doubt.

But she holds me in that hallway for so long my legs start to ache from standing there. Then without a word, she guides me downstairs and sits me down on her bed. I vaguely register the crisp new linens and curtains she's added to the otherwise unchanged room. I spot a Maggie's Grocery basket with clean towels rolled and perched atop the counter in her teeny bathroom.

I sit upright on those fresh new linens until exhaustion finally takes me, and I fall over and curl to the edge of the bed while she lies beside me under the covers, both of us staring into different shadows of a house neither of us really knows what to do with.

"How did you know?" I ask her, the stillness of the room the only indication she's still awake, too.

"Hmm?"

"How did you know to come upstairs? Did you hear the curtain rod fall?"

She's quiet, and if I weren't so tired, I would roll over to look at her. Her silence is more prolonged than it should be.

"No, I was already awake," she says. "The toilet . . ." and she drifts off, and pretty soon, so do I. Just before I doze off completely, I feel the mattress shift, and then April's weight is absent.

15

APRIL IS WEARING HER GLASSES, so I know she means business.

"We're just going to go in, get what we need, and get out. I will not get swept up in the history. I will not get swept up in the history. Say it with me."

"History. No sweeping. Got it," I say, my head to the jeep's window.

I don't think April went back to sleep last night. I think she stayed up all night, pacing the uneven floorboards of the Carver House, evaluating all that is wrong with it. I think for the first time, I'm seeing a different April. One who finally feels the immense weight of a broken-down house resting squarely on top of her. And it's heavier than she thought it would be.

When she practically tackled me this morning with the plan to visit the Point Finney Hall of Records for details on the house's history, I sensed a shift in direction. Her new strategy is evidently to play up the house's historical "charm" to distract from its decrepit plumbing and fire damage that she still hasn't had any luck finding contractors to fix. This is obviously the part of this whole summer project that April's been the most excited about anyway.

I only agreed to go along on the chance there's a public computer with a fully functioning connection to the Internet. I found a missed call from my mom this morning from who knows how long ago. My phone never rang, not that that's a shock given our nonexistent cell service. I should at least drop her an e-mail to avoid the inevitable guilt trip I'll be subjected to if I don't respond at all.

And if I'm being truly honest, after last night, I have no desire to be in that house by myself. April could have declared that she was going on a cockroach hunt this morning, and I would have grabbed my boots and told her to lead the way.

The Hall of Records is actually the Registrar's Office, which sounds way less dramatic and historical than April made it out to be. Not that it makes much of a difference to me either way, so long as they have a computer I can use. But April seems disappointed, and her disappointment deepens as we walk through the doors of a bland, one-story office building that smells vaguely of those pinecone car deodorizers. The Registrar's Office shares space with the Department of Education's local branch, a chapter of the Elks Club, and Pierce County Vehicle Licensing Services.

April turns to me, her brow pinched.

"You know, as long as they have the information you're looking for, it really doesn't matter if it isn't pretty."

It's clear that absolutely nothing but the oven in the kitchen is shaping up to be the treasure hunt of historical significance that April thought it would be.

We follow the marquee pointing us to the Registrar's Office and stand in the Real Estate Inquiries line. According to the nameplate on the desk of the only working employee in the office, "It's Cynthia Doom's Pleasure to Help You!"

"Doom? This just keeps getting better," April says as I nudge her forward. We're next.

"I'm looking for some history on a property—"

"Form B12, fill out the front and back, sign and date the front, *not* the back. Bring it here when you're done. Next!"

April shakes her head. "Sorry, that was a lot of information. Did you say—?"

"B12. Like the vitamin. Next in line!" Cynthia Doom

beckons the next customer with her chapped hand while pointing April to the corner of the room where stacks of forms live.

"Do you have a computer in here that I can use?"

Cynthia Doom turns to me, making it clear that we've exceeded her patience with two more questions than she's allotted us.

"Library across the street. Is there anything else I can help you two with?" I've never heard that question asked in a more threatening manner.

April and I shake our heads, retreating to the form table.

"I'll be back in a few," I say.

April looks at me like I'm leaving her to fend for herself against zombies.

"Please, April. I need to reconnect with civilization. I'm woefully behind on my celebrity gossip. And I haven't been able to get my e-mail to load on my phone since we got here."

She sighs. "Fine. It's not like you could really help me out here anyway. Sort of a one-person job."

I'm halfway to the exit before she says, "One hour, okay? Meet me back here. If you don't see me right away, call for help; I've fallen down a bureaucratic hole."

The library across the street is exactly what April was looking for in the Registrar's Office. It's small, but the building was probably built fifty years after the Carver House was, only I'm guessing the library's toilets don't flush arbitrarily. The entire place is paneled in wood, and the air is a mixture of oak and old paper. The librarian is younger than I feel like she should be in a place like this. She can't be more than twenty-five.

"Do you have computers people can use here?"

"Do you have a library card?" she asks.

I try to remember the last time I set foot in a library. It involved a canvas bag and a summer reading list. My parents were still married.

She smiles warmly, and after Cynthia Doom, I want to hug this girl.

"You can sign in as a guest for thirty minutes. Just put in this code," she says and slides a piece of paper toward me. I thank her and grab a seat next to a middle-aged man in khakis and a bright blue rain jacket who smells like bubble gum.

I sift through celebrity news in a matter of minutes and get bored faster than I'd expected. I log in to my e-mail and shoot my mom the obligatory note, then surprise myself by deleting the entire contents of my inbox without reading a single message. I can't actually imagine wanting to hear from anyone I haven't had contact with in the past three months.

Most of it is probably just spam and more empty questions from fake friends in Phoenix wanting to know if I'm okay. Translation: *Can I get some more details about how your best friend died?*

I go into a trance thinking about Rae. Thinking about all the times I almost reached out to Melissa Corey after she transferred. But what would I have said? How do you beg for forgiveness for the crime of standing still? Thinking about that night in the desert, how I blamed Rae for all of it. Thinking about how I want, with everything straight through to my bones, to stop thinking about all these parts of a life I traveled three states to get away from.

And eventually, my mind shifts to more recent horrors.

After sitting in front of the screen until it falls asleep, a little Pierce County Library icon bouncing from wall to wall, I have used up fifteen of my thirty minutes on the machine while reflecting back on the events of last night.

That hand, frozen in midair, ready to slap the face of a young, terrified Miller.

The boys in their curtain disguises.

Jack's eyes staring from the mural.

I think back to previous nights, to the girl in the woods I've been trying to convince myself this whole time was Rae. To Miller's uncle. To Roberta and George. To the plumbers and engineers who won't set foot in the woods.

Before I know what my fingers are doing, they've woken the computer and started a news search on "Point Finney missing kids."

A flood of headlines fills the screen, most dating back nine or so years, with a handful reflecting on the anniversary of the kids' reappearance from the years that followed.

I try "Point Finney North Woods" in an effort to narrow the results.

I'm rewarded with almost the same number of results.

I erase and try "Point Finney Jack Dodson."

This narrows the search slightly, though with a few new headlines emerging that didn't pop up in the initial two searches. I sift through the stories about a Gail Dodson from Omaha who won the Pick 5 back in 2009 and a disputed election in Dodson, Texas.

The timer in the corner of the screen is clicking down. I have twelve minutes left.

I choose the first story, the one that has come up in every search, from the *Tacoma Weekly*. It looks to be the first article written about the kids after they went missing. The same row of school headshots is used in this article as was used in the one in Ripp's newspaper clipping.

"At the edge of the North Woods," I say.

"What?"

The bubble gum guy next to me is leaning over, trying to hear me better.

"Sorry, I was—"

"This ear," he says a little too loudly for a library. Or to someone he doesn't know. "Can't hear so great in this one."

Someone shushes him from across the room.

"I was talking to myself," I say, one eye on my computer timer.

"Uh oh. First sign you're gettin' old," he says.

I smile and position myself away from him.

The second article is an update offering little information, aside from interviews with the investigating police and surrounding families after the kids had been missing for several days. The third article is the electronic version of the one on Ripp's wall.

TACOMA—JULY 16, 2004—The small township of Point Finney is celebrating tonight as the last of four missing minors has returned home after a harrowing six-month stay in the densely wooded land on the outskirts of town. Anna Riley (12) was found not far from the edge of the woods where the kids were last seen, before disappearing on January 19 of this year.

Found by her own father, a teary George Riley told reporters, "It's a miracle to have our kids back." Asked what he planned to do now that Anna has been found safe, he simply said, "We're going to go home now."

Mr. Riley's words mirrored those of the other two sets of parents, whose repeated requests for privacy have left followers of this remarkable story of tragedy and miraculous recovery of Jack Dodson (14), brothers Russ (11) and Blake (12) Torrey, and Anna Riley (12) baffled.

Marjorie Torrey, mother to brothers Russ and Blake, whose returns marked the beginning of the end of the terrifying journey for four Point Finney kids, was the first to comment, saying in almost the same words that her sons' return was a miracle, and that they wished to be left alone while they waited for the remaining youths to come home.

Sergeant James Meckel of the Pierce County Sheriff's Department—who has led the investigation from the beginning—has assured the public that after talking to the children, parents in the area have nothing to fear.

Says Sergeant Meckel, "I've spoken with each of

the kids in detail, I've talked to the parents, and this is basically just a case of kids wandering off where they're not supposed to and getting lost. They're lucky to be alive. We're still investigating the precise location of where they disappeared and have apparently been living for the better half of a year."

No arrests have been made in the case, and no suspects have been identified in what police are saying is an ongoing investigation.

Adds Sergeant Meckel, "We'll have more questions for the kids, of course. We'll want to know how they kept alive in that sort of weather. It really is a miracle that they've come back in such good condition."

But police and the press will have to wait for now. As the families of each of the missing children continue to request privacy, many are left wondering how the parents knew where to find their kids upon their return, leading some to wonder if it was all an elaborate hoax for media attention.

Janet Brewer of Port Orchard is skeptical: "There's no way those kids were missing that whole time. They came back one after another, right in a row, like they were being called back by a dog whistle or something. And now those parents don't want to tell the police what happened? Come on."

Still, some locals are quick to point to long-standing superstitions about the dangers this section of the Kitsap Woodlands Reserve—better known as the North Woods to Point Finneyians—holds for children who misbehave.

"Nobody from around here would dare to let their kids go anywhere near those woods. Everybody knows that. Ain't no place for children. Ain't no place for anyone, really," says Delinda Major, whose family has lived in Point Finney for five generations.

Roberta Wallochuck, who clerks for Point Finney's only grocery store, agrees. "We've got a saying here. You do something stupid, that means you're taking the fork on the right." The fork on the right, according to Ms. Wallochuck, leads to the North Woods from the only road in town that travels in that direction.

But superstition or not, few can argue with the relief felt across the small, historic township of Point Finney now that the youths have turned up.

In addition to the four pictures of the kids used in the print version of the story, one more picture is included in the electronic version, this one capturing all four kids together after their rescue, at least one parent at each side.

Even as a digital image, the picture is slightly out of focus and taken at a distance. It's difficult to make out much, but what isn't hard to see is that each of the four kids is staring in the same direction, off to the side, as though someone made a loud noise somewhere outside of the frame right before the camera clicked. The only thing visible from the frame in that direction is the woods.

And while each parent holds the child who belongs to them, not a single kid holds their parents in return. Instead, their arms are limp at their sides, their faces slack.

I stare at the picture for another moment, unable to tear my eyes from what it's showing me, which is basically nothing. But something about it is so unsettling, I can't seem to look away.

My timer is down to seven minutes by the time I click on one of the last stories, which is the shortest of them all. Barely enough to justify space in a newspaper.

POINT FINNEY—AUG. 23, 2012—A Point Finney man died in the early hours of August 22 after veering into a tree on the Magnolia Parkway. Burt "Scoot" Dodson (52) of Diamond Creek Road was last seen by acquaintances at The Washingtonian,

a bar located less than a mile from the scene.
Owner of Scoot's General in Point Finney, Dodson
was the father of Jack Dodson, one of the Point
Finney Four, whose disappearance and miraculous reappearance in 2004 remains a mystery to
police to this day. Jack's whereabouts have been
unknown for some time, according to neighbors.
He could not be found for comment. Burt Dodson's wife, Doris, took her own life in 2010. The
Pierce County Sheriff's Department offered no
statement on the matter, only responding that it
was a tragic accident. When questioned about the
Point Finney Four case, a sheriff's deputy stated
the case was closed, and that the officer heading
up the investigation was no longer available for
comment. Sergeant James Meckel retired in 2009
to the Toronto area.

I blink at the screen while the timer in the corner blinks
back. One and a half minutes left. I return to the first article
listing all the kids' names and paste each one into the search
bar. Aside from random articles featuring different kids with
the same names, the same articles appear as did for Jack.
Nothing more comes up about the lives of these kids beyond

the day they came back, aside from vague speculation.

I watch the clock count down from ten. From five. Three, two, one. And as though the sweet librarian who first gave me the code has been hiding under the desk ready to pull the cord the minute the clock ran out, the screen goes black, not even the Pierce County Library icon left to keep me company.

"They're not fooling around," Bubble Gum says. Apparently, even repositioning myself with my back to my computer neighbor couldn't do the trick.

"Yup." I stand, crumpling the paper with the code and tossing it into the nearest bin.

"Crazy thing about those kids, huh?" he says, getting shushed by the same person across the room.

I turn toward him, suddenly a little more interested in what he has to say.

"Oh shush yourself, Frank. It ain't like you're over there workin' on your dissertation," Bubble Gum hollers, raising more than just Frank's head in response. He turns back to me, winks, and says, "Crosswords. The guy acts like he's researching the cure for cancer. Anyway what was I . . . oh yeah. Those kids. The darndest thing. The dad of one of 'em—the little girl? He used to be a drinkin' buddy of mine. He did a lot more drinkin' after she came back, that's for sure. The Washingtonian. Now that place has seen a few sins. I can't drink like I used to, lordy no."

I sit back down on the bench, not certain I want to hear more of what Bubble Gum has to say but unable to walk away.

"One night after—" He stops himself, looks up, looks back down, twists his mouth. "Maybe a few too many," he says, choosing a strange time for discretion, "George tells me this story about how he heard this sound in his daughter's room one night. He goes to check on her, and what he sees, he can hardly even describe it to me without his hand shakin.' Says her eyes were huge, whited out like she had cataracts or somethin.' Says she's facin' the window, lookin' out at the trees behind their house, and she's got her mouth so wide open he thinks maybe she broke her jaw or somethin.' But she's not sayin' a word. Just standin' there with her mouth open and her eyes lookin' like that. Says he ran from the room—ran from his own daughter—and when he sees her the next mornin',' she ain't sayin' a word. Just sittin' there eating breakfast like nothing happened, lookin' normal. But not normal, you know?"

I do know. And I shouldn't know. But I can't make sense of how this man I have never met has just described what I'd promised myself I hadn't seen last night.

I recall with crystallized clarity the image of those two

boys, the curtains billowing from their faces, exposing their wide, white eyes. Their hanging jaws open in a suspended, silent scream.

I've never remembered any image from a nightmare that clearly.

"Shame, you know? Everyone sorta drifted apart after that."

"I don't understand," I say.

"Well, ya know. All those families. They used to be pretty tight before that whole mess. But after their kids all went their own ways, or went no way really, no one really heard much from any of 'em after that . . ."

I shake my head against a slowly forming realization. It's not possible. It can't be those kids. They came back nine years ago. But then, what is it I've been seeing? What is it Jack insists on showing me, dragging me out of bed and into his nightmare, like I needed another to add to my collection?

"Yeah, well, kids, they go off, they get into trouble," he continues. "But these kids. I dunno. I don't think any of 'em live here anymore. Small town, you know? You'd think we would've run into them by now. Margie Torrey—those boys' mom—she mostly just drinks where we all used to. Like she never really left, you know? Poor thing. But you know, life goes on."

I think back to the article. George Riley. The little girl's father. And suddenly, my brain pieces together a man with a tan jacket, gin-blossomed nose over a mustache that weighs on the mouth of a man who just wanted to buy groceries without facing the memory of losing and never really regaining his daughter.

"Hey, you mind if I use that computer?" Bubble Gum says, changing direction quicker than I can register.

"What?"

"It's faster than mine. This thing moves like a dinosaur."

I peer at his screen, the words "massive government conspiracy" in bright red slathered across the page.

I've been talking to Government Conspiracy Guy for the past five minutes.

I leave without another word to Bubble Gum and give a half wave to the kind librarian. I walk back to the Registrar's Office in a daze, my head swimming with the information a paranoid schizophrenic just assaulted me with.

But even skeptical me knows that's not true. I've seen what that poor father saw, the one who watched his daughter turn into a monster before his eyes and wondered how to eat breakfast with her the next morning.

I wonder if there's a single person in this town other than him who might understand what sorts of secrets are trying to crawl their way out of the North Woods. I wonder if those secrets will leave me alone before I hear them out.

Back at the Registrar's Office, April is yucking it up with Cynthia Doom at the only cubicle designated for public use. I approach with caution, certain I can't be correct thinking those are the sounds of laughter. But the closer I get, the easier it is to make out the muffled cackle of a woman who is long out of practice at making that sound.

Cynthia Doom is doubled over the cubicle wall, my stepmom matching her hysteria.

"What the hell?" I ask, and both of them turn to me.

"Language," they admonish in unison, then bust up all over again.

"Honey, your stepmom is a bad, bad lady," Cynthia declares, and April throws me a wink that says she can literally win anyone over.

Anyone but Ripp. Or Roberta. Or George.

"Hmm," I agree as much as I can without the benefit of their backstory. "Find anything interesting?" I direct the question to April while Cynthia tries to recover her composure. People are starting to stare.

She cuts her eyes to me, gives a nearly imperceptible nod to Cynthia, and puts her hand on the massive stack of yellowed papers in front of her. "We've been having so much fun, I haven't even gotten started!"

I glance at the line of waiting Registrar Office customers.

It's seven people deep, and each person looks more exasper-ated than the last. One of them even gives *me* the stink eye.

The stack of papers under April's elbow is four inches high. It could take hours to go through. I search the office for a place to get comfortable and find a row of three plastic orange chairs lined against the wall like inmates.

I slump into a chair and beg my brain not to rehash Bubble Gum's story. But my brain has not cooperated with me for at least nine months, and there's little hope it's going to start now.

I've almost decided to curl up across the three empty chairs to take a nap while April extracts herself from Cynthia Doom when I feel a vibration in my bag.

It's Rob's face on the screen.

"Are you on a break or something?" I ask, relishing the full bars of cell range afforded by the Registrar's Office.

"Or something," he says, sounding distracted. And while my reception is crystal clear, his voice is crackling for the first time all summer.

I sink lower in the seat, as now half of the line of waiting customers stares me down, apparently deciding their death rays are wasted on the real culprits behind their misery.

"Where are you?" he asks.

"A fresh level of hell, I think."

"How fast can you get home?" he says a little breathlessly.

"Not fast enough. Wait, are you back in Seattle? I thought soccer camp went through the middle of August."

"No, I mean home here," he says.

After a few seconds of struggle, my brain wakes up.

I edge past the line of customers and interrupt Cynthia Doom's story about her coworker and the UPS man.

"Hey, April, can I borrow your car for a little bit?"

April looks like a caged animal. Cynthia casts her large shadow on April, giving me the same look her customers are trying so desperately to give her. Evidently, I'm interrupting.

"I'll be back in a couple of hours," I say. Then a little louder, "Remember, we have to meet up with Dad by five at the latest. You told me to remind you."

April looks a little more relaxed under the cover of my lie, then turns to Cynthia. "I completely forgot. Wow, guess I'd better get started on this research."

Then she puts a hand on Cynthia's dry, withered forearm. "Don't you take any shit from Mary Jo. She might have gotten the UPS guy, but she doesn't have what you have." She pauses while we all wait for it. "A pension!"

April and Cynthia Doom bust a gut while April slides me her keys, squeezes my hand in a way that begs me to come back before five, and releases me.

16

BEFORE I CAN EVEN GET out of April's jeep and say hi, I notice Rob staring at the house. He's looking at it like he doesn't want to go near it. I follow his bony shoulder down his long arm to his knobbly hand, fingers twitching but otherwise unmoving.

"Where's Alfredo?" I ask from the open jeep window, pointing to a car that isn't his.

He looks startled to see me, and I wonder for a second if he even came here looking for April and me, if maybe he just stumbled into a random forest in a random town several random towns away from Seattle.

"Borrowed it from a friend," he says. "Alfredo's in the hospital."

"Is it serious?" I ask, trying to find comfort in our easy

banter but distracted by his unfocused gaze and the fact that he's here at all. Not that I'm not overwhelmed with relief to see him.

"He'll live."

We both get quiet. He goes back to staring at whatever he was staring at, and this time I have to look because his lack of focus is starting to weird me out. But when I look at the house behind me, all I see is the same wood, the same glass, the same place that should have been a two-month escape from this type of feeling.

I try again. "Well, he's going to be lonely."

This seems to get his attention because he walks away from the house, and I walk toward him, and we meet somewhere in the middle.

"He's been acting like an asshole for a while anyway," Rob says. "Needs a new transmission."

"That sucks," I say. All he'd have to do is lift one eyebrow giving me the signal and I'd get into the beige compact car he's borrowed from his friend, and I'd go anywhere with him. Absolutely anywhere but here. I wouldn't even need to know why he came.

"Come on," I say. "April—um, your mom—is living the dream over at the government building. We've got sandwich stuff inside though."

But Rob just shakes his head, looking up at the house with that faraway stare again. "Nah, I'm not hungry. Let's just take a walk or something."

The trees are whispering. They do that a lot here. It's not all that different from high school.

When we first moved to Phoenix, I gave myself this fantasy. It was the only way I could bring myself to walk through the double doors of the hallway that led to my locker without passing out from fear. In my fantasy, a girl with a face I could never fully conjure offered me her name—something else I could never make materialize, even though it was my fantasy—and she would turn out to be the most fascinating girl in school. That nonexistent hybrid that is able to move easily through every crowd, envied and loved, disarming and self-assured. And her single gesture of recognition would enshroud me in the kind of protection that would sustain me throughout the rest of my new existence in this new school, this new city, this new climate that had me sweating before eight in the morning.

But that no-name, no-face girl didn't exist. I had Rae, whose first gesture to me was a smile resting over a raised middle finger. And once she'd claimed me as her friend, so began the low grumble of hallway murmur, the act of measuring me for the box in which I'd eventually have to fit so everyone would know how to identify me.

If I wasn't the scary girl, I was the scary girl's friend. Close enough.

Now as Rob walks beside me through the woods behind the house, the trees start up their chatter, and I lean in closer to hear. It's a habit that's grown stronger since we got here, that need to hear what I know won't bring me comfort.

"What did people say when I first moved to Seattle?" I ask him.

He shakes his head like he knew I'd ask that question someday. "I was a sophomore," he says, as though that explains everything.

"And I was a junior. So?"

"Come on, Penny. You know what it's like. Sophomores are innocent bystanders in a mafia shootout. Nobody saw nuthin'. We're all just trying to get by until we become upperclassmen."

"Yeah, but you did hear things."

"What do you want me to say, Penny? It's the same with every new kid. Especially girls. Guys talk about whether or not they're going to bang her, girls talk about whether or not she's a slut, nobody says anything to the new kid directly, and eventually some other new kid moves in, people start talking about her instead, and that's the end of it."

Most people have certain "tells" when they're lying. Like they get all twitchy or something. Since Rob doesn't lie, he has those same tells when he has to be honest about the painful things. He's fidgeting now.

"Did they know why I was there? Did they know about Phoenix?"

He chuckles a little. "They thought you were a pyro."

"What?"

He ducks under his embarrassment. "I heard one guy in the locker room talking once about how you got kicked out of your last school for trying to light it up. You know, people just make shit up."

I remember what Rae said about how teenagers are sociopaths. I try to decide what makes a kid worse—being a pyro or being a liar.

Or being the girl who lets another girl get beat up for something she didn't do.

"Don't worry, I set him straight," Rob says quietly, and I feel maybe my first glimmer of summer warmth. I know I can make it stay as long as he's walking next to me, this strange nonsibling I never thought I wanted.

"Why are you asking me all this now?" he says. "I mean, what does it matter? You'll come back. You'll be a senior, and part of that will probably be independent study anyway—assuming your grades don't totally suck—and then you'll be done with high school forever. I'm jealous."

I step over a high tree root jutting from the ground, and Rob follows my lead.

"I guess I just wanted to know how bad it really was. And my grades do suck, by the way."

He sighs, a gesture maybe more mature than I think he's ready for. It's only occasionally that I look at Rob like an actual little brother. He's too close to me in age, and of course not actually related. But every once in a while, I find myself fighting the urge to turn his shoulders and steer him down a certain path when he looks like he might be veering, which is practically never. I wonder not for the first time how often he feels the need to do that to me. I wonder if that's why he's here now.

"I think what you want to know is how bad *you* were when you first moved out here. But see, that's the thing. You don't have to be in that place anymore, you know?"

I don't say anything, but I slow my stride, and he almost bumps into me.

"I mean, I'm not going to be all 'move on with your life.' I know you've heard enough of that by now. I guess I'm just asking why you don't feel like you can yet."

The trees are gossiping louder than ever. We're giving them a lot to talk about, I guess. But there's that maturity again, only this time, it feels like he's the one turning my shoulders straight.

"I think we're kind of close to where they went looking for those kids," Rob says, and I do stop now. Fully. And Rob does walk into me.

I lose my balance and catch myself on a tree, and when I pull my hand away, I take a sharp sliver of bark with me. Pulling the sliver out, I release a fine trickle of blood down my palm.

"Damn, I'm sorry," Rob says, pulling the edge of his shirt up and pressing it against my hand, squeezing.

"What did you say about those kids?" I ask, barely feeling my hand or anything else. "How do you—"

"Huh?" Rob is pressing harder on my hand, and now I do flinch a little.

"Hey, how bad does that hurt?" he asks, ignoring my question and checking my hand again.

"It's fine," I say.

"You don't look fine. You look kinda pale. I think we'd better start walking back."

I let Rob turn us around, and we trace a path back to the house and enter through the back door and into the tiny kitchen with April's cherished oven.

"I think there's a first aid kit in that second box from the bottom," I say, pointing to a crooked stack of sagging cardboard boxes. Rob unpiles them until he reaches the bottom of the tower.

"There, next to the vodka," I say.

Rob pulls the bottle out, lifts an eyebrow, and sets it aside gently.

"I don't suppose that's gotten any use lately," he says, only half turning toward me. Then he guides me to the sink and orders me to wash the cut out.

"It's not that bad," I say, but I can't stop my hand from shaking, so of course he doesn't believe me.

"Peroxide," he grumbles and digs out a brown bottle, unwraps a cotton ball from the tiny white kit, and exposes a fresh bandage, prepping it like a surgeon.

I can't help but smile at him, but he doesn't seem convinced.

"I feel bad," he says. "I practically body-slammed you into that tree. I wasn't expecting you to stop so fast. Did you trip or something?"

My smile drops, and he snugs the bandage over my wound before crossing his impossibly long arms over his chest. And he waits.

I slide the bottle of vodka around on the countertop for a second before I confess.

"It's a little weird here," I say, wondering how vague I can be without sounding completely crazy. Not that complete honesty will make me sound sane.

Rob doesn't say anything. But I think I see his arms tighten across his chest.

"I keep thinking . . . sometimes when I'm alone, it's like . . . I'll hear . . ."

I focus intently on the bottle of vodka. "Sometimes I think I hear things. And . . . see things. Like, maybe . . . Rae."

For a minute, I think I've imagined Rob, too. Maybe he's one of the kids I've conjured along with Rae and the girl in the woods and the boys behind the curtains.

And that thing under the mattresses.

He's so quiet, I almost don't want to look up to see if he's really there. If he wasn't, I think I'd bolt into the woods and run as far as my legs and lungs would let me, and once I couldn't run any longer, I'd sink to the ground and die, numb and breathless.

But he is there, and I'm glad I looked up because his arms aren't across his chest anymore, but he's rubbing his chin. Both hands, just rubbing and smoothing out the skin around his jaw, like maybe the answer of how to fix me might appear like a genie.

"She's gone, Penny."

"I know."

"I know you know, but I don't think you're letting yourself feel it. Any of it."

I nod. I know.

"I don't even know if you're hearing me right now," he says, growing frustrated, something I've never actually seen on Rob. I'm getting that feeling again that this emotion is too mature on him. It doesn't fit.

"What do you want me to do, Rob? You asked, okay!"

"I shouldn't have mentioned anything about those kids." He's shaking his head like he's blaming himself, but he still sounds upset with me.

"Why, because I'm too fragile to say the slightest thing around? 'Oh, nobody say anything about anything. It might set Penny off. Oh, nobody talk about her like she's in the room. We might spook her!'"

"Not me. I don't pull that shit with you, and you know it," he says, taking a step back.

"You just did."

And now we're both quiet. His arms are back across his chest, and I'm fiddling with the vodka bottle again, and even though I haven't wanted to drink since that night in the woods, I would love nothing more than to struggle to focus on this moment, to have to squint to pull my thoughts together. I would love it if I could act exactly how I feel around the only person I thought I didn't have to pretend to be okay around.

And then, just when I'm considering uncapping the bottle and pouring a burning stream down my throat, Rob sinks into a squat beside one of the boxes, then lowers himself to the floor like he can't bear to stand a second longer.

"I didn't know her," he says after a few false starts. "Hell, until March, I barely knew you."

He's not wrong. Aside from the occasional e-mail, which I'm pretty sure was initiated less by Rob and more by April, Rob and I only ever saw each other on the rare visits I'd make up north to see my dad. And I'd made every effort to associate Rob with April, April with divorce, divorce with the way Mom is now, and everything else that went wrong all those years ago.

"But maybe this doesn't have as much to do with what happened." And he stops here and looks at me pointedly. "Whatever that might be."

He knows most of it. Maybe not all, but most. He's giving me a pass on the rest, and I'm positive I don't deserve it.

"But maybe," he continues, "it has more to do with how much of it you're not sure you would take back."

And this surprises me. Because up to this point, I would

have told him the same thing I told Miller that night in his trailer. That I'd take it all back. Every last ounce of it from the moment I locked eyes with Rae.

"When I went through that stuff with my mom," he says, unearthing the conversation about his dad that he vowed would stay buried, "I regretted a lot of what I said to her." He stops rubbing his chin, and I see red splotches in place of his hands. "But not all of it. And once I figured that out, I knew what I could let go and what I'd have to keep."

I consider the prospect of inventorying all those moments with Rae and start to feel a little dizzy.

But I nod anyway.

"It'll probably take awhile," he says, divining my thoughts not for the first time. "Just . . . I don't know. Give yourself the time."

It's maybe the most reasonable advice I've ever received, and because I now feel that distance shrinking between us, I nod again. Just once. But I think he believes me because he drops the conversation into the box with the first aid kit, then slides the vodka bottle out of my loose grip without a word and buries it in the box too.

"You never told me why you ditched out of soccer clinic," I say, ready to lift the weight of this conversation.

He shrugs, clearly not prepared to answer that question.

"You just sounded funny the last time I talked to you. Actually, you and my mom have both been sounding funny. I guess I wanted to see for myself if everything was cool. You know, make sure you two weren't going all Jack Torrance up here or something."

I try to laugh, but it feels impossible. I picture April cackling away with Cynthia Doom at the Registrar's Office. I reflect back on her pinched face, the dark half moons under her eyes, her shortness with me when she's normally nothing but patience personified. And today with Cynthia, that wasn't anywhere near her real laugh.

"Hey," I say, dark inspiration seeping in. "Do you want to take a drive with me? I need to talk to someone."

17

Rob and I sit in the parking lot of The Washingtonian, staring at the front doors like the answer of what to do next might be written on them.

"I can't count all the ways that this is a bad idea," Rob says, running his hand up and down the seat belt absently. The flashing Bud Light sign reflects off the surface of his eyes.

"I could have come alone," I say. "I'm sure you have to get this car back to your friend. He's probably missing it. Plus, don't think I haven't noticed how you've managed to avoid explaining how you snuck out of soccer clinic without being noticed."

He looks down, a tiny smile fighting its way to his lips.

"She doesn't need the car back for a couple of days."

"Ah. I see. She," I say, arching an eyebrow at him. "And I suppose *she* is also the one covering for you while you play hooky from your very expensive summer camp?"

"Okay, one? *She* is Gwen Brzinski, and she's really funny and smart and beyond gorgeous, and she's a better forward than me. Two? When you say summer camp, you make me sound like I'm nine. Three? I'll give you a ride to school every day this year if you promise to let me be the one to tell my mom about her *if* I ever get anywhere with her."

I'm getting that feeling again: the urge to take him by the shoulders.

"You would have given me a ride to school regardless," I say.

His eyes plead.

"Okay! Yes. Besides, I'm not really sure how I would have told her about your maybe-girlfriend without somehow involving the story of you actually being here. Which, according to me, you never were," I say before he can beg me not to tell April that part, either.

"And not Dad either," he adds, which only gets a grunt from me in return.

"What?" he asks.

"Oh, come on, Rob. When am I going to confide that little secret? During one of our daily chats?"

Rob isn't as good at ignoring sarcasm as April. "Well, when's the last time you tried talking to him?"

"Don't you start on me too. April's tried," I say, though I try to think back to her nagging me about my relationship with my dad, and I can't think of a specific instance. Maybe it's just the way she cocks her head at me whenever I blow off a message my dad has sent through her.

Because he can't say anything to me directly.

"Sorry," Rob says, and for a second I forget what he's sorry about. "It's just . . . why would a guy who doesn't care about his daughter carry that stupid penny around in his wallet?"

"I have no idea what you're talking about," I say, because I'd rather not be having this conversation at all right now. Since when is my relationship with my dad on the table for discussion?

"The one he keeps in the picture part instead of a picture. He said he got sick of never getting school pictures from your mom, so he put the penny in there instead.

A penny. For Penny.

I stare at Rob for a full minute, and he starts to look supremely uncomfortable. But I am searching for the lie I know he's incapable of telling me, even if he suspected there was a chance it could make me feel . . . it's a thought I can't possibly finish. I have no idea how I feel right now. But there's that sensation in my throat again. The one I can't swallow away.

"I keep telling him nobody actually prints pictures anymore," Rob finally says, trying to cap the conversation he looks like he's regretting starting.

We sit for another strained minute, searching for a life raft in all that silence we're swimming through.

Finally, I can't take it anymore. "So can we go inside now, or what?"

I'm totally faking confidence, of course. I have not a single clue what I might say to this poor woman once I get in there, assuming she's there at all. I only now start to think of all the ways this could go horribly wrong, the smallest consequence being that I force a mother to rehash what was likely the worst event in her life, the thing that keeps her coming back to this weather-worn building with tiny windows that blink beer advertisements. I think about the last expression on George's face as he stood in line and waited for Roberta to change the topic no one meant to bring up.

I remember Ripp's warning to me, the wish he made that I would not disturb the soil of a long buried past with Miller. The wish that I have already made sure wouldn't come true.

"Tell me again what that guy said in the library," Rob says, but I know he's just stalling.

I told Rob most of it, but not everything. I left out the story the little girl's father told.

And I haven't told Rob about any of what I've seen. I can't seem to find the right time to say something like that.

What's strange, though, is that Rob didn't seem too surprised when I told him that one of the parents still hangs out here, and that I wanted to talk to her.

"Rob? Why did you bring up those kids when we were in the woods?"

I expect him to take a little longer to follow my thought, but he seems to arrive at it almost before I do. He looks down at his lap.

"Rob?"

He looks up at me, the blinking beer sign now lighting the side of his face. "I saw the articles online when I was looking up how to get here," he says. "It was weird and all, but I didn't really think much of it. And you know, Mom knew some of it, but she just thought it would add to the intrigue or whatever. And the house is kinda . . ."

Now it's taking me a second to catch up with him. But just a second. I suddenly remember the look on his face when I pulled up to meet him in front of the Carver House. How he was looking at it. Couldn't *stop* looking at it, actually.

"What did you see in the house?" I ask, cringing against the answer I'm already expecting.

He shakes his head. "Nothing."

I keep looking at him. It's the first time I've ever seen Rob lie, and now I know why he never does. He's terrible at it.

"You saw one of them, didn't you?"

"Nah," he says, and the red light on his face looks even darker. His own color has drained entirely.

"Someone was just in the house," he continues, denial looking ridiculous on him. "A repairman or something. Mom said she was trying to get a plumber out—"

"No repairmen will come to the house," I say, and now we're both quiet.

"I didn't see anything," Rob says again, as though maybe the lie will sound more convincing the second time. "But maybe you guys should just come home."

"Are you kidding? Do you have any clue how invested your mom is in this? I mean, it's not just the money. She's obsessed."

"So she'll be disappointed," Rob says, his conviction disproportionately strong for someone who just saw a repairman. "But I mean, if the whole point was to help you recover by bringing you out here, and she can't get anyone to work on the house anyway, then what's the point?"

"What am I supposed to do? Tell your mom to drop everything because I'm seeing things? 'Hey, April, remember those hundreds of thousands of dollars you sunk into this dream of yours? I've got a cool idea. Let's ditch it and get the hell out of here! See, I'm kind of afraid of the dark, and—'"

"Who cares what she thinks?" he says, but his voice cracks under the weight of doubt.

"Rob, I have no place else to go!"

And here's where we finally understand each other. He knows as well as I do that there's nobody left to pass me off to. If I can't make it work here, with April, who else will take me?

"What if they're trying to tell me something?" I ask. I've been so wrapped up in denying they were there at all—that Rae was the only one haunting me—I hadn't wanted to consider this possibility. But what if these kids who disappeared for six solid months are screaming to be heard, to be understood?

To be needed.

The little girl. Those boys behind the curtains. The articles referenced two brothers, a girl, and . . .

"Jack," I whisper, too quietly for Rob to hear.

And Margie is my last hope to find out what it is they might want.

"There's nobody trying to tell you anything because there's nobody there," Rob says, his tone flat. But I can't see his face. I just see the back of his head as he stares at the front doors of The Washingtonian again, and he must be thinking the same thing I am: Going in there feels like a worse idea now than it did before.

And now I've given him my sanity to worry about, too.

According to the bartender, the woman named Margie is the one sitting on a stool at the far side of the bar. In profile, she looks like a reversed C, her back and head curving toward a nearly full martini glass. Rob and I look back at the bartender, who warily eyes us from his post behind the counter. He's been toweling off the same glass since we walked in. Rob engages him again, as though he's done this a million times—talking to bartenders in shadowy dives.

"We're just here to talk," he says, then turns toward Margie, whose head looks a little closer to her drink than it was a few seconds ago.

"This isn't exactly a 'talking' kind of establishment," the bartender says, still working his glass over with a towel. Then he sees me staring at Margie. "But you're welcome to try. She's about three deep already."

I lead the way toward Margie. From farther away, she

looks like she might be sleeping sitting up. Upon closer examination, her eyelids are drooping but open, focused on nothing in particular.

"Well, you found me," she says, slurred and slightly amused.

Rob and I look at each other.

"Hoping we wouldn't?" Rob asks, playing along.

"Yes," Margie replies without hesitation.

I look at Rob again, but he just frowns and continues to study the woman in front of us. I don't know if he's seeing what I see: black jeans faded to greenish, black shirt faded to brownish, boots creased as deeply as the skin around her lips. Her hair might have been black at one point too. But so many gray corkscrews of frizz halo her head above the loose elastic pulling the rest of her hair back, who could ever say how she might have looked ten, twenty years ago?

"Let's have a seat in my office." Margie's voice crackles, and she coughs to clear whatever lingers in her throat. She slides from the stool and lands with a surprisingly sure foot on the sticky floor, knocking back the martini with a single swallow and raising the glass in the direction of the bartender before returning it to the bar top and guiding us, a little slowly, to a shadowed booth at the back of the tavern.

"Ask what you want," she says, her eyes on the table first,

then on Rob, then for a long time on me. She squints at my forehead, my eyes, my mouth. She looks like she's trying to mentally reassemble my features.

"I'm sorry, but who is it you think we are?" I ask, uncomfortable with the amount of time this unsolicited charade has already gone on.

"When a snake eats a, oh, I don't know, a gopher," she says after a long pause, "did you know it can go for months without eating after that? Months."

Rob said he couldn't count the ways this was a bad idea, but I'm thinking I can. I've already counted one.

"You people," she continues, "haven't been fed a good story in years! Guess you had a nice fat rodent to feast on last time," she says.

I duck my head toward Rob. "She thinks we're reporters."

"We aren't—" he starts.

"Do you really think it matters?" she asks, and I've just counted the second reason this was a terrible mistake.

"If I'm talking, I'm talking, so just ask me what you want to ask me, and let's get this little chat over with."

"The Carver House," I say. I consider saying more, but wait for Margie to fill in the blanks first.

She does not. Instead, she stares at my face even harder, her head looking heavy on her neck.

"It's near where . . . where . . . ," Rob tries now.

"I know where it's near," she interrupts his efforts. Reason three.

Margie continues to stare at me. I find a groove in the wooden table and run my finger along the crevice, dropping my eyes to get a closer look. The bartender appears beside us with another martini for Margie. He plunks two beer steins in front of Rob and me, filled three quarters of the way with cloudy tap water.

"Thanks," I say, but he's already gone.

"Joe's the thoughtful type," Margie says into her glass before taking her next sip and lifting her cocktail in salute to Joe the bartender. She laughs a little at a joke in her head.

"So ask what you really want to ask," Margie says. "Or we can drag this out for another ten years."

Margie's words are crisp and clear now, the kind of sudden sobriety that occurs when emotion regains control. Her hand shakes a little on the table, and I have this sudden urge to put my hand over hers, an urge I fight because I know that's not what she's looking for.

"How did you find them?" I delve in. What else can I do? We came to ask her a question, and she's just demanded we do that.

Margie shifts her suddenly clear gaze to me. "It was a miracle."

She smiles the worst smile I've ever seen. It's like facial scar tissue, like an old wound never healed right, and her features have had to maneuver around the wreckage for years but never quite learned how to avoid the worst of the damage.

"I keep hearing that. It's just . . . it feels like maybe there's . . ."

"Just ask, goddammit!" Margie slaps her hand on the table.

Our respective drinks tremble under the force. I gasp before I can stop myself. Rob grabs my free hand under the table, and I hear Joe the bartender clear his throat from across the tavern. But Margie holds me with her eyes. It's like Rob isn't even there. She's dismissed him. It's me she's having this conversation with.

"How did you get them back?" I ask, my voice clear and steady, even though I'm having a hard time catching my breath.

"There it is," Margie says. Her voice burbles from someplace deep inside her.

"So then they didn't just come back?" Rob asks, but we all know that he doesn't need to. He does out of obligation, a final wish for the convenient truth.

"Why'd you ask me about that house?" she asks, thrusting the interrogation back at me.

"I'm living there for the summer," I say. "While my . . . I'm living there," I say. It occurs to me this has become a sort of quid-pro-quo questioning.

Margie's face darkens under the shadow of her tilted martini glass.

"And why on earth would you be doing that?" she asks.

"What happened there?" I say. It's her turn to answer.

But she only smiles. "I haven't the slightest clue what happened in that place," she says, and for some reason, I believe her. It's something in her mangled smile. Like this is one truth she can bear, but she can't feel any pleasure in it.

"So then what happened in the North Woods?" I ask, trying again even though it's not my turn.

"What's the point in asking pointless questions?" she snaps, snatching an olive from its toothpick and grinding it between her teeth to a vodka-soaked pulp.

"I don't think they're pointless," I say, pressing my luck. Rob must think I am too, because he's squeezing my hand under the table a little harder now. "Actually, I don't think you'd be acting like this if you didn't know I was asking for a reason."

Margie stares at her drink for so long, I'm certain we've lost her for good. The alcohol has taken hold, and we have officially gotten all we're going to get from Margie.

"My grandma used to talk to us about those woods," she says, startling me. "She used to say, 'Marjorie, those woods are older than time itself. They've been around longer than any other living thing.'"

Margie continues to stare at her drink, her brow furrowing under the strain. "Something that's been around that long, it has a long time to get lonely. Too long of a wait for something to keep it company. Nobody should've been living there back then, and no one should be doing it now."

I chance a look at Rob, but he's staring somewhere past Margie now, someplace into the dark of the shadowy pub. I look back at Margie.

"From the time I was little, I knew about those woods. We all did."

I have to lean in because Margie's practically whispering now.

"They knew not to go in there, but kids are so damned smart. Always know better than their parents."

"How did you get them back?" My own voice is barely above a whisper, but it's not because I'm trying to match Margie's tone. I couldn't make more sound even if I wanted to.

"We gave the woods what it wanted," she says, her own words sounding like a surprise to her. "Company."

Rob and I look at each other now, his eyes searching mine

for what we apparently both missed. He opens his mouth, but I squeeze his hand. I don't think Margie's done.

Her lips fall open, and the next sentence tumbles like a prisoner suddenly unchained and wild. "We brought the ones no one would miss."

Rob's hand goes limp in mine. Or maybe I can't feel my fingers.

I pull Margie's sentence over the coals of my mind, see if it'll catch fire. I wait for it to ignite a revelation other than the only one I can form in this moment. Because what she's saying can't possibly be true. Because no one—no person, no monster, no one—could have done what it sounds like Margie is saying.

"You . . . brought . . . you brought *other* kids . . . ?" My mind is still on fire.

"They were a . . . miracle," Margie says, her mouth moving over the debris of ten years. "The old story was right."

I'm shivering, but I don't feel cold. I'm having a hard time feeling anything, and I think back to the last time I felt this way. It involved a bonfire and a desert. It involved a furious Rae, a notepad that looked familiar, but I couldn't quite place it. A pad I knew was mine, but my mind couldn't own it at that time. My mind couldn't own a single feeling outside the one that shrouded the rest of me in the numbing warmth of total and complete denial. It couldn't have been me who wrote those awful things about my best friend. It couldn't have been me.

"That's how you got them back," Rob says more to himself than to Margie.

"No," she says, drawing the word out so it sounds like "Nooooeee." She takes a long sip.

"You didn't get your—"

"I got the boys back," Margie answers him, her eyes on the table again. "Not my sons, though. Not *my* boys."

"It must have been so hard," Rae said. *"Pretending this whole time to be my friend. It must have just killed you to put on another face every day around me."*

"Looked like them," Margie says, her voice barely audible. "Smelled like them. They have a smell, you know. Kids do. Each one their own. Blake smelled like wheat. No matter what you fed him, that's what he smelled like. Russ was more like . . . vanilla and sand. Eyes like sea glass."

I watch Margie so closely I'm afraid of what I might see. This hard woman, so weathered she looks like she's lived fifty lives already, weaving a delicate poetry about the boys she wanted back so badly she was willing to sacrifice someone else's child.

"I got my boys back, but not really. It wasn't them."

"What happened to them?" I ask. I know I shouldn't. I

should stop where Margie stopped it. This is her living nightmare, not mine. Except I know that's not entirely true.

"Don't know," Margie says, resuming her conversation with her drink.

"You mean—"

"I mean I haven't seen either of 'em in six years," Margie says, lowering her glass long enough to make me read her lips.

"I don't understand," I say. "You mean to tell me you went through all that . . . *did* all that, just to lose track of them? Just to say you don't know?"

I should have stopped long ago. Rob is already trying to push me out of the booth. But I'm in far too deep, and I can't possibly leave without hearing her say it.

"Don't you dare preach your gospel to me, little girl," Margie says, her words dousing the burning coals in my brain. "Don't you dare until you have something so precious, the ache of losing it is enough to pull you to pieces. Don't you dare. Nobody was going to miss some abandoned child wasting away at Our Lady of Grace. Not the way I did my boys. If you'd been swallowed whole by that kind of grief, don't you tell me for a minute you wouldn't slit the belly of it open to get free!"

I see Rob nodding to someone as he finally pulls me off

the bench of the booth and onto my feet. It takes me a full moment to understand that he's apologizing to Joe the bartender for upsetting his patron, the woman named Margie who I finally pull into focus, my vision blurred through the smoke of a bonfire that burned nine months ago.

"We're leaving," Rob says as Joe hands Margie a cloth handkerchief from his pocket.

Once we're outside, the glare of the sun behind its silver clouds is enough to make my eyes throb.

"It can't be true," I say to Rob once I'm behind the wheel of April's jeep and we're back on the road. The glare from the sky is killing my eyes, and I wish I could look down at my lap like Rob is. At least then I wouldn't have to face the vision of the North Woods the closer we get to the Carver House.

"There's no possible way that could be true."

And I wouldn't have to contemplate what it means if Margie was telling the truth after all, and the woods really are as lonely as she says.

18

Dear Rae,

You lied to me every single day that we were friends.

It started that day in the gym. There was that assembly, the one where Principal Pittman told us all where to go in case of a natural disaster, even though Phoenix doesn't get earthquakes or hurricanes, and the last tornado was in 1996, and there are tons of people who say that wasn't even a tornado.

But Principal Pittman told us we needed to go to the locker rooms, and you leaned over and told me something I can't even remember now, but it was hilarious enough to make my stomach hurt from laughing.

That was the first day we became friends, and I know that because you told me so. You said, "So you and I are friends now." We'd hung out before that, and you'd called me or texted me practically every day since the first day we met, but you'd never called me your friend. And because no one ever says things like that, I believed instantly that you were right.

So when you came to get me the other day and said, "This is the perfect night for a drive," and I knew it wasn't because it was raining, and the roads were slick after ten months of draught and the gorges were high with rushing water, I still didn't believe myself.

I believed you instead.

And when you drove up to that wash and said we could make it even though the water was up to the tops of the tires and your eyes got wide and you looked like the fear was what was keeping you whole, I wanted the same fear to fill in my gaps, too.

So how come all I feel now are big, drafty spaces?

That's how I know now that you've been lying this whole time. Because if we were really friends, you'd be able to hear the wind whipping through those gaps in me, and you'd want to insulate me against it somehow.

I know you've been lying because you told me after we got through the wash that the car had lifted off the ground and almost rushed away with the water. You told me that even though I was in the car with you and felt no such thing. The wheels stayed on the ground. We weren't almost carried away. But I agreed with you anyway. Because I knew how much you needed me to.

I'm making a story for you, Rae, but it's actually a story for me. I'm building up the walls of what you called our friendship because you actually never built the walls yourself. I guess you figured I'd get around to that eventually. And these are only paper walls, and each one is pinioned to the ground with "Dear Rae," but that's all I really need them to be because they aren't permanent anyway. They just need to stay up long enough for me to tear them down. Sometimes a story

has to be ripped to shreds so you have pieces to build
something new out of it.

And I think I'm just about ready to build something new.
These pieces aren't for you, Rae. They're for me.

Love,

Penny

I don't remember rescuing the notepad from the bonfire. I remember Rae throwing it in there after she unearthed it from her bag, a found artifact from the ruins of my life I hadn't seen starting to form.

I can look at the notepad now, its singed edges still smelling of smoke, sitting there underneath a patiently waiting Linda, and know that I did indeed pry it from the hands of flames that night. I might have used a stick or my foot to kick it out of danger. I might have stomped the glow from the pages until it was nothing but desert scrub and shoe prints, although I see traces of neither as I look at the pages now.

All I know is that when I saw it tip from Rae's fingertips to the edge of the rock-rimmed fire, I couldn't bear the thought of it burning yet. I couldn't comprehend that the notepad would perish at her hand instead of my own.

The notepad lived, and Rae died.

My phone buzzes again, nagging me to check the text that came in several minutes ago. I've ignored the last three, and it seems I won't be able to get away with disregarding the fourth. I know it's Rob checking on me again. He hasn't let half a day go by without texting me since he went back to soccer clinic and Gwen Brzinski and a life much simpler than the one that faces his mom and me in the North Woods. We argued for at least another hour after we got back to the Carver House, sitting in April's car while I watched the minutes tick away, becoming increasingly aware that she was mere seconds away from officially becoming a prisoner of war at the Registrar's Office, Cynthia Doom the key master.

But really, we both knew that what he was arguing for—that we both leave with him that night—was a ridiculous proposition. Aside from Margie's likely made up (or alcoholically imagined) story, nothing had changed. April was still in this house up to her eyeballs, I still had nothing of substance to tell her aside from ghost stories, and neither of us could point to any reason that she and I might be in any kind of actual danger.

So off Rob went, shaking his head as he backed out of the

in-road to the house, but we both knew all that head-shaking that made me look so unreasonable was just so he could feel better about wanting to get the hell out of there and back to a happier place without people like Margie and with people like Gwen Brzinski. We bartered secrets: I promised not to tell anyone he'd escaped from soccer camp (borrowing his maybe-girlfriend's car), and he promised not to tell my dad I was cracking up.

So now he texts me every several hours to make sure we're still alive. Some of the texts make it through the black hole of cellular connectivity I'm quickly growing used to. I know when some haven't because the ones I finally do receive show Rob's increasing anxiety at my nonresponse.

"Yes," I say to my phone. "Yes, okay? Still kicking."

But when I see the screen light up with a fourth text, I'm surprised to find a 253 area code behind it.

There's more 2 it than u know.

I back up and read the first three.

I was an asshole the other nite.

I'm sorry, k? But I need 2 talk 2 you.

I know what u heard.

I reread the texts three more times. Miller hasn't so much as called since I left his house the other night, and now he's suddenly sorry.

But that's not all. He knows that I talked to Margie.

And though I should be happy that there's more to the horrible story than what she left me with, I had been trying to convince myself ever since hearing it that I didn't need to know any more. That so long as April could get this stupid house fixed up well enough to sell it and get us out of here without me having to see anything else in the middle of the night, whatever happened or didn't happen in these woods could remain the business of the trees and weird little coffee shops and shadowy dive bars in this closed-up town.

And even though April didn't learn much about the house itself in all those papers that Cynthia Doom gave her, she did learn that it'd had only a few owners in all its years, with decades passing between ownership that never lasted more than a year or so, all the remaining years taken up by bank ownership. She surmised that the cost of tearing the house down was too much for anyone to actually take on, especially since nobody really came to these woods anyway, and most seemed to rather just pretend the house didn't exist at all.

Then she erased voice mails from the sixth plumber who refused to come and take a look at the toilet and the at least apologetic lady from the cable company who basically told us we should give up on ever getting decent Internet access out here.

In the meantime, I'd spent the last couple of days convincing myself I could go the rest of my life not hearing from that guy with the burnt red hair and evergreen eyes and be perfectly fine with it.

Now I stand with my cell cradled in my hand, staring at the texts that somehow managed to get through while I pace the upstairs hallway back and forth and contemplate my response. If I respond at all.

I'm almost to the end of the hall when I hear the faintest groan of a door on a hinge.

I look up, squinting to hear better, a habit I'll never be able to break myself of. As though seeing what I can't see will help me hear better.

After another several seconds of silence, I hear it again, this time more pronounced. And this time, I'm positive it came from the room at the end of the hall, the one with the boy Jack on the wall.

I enter the room with new caution, my experiences in this corner officially making me wary.

Jack's eyes are on the closet across the room, the mattress tunnel still destroyed, the random furniture and blankets and papers that were once strewn everywhere now piled in semi-organized columns in corners and against the walls.

April must have been doing a little cleaning up in lieu of

the real work she can't have done. I heard her moving around again last night. Even though all my stuff is still upstairs, I only sleep in her room now, which means I'm acutely aware of when she sleeps. Or when she doesn't sleep, which I'm finding is often. I wonder how long she's been an insomniac. Not ever having lived with her before March, I don't know if she goes through spells like this, but thinking back to the spring, I never remembered hearing her shuffling around in my dad's house in the middle of the night.

Now as I watch the boy on the wall for clues, I hear the creak of the door up close, turning abruptly to see the closet door sway slowly on a breeze that can't possibly exist in this room with all the windows upstairs shut tight.

But there it is, plain as day, groaning open with such patience, I swear it's waiting for a reaction from me. I shift my gaze cautiously to Jack, but his stare is as fixed as ever.

So I try something new.

"What else is there? What are you trying to say?" I ask him. I cram my heart back into my chest before it can creep up in my throat. "What?"

I hear a creak of floorboards behind me and spin, releasing a tiny shriek before I can catch it.

"Don't shoot!" April jokes, but I know she's not kidding exactly. Her eyes are bouncing between me and the mural.

"April! Seriously, your new name is Creeper."

"Who were you just talking to?"

I hold up my phone, the lies coming more easily now.

"Boys. Cryptic messages. I'm sure you don't miss those days." I laugh what totally doesn't sound like a nervous laugh.

"No, no I don't," she says, still looking at the boy in the wall. "So you weren't just, you know, talking to . . ." She looks more nervous than I do.

Great. I've officially made her afraid of me.

"The wall? Wow, what is that, the third symptom of cabin fever?" I say, turning from the mural and April to text Miller back.

"Can I borrow your car?" I ask.

"Hmm?" April is nibbling at the dry flakes of skin that have begun to form on her normally glossed lips.

"I need to run out to the store," I say, not entirely lying this time.

"Uh-huh," April says, and it appears I've finally grasped her distracted attention. "The store. Got it. Need to go buy a little clarity then, I take it?" she says, and suddenly I'm embarrassed for us both. Guy talk isn't exactly an area we've ventured into yet.

"Right," I say. "Are your keys . . . ?"

"On the table downstairs," she says, rolling her eyes.

But she looks worried, and I wonder if she really is concerned for my sanity. I might actually find that comforting if not for the fact that I'm a little worried about it myself.

"You okay?" I ask. Suddenly I'm the one embarrassing us. What would I know about the kind of stress she's under with the hefty weight of this expensive mistake?

"Oh, sure," she says. "Nothing a pint of Ben & Jerry's and two hundred thousand dollars won't fix," she says, and we swirl in the wake of her massive admission for a second before I pull myself from the water.

I slide her keys from the table and leave the Carver House with April in it, wishing the woods would leave me a little more breathing room than the house does, even though I know they won't. I wonder if April's slept more than one full night total since we moved in.

19

THE BELL AT SCOOT'S GREETS me on entry, and I search its sound for some of the comfort it brought me the first time I heard it. But all I can locate is the tiniest flicker of anticipation at seeing Miller, and that seems a poor substitute for the quiet that I was actually hoping to find. In fact, I haven't felt this much noise crowding my head since those blurry months following that night in the desert.

Or that day at the rest stop.

"I know you don't want to be here," I hear his voice say from somewhere at the back of the store. Why is it his voice always precedes him when we're here? I suddenly want nothing more than to be in his cozy trailer where I can see from one end to the other from the front door.

And then, as though divining my thoughts, he says, "I was just about to close up. Will you come back to my place with me?"

I find him now, crouched behind the register. He slides the drawer closed with a click, the chime of the machine filling all the spaces of this store with an echoing *ching!*

I watch his face change as he finds me, too, and he follows quickly with "I mean, I just want to show you something."

Now I understand his embarrassment, and I cross my arms over my stomach because he hasn't made it much better by saying that, either.

"I mean, I . . . look, you don't have the whole story, and I just want to be sure you do, okay?"

I'd managed to shove aside the real reason he asked me out here in favor of the sliver of a chance he just wanted to apologize, and we could go back to being people who maybe, possibly, might have enough in common to be comfortable around each other, maybe more than comfortable. I thought that there was a speck of hope we might be able to pretend something horrible hadn't happened to both of us. But I should have known the minute I left The Washingtonian that I was kidding myself to think that. This is a small town, and from what I've heard, word travels at light speed in these places.

Besides, what else do we have in common but our respective secrets?

Miller finishes locking up the register and flips the sign on the glass door of Scoot's before switching the light and bringing the entire store to a shocking darkness. He holds the door open for me and walks me to April's jeep before climbing into his own car. Even though I know where I'm going, I let him pull away first, content to lag a little behind. I'm in no hurry to discuss more of the story Margie started.

I'm nearly out of the dirt parking lot before I see Ripp's face hovering in one of the many panes of glass that face Scoot's, as though the building was designed especially to watch over the one it neighbors. We lock eyes before I turn to see Miller's taillights disappear around the corner.

For maybe the first time in my life, I turn down coffee. Since I was a kid, I've always loved the taste of it. Mom must have thought it was just strange enough to let slide because she never kept me from drinking it, despite the warnings of stunted growth and other dire consequences.

But maybe it's the memory of Ripp's face in the window of his own coffee shop, clearly wishing he could somehow teleport me back to wherever I came from, that's making my stomach turn against it. Or maybe it's the fact that I haven't been able to keep my hands still since talking to Margie, no matter how many times I tell myself it couldn't possibly be true that these parents did the horrible thing Margie implied to right the horrible wrong that was done to them.

Without a word—and without taking a cup for himself, either—Miller walks straight to the artwork tower and reaches to the top of the stack, lifting from it the tiny canvas that fell and marred his carpet the last time I was here.

He places it on the little folding tray to the side of the recliner where he's insisted I sit.

I stare at the painting and unsuccessfully fight the urge to pick it up. The tiny bits of carpet fuzz have been plucked from the once-damp pools of color, and new brushstrokes smooth the surface where they'd once stuck. The sky, the trees, the dip and curve outlining his brother's face—all of it is so perfect, I want to drag my nail across it. Just to chip away at the edges a little bit. I think about the streaks of paint frantically slapped against the old walls of the corner room at the Carver House. Their uneven smears and colliding images, detailed and intricate, but painted in a frenzy. There's so much more about that mural that feels so real.

Maybe that's because it keeps changing.

"I know you've been wanting a closer look at some of

these," Miller says, but it sounds a little more insistent than an offer.

"Miller, I'm sorry if you feel like I was prying. I know what happened to you and your family isn't any of my business. I was just—"

Miller starts shaking his head, clearly tempering some frustration. He closes his eyes for a second, then opens them, and says slowly, "I just need you to know what you heard, okay?"

His eyes are on the miniature painting like he's afraid to let it out of his sight. But after I've been looking at him for a moment, he finally finds me, and for the first time since that night in his car, I think maybe I wasn't imagining that thread connecting us.

"Can I show you a different one?" he asks, sounding needier than I think I've ever heard him sound.

"Miller, really, you don't have to. It's none of my bus—"

"No, I—" He cuts himself off, stifling a hot burst of impatience that closely resembles anger. He takes a quick breath before saying, "I need to show you."

And even though Miller's never said anything like that to me before, someone else has, in a dream that couldn't have been a dream but couldn't have been real, either. It suddenly feels very cold in his once cozy trailer.

Miller is in front of me again, and this time he's holding a slightly larger canvas. He carefully extracts the palm-size portrait from my hand and replaces it with the new canvas. I grow even colder at the sight of this one.

"I just finished it the other day," he says, not so much with pride as with relief. Like he's been holding his breath for days and finally found a reason to exhale.

The painting is a nearly perfect replica of the little wooden shed just past the clearing in the deepest part of the woods I've been to. The fine brushwork even manages to depict the age of the wood somehow, with tiny splinters fringing rusted nails.

The only difference between the shed in real life and the shed depicted on this canvas is the little green door, the one I couldn't manage to open the night I chased the girl through the thicket before Rae chased me all the way back to the Carver House.

In Miller's painting, that door stands ajar. And though the shed's interior is shaded, I get the impression it's shaded on purpose. Miller has no desire to illuminate the inside. Not yet, and not for me, not that I'd want him to.

"Why are you showing me this?" I ask him. It doesn't come off mean, I know that. But part of me wishes that it did, just so he wouldn't continue this confession. I know how unfair it is for me to not want to hear this after my meltdown in his car, but after the horrors Margie relayed, I'm not sure I can bear to hear any more.

"You've seen the mural," he says, eyeing me closely. Too closely. Like he can read something deep and dark inside of me. And I thought I'd already shown him all my darkest corners.

"You've seen it . . . you've seen how it . . ."

It's the first time I've watched Miller struggle for words. He always seems to know exactly how to land a sentence, his words sketched out before making their way to the canvas. He wants me to finish, and I almost do. But he can't possibly mean for me to say what I actually see: that the mural changes. He can't possibly mean for me to say that because he can't possibly know that. I don't even know that.

When I don't finish, he sets it aside. Not giving up exactly, but it's obvious I've disappointed him again. Still, he tries a new direction.

"Kids went into those woods all the time. They went on dares, you know? Mostly just because some of the parents told them not to. Probably afraid they'd get lost or something. Some of us just went because we knew we could get away with it . . . because no one would come looking." His eyes lose their hold on mine for a second, and that's all it takes for me to understand which category his parents fell into.

Then his eyes are back. "Nobody really believed the stories. I knew my brother used to go out there. He never let me come with him, but I knew where he was going. So one time, I followed him, and I found him at this shed."

I hold my breath because I get the sense Miller would prefer to be doing that too. Except he can't because he's confessing to me, the same way I had to confess to him in his car that night it poured so hard we couldn't see the road from behind the windshield.

"It's not like he was . . . I mean, they were just animals, and maybe they were already dead before he . . ."

A conversation I should never have heard meanders into my memory. *He needed help, not . . .*

I look at the shed in the painting and run my finger over the shaded entry. When I do, I swear I see just a smidge more light shine on the hearth than was there before. My eyes are burning they're so tired.

"I don't understand. What does this have to do with what Margie said?"

"I told my pop," Miller blurts, his voice loud on the stiff air around us.

I shake my head. "Miller, what're you—"

"I told him, don't you get it? I started the whole thing." He looks at the painting like it's a living, breathing creature he'd like to step on. But the instant I see that hate burn in his eyes, the fire is snuffed out and he looks up at me, the thread between us tugging.

"I thought I'd make him proud if I told him." Miller drags his hands through his burnt hair and tugs, the skin around his eyes lifting. "It's just . . . I was only eight."

I want to say that I know, that I completely understand, that the thread isn't tugging too hard on me now. But suddenly I'm understanding a little bit more about Miller's specific pain in losing his brother after that—even if some part of him returned.

The little boy standing in the doorway, scratching at his arms, waiting for someone to notice him.

"Miller, you don't think—"

"I made it happen, Penny." The fire that burns his hair now looks like it's traveled someplace behind his eyes. "It's my fault. Everything that happened after I told my pop, it's all my fault."

I think of the man, Burt, returning with Jack, the boy left in the woods for six months. I think of the woman, Doris, her hand raised high in the air, her eyes wild. Her eyes finding anyone but the eight-year-old Miller standing in front of her, ready to receive the blow. But none of it makes sense. Did they send Jack into the woods as punishment before they realized what they'd have to do to get him back? Or did they know and do it anyway? The thought is almost as horrific as the confessions Margie laid on me in The Washingtonian.

"Miller, you didn't make any of that happen. Whatever your brother did. Whatever your parents did. None of that was your fault."

I wait for second before I add, "You were just eight."

But his words repeated back to him do nothing to comfort this eight-year-old boy who is a young man now. He's shaking his head before I can finish, and I know I'm not understanding what he needs me to understand. And he's right. I have no idea what it was like to grow up in his house, though if whatever Jack's been showing me at night is even half of the reality Miller lived and not just a figment of my own messed up imagination, I'm starting to get a better idea.

I look down at the painting with the mark of Miller's troubled childhood memory all over the canvas. I trace the brushstrokes and read the thoughts an eight-year-old Miller must have had when he was waiting for his missing brother to come home, watching his parents grapple with a reality few have ever had to face. I feel stabs of guilt for my outrage at Margie the other day at The Washingtonian.

Then I remember the rest of her story, the story of what she did to ease the burden of her pain.

I set the painting down on the folding table before looking back up at Miller, and I'm not at all surprised to find him entirely deflated when I raise my eyes. The thread snaps.

"It wasn't your fault. However horrible the whole situation was, you weren't the one who made it happen."

"Penny, don't you get it? There's something going on in those woods. You know it too, or you wouldn't have gone around asking."

"What I know is that if Margie was telling the truth, some horrible things have gone down in those woods. And I'm not sure I can believe something that awful . . ."

"It happened," Miller says, and the sadness that soaks his already faltering voice is enough to make me buckle.

We share the silence, searching for each other in the murky depths of it. Because he said it—because his parents lived it, and that means he did too—I can't deny that Margie was telling the truth anymore. Whatever those woods are or aren't, I have to hold up at least one truth as a light through the trees. A bargain was made, the "miracle" that brought those kids back one by one from the North Woods.

And whatever remains there now isn't what the Point Finney Four left behind. It's whoever was left in their place.

"It wasn't you." I finally say to Miller.

But he doesn't say a word. He simply hooks his finger gingerly under the canvas's wooden frame and pulls it toward him.

"It wasn't you." I say it again because I can't think of what else to say.

He takes a while to answer. And when he does, he sounds more assured than he has the entire night. "Maybe not," he says, "but I could be the one to make it right."

I search his face for answers, but I can't get past the smoke from all that fire around him.

"Miller, what do you think you could possibly do now—"

"You know," Miller says, his eyes widening. "I *know* you know. You've all but confirmed it. What I'm doing is making a difference. It *changes* things."

His eyes are wild with a kind of mania I've never once seen in Miller. They drop to the painting of the shed, and I wonder if this is how everyone's been looking at me all these months since Rae died. The way I want to look at

Miller now. To convince him not to believe all the things his bereaved brain is telling him.

"The painting? Miller, that's just a coping mechanism. It's like therapy. It's not real."

I don't mean to sound like I know better. I write letters to my dead friend. But it comes out like that anyway, which is why the fire burning all around him snuffs instantly, and he walks me to the door sooner than I'm ready to go.

"I just wanted you to know," he says, unlocking the bolt and ushering in the June night's breeze. "I thought you'd want to know there's more than just a horrible mistake behind what happened back then. Whatever you've heard—whatever you've seen—it was more than just a mistake. There's blame, too. And we all share a piece of it. It's not just bad people who do bad things."

I consider what he says from the step outside his trailer.

"There's always more to a horrible mistake than what happens after it," I say just before Miller closes the door behind me.

I walk slowly to April's jeep despite the chill reaching toward me from the woods.

Even though the sun has finally set and the moon is fighting for a space to shine between the dense trees, I don't feel nearly ready to go back to the Carver House. I check the dash and find that April's tank is three-quarters empty. And because it's the closest station to the middle of nowhere, I get back onto WA-16, ignoring the impossible lure that tempts me toward I-5 North and back to Seattle. Instead, I pull off at the same concrete-laden gas station April and I stopped at the day we arrived in Point Finney after leaving the rest stop. April's jeep is shuddering as I depress the brake, and I notice that the thermometer is climbing toward the *H*. I make a mental note to buy coolant, but not before I enjoy this moment outside the car, surrounded by concrete. It feels good to be in a place free of the encroaching trees, just for a second.

I slide my card and situate the pump, tapping my foot absently to the tinny music playing through the speakers overhead. The same inane jingle I heard the last time.

I look up at the convenience store, its brightly lit entrance marred only by one flickering light that can't manage to keep up with the glow of the rest of this place, with its sparkling red fixtures and absence of oil stains that haven't yet formed on the concrete. The convenience store is closed, the pumps set to accept only cards.

"Not exactly the most convenient convenience store," I mutter.

The same boy sits just off center of the entrance,

crouched with his knees under his chin. His cardboard sign is lettered neatly in all caps: NEED $5 FOR BUS RIDE HOME. HUNGRY. WILL WORK. GOD BLESS.

The pump clicks to a stop behind me, but I hardly notice. All I can think about is what Miller said, the singular focus of his pain. I can practically feel the textured paint of the little brown shed under my fingers.

"I thought you'd want to know there's more than just a horrible mistake behind what happened. There's blame, too. And we all share a piece of it."

I can't shake the feeling that I let Miller down. That I didn't meet him at the conclusion where he's been waiting for me. But all I learned tonight is that Miller thinks he *is* the canvas on which the rest of this story is painted. That somehow he was the architect of the events that led to his brother's disappearance and reemergence from the woods six months later. A fraction of his former self, but enough to satisfy anyone looking from a distance. That he thinks he can repaint the saddest picture in the world to somehow make it a happier one.

And while I have seen enough over the past few weeks to open my mind to a lifetime of horrific possibilities I would have dismissed as insanity prior to that, I have to remind myself that I've had a constant companion in Rae for the last nine months.

I think back to the night she turned me by my shoulders, pleading with me. *"Then why am I still here?"*

"Because I keep you close," I say, and I see the head of the boy by the entrance lift in response to an answer that isn't his.

Rae is so close, I can smell the vanilla bean lotion she used to wear.

"Because I'm not ready to let the pages burn yet," I say to her.

20

THE WOODS ARE SO QUIET by the time I pull up to the Carver House, I almost feel like they're waiting for me to do something.

"Nothing to talk about tonight?" I say, knowing I'm insane for taunting whatever might be listening, but I am delirious from lack of sleep and I've heard enough horror stories in the last few days to numb me for the moment. It feels good to be a little pissed, and I let the shell of that anger shield me all the way to the front door and through the living room.

Even in the shadows and the silver light of the moon, I can see that April has rearranged the furniture and done a respectable job of scrubbing and polishing the floors. I feel a pang of guilt for not being here for that, and I vow to be of more help starting tomorrow, even if all we can manage right now is to make the place look prettier.

A large eye winks at me from the side table by the couch, and I recognize Linda's blue and white strap dangling from the edge like a tail. A pink Post-it in April's handwriting reads: "Borrowed your camera for some before and after pics. Nice, huh?"

I advance backward through the pictures, seeing the "after" before the "before," and I have to say that I'm impressed. It looks like she took some magical lint roller to the couch, and what she uncovered, at least according to Linda's digital record, is something less mauve and more like a cranberry color. She left the gray coat hanging on the hook by the door, and it's the only thing that disrupts the room's appearance of antiquity.

I scroll backward and find a couple more pictures reflecting the work she did in the first two rooms upstairs, the ones closest to the stairs. With the beds made, the mattresses in place, it actually looks like this house could serve as a bed-and-breakfast to a buyer with just the right kind of imagination.

One who doesn't care about small things like plumbing and electricity.

And uninvited visitors.

I click back once more to find the room with Jack in his mural, and as always, my eye travels straight to him. Everything looks as it should. His earnest green eyes fixed on the closet across the room. The clumps of trees growing thicker as they travel to the top and back of the mural. I'm sure if I zoomed in close enough, I'd be able to make out the little wooden shed—the one I've seen not only in person, thanks to Rae, but centered on its very own canvas thanks to Miller's eternal guilt.

But I don't want to see any more.

April is in bed. I can see her room from where I stand in the living room, her back to me in a position that feels oddly familiar, and it's not until I'm almost taken by sleep—my body finding the curves of the newly cleaned sofa—that I remember another woman lying on her own bed, staring at the reflection of her face in a vanity mirror that refuses to give her any comfort instead of staring at a little boy standing in her doorway, waiting to be noticed.

"Just for a second," I say to no one in particular, but I know someone is listening. Someone is always listening in this place. "Just for a second, give me some quiet."

I allow the heaviness of sleep to press me into the sofa, its tufts of fabric cushioning my head. My body is limp from exhaustion, and I let sleep swallow me whole.

. . .

Jack is waiting for me on the edge of consciousness.

"Please," I beg him, but I know it won't do any good. "Please, just a few hours. I can hardly breathe I'm so tired."

But my hand is already on the mural as I say it, and his smile, too knowing for his young years, deepens grooves into his soft face. His eyes glow bright green under the shadows of the room.

"You're already here," he says. "Just a few more steps and you'll see."

"I don't want to see any more," I tell him, but he's walking away, and I know I have to follow. The painting pulls me in, the dried dust of greens and midnight blues and the fire red of his hair blowing in a gust that reaches my face, watering my eyes.

"You'll see," I hear him say, and I believe him, though I don't want to.

We're back in the house—in Miller's house, when he had one. This time, I don't see anyone. This time, I only see a closed door. And behind the door, I hear the inescapable sound of a man crying. It comes out in stunted gasps that sound like choking at first.

The little boy Miller wanders from his room, eyes shaded in freshly disturbed sleep. He approaches the closed door with caution, holding a shaking hand to the knob before dropping it to his side and turning toward the basement door instead, opening it with an almost imperceptible creak and slipping down the stairs on socked feet.

He finds the same corner as before and sits on the cold concrete, tucking his legs under his chin and pulling his thermal shirt over the thin fabric of his pajama pants. The whole of him looks so small, it seems he could fit into one of the boxes he's now unpacking. And by the look on his face—the one that desperately seems to be searching for something—he might just choose to curl himself up and hide in one of those boxes for the rest of the night.

But he's searching for something else, setting aside the same Christmas decorations and old tissue that's long since lost its padding for precious ornaments. He once again finds the purple Huskies cap that must have been restored to the box at some point. He pulls it snugly over his head and bends the tops of his ears down. I can hardly see his face under the bill, but his chin stiffens in fixed determination. He pulls out a partially finished model of a 1955 Cadillac El Dorado, or so the box it comes in says. There's a smooth, flat stone perfect for skipping. There's an early model iPod, its thick white body bound by a pair of white earbud wires, its jack still plugged in, its screen probably long since black and chargeless.

And this time he pulls something new from the box: a sketchpad. Handling each page gingerly, as though it contains holy documents, Miller turns page after page to reveal detailed, shadowed drawings of castles. One has a moat that winds around the back and all the way into the deepest point in the woods surrounding the spires. Upon closer examination, the moat depicts reflections in its water, rippling trees and towering structures twinkling back up at the massive castle drawn above it.

And something different happens this time. Instead of receding to the background as he has in the past, Jack emerges from behind me now, standing at first next to the younger version of Miller, then crouching, leaning against the boy's ear that pokes out from his hat.

"You know, one day you'll be bigger than Pop," he says to Miller.

Miller jumps, and he looks at Jack with the kind of anxiety no boy that age should know how to feel.

"He's crying again," Miller tells his brother.

"He should be doing a lot more than crying," Jack says with an anger that surpasses Miller's anxiety. "We were all supposed to be his sons."

Jack traces a finger along the cracks drawn across a picture of a cement wall, a looming obstruction made mostly of shadow and lead shading. But every inch of space across the page is branded with graffiti so lifelike I'd swear it was a photograph.

"I know," Miller tells him.

"You'll never be Jack, and he knows it," the boy from the mural says. "That's why he won't ever look at you the right way. Just stop expecting him to. It gets easier when you stop expecting him to."

I take a step forward, knowing I can't be a part of the scene like they are, but now I feel like I need to be. Because I can't make sense of what I just heard the boy from the mural say.

The boy who is supposed to be Jack.

Young Miller nods and turns the page of the sketchbook, the older boy looking at the pages protectively, his hand inches from jerking the sketch from the small hands of Miller.

"This one's my favorite," Miller says, finding a page with a face.

It's actually just eyes. There's a face there—at least you're supposed to think there is—but it's only implied. I have to walk even closer to see, but up this close, I don't like the eyes staring back at me. Even upside down, they make me uncomfortable. And maybe it's because they evoke the eyes of too many stares I've seen over the past nine months.

The boy from the mural holds the corner of the page so he doesn't smear the pencil lead across his fingertips. The shadow shading looks like ash left over from a fire. The eyes rage against the darkness that practically swallows them.

"I never got to finish it," the boy from the mural says, anger spilling from his voice at a rapid boil.

"I didn't know," Miller says, his voice so childlike he could be three years old. "I didn't know what they would do to get him back."

The boy from the mural snatches the page with the eyes from Miller, the edge of the paper slicing a cut deep enough to make Miller cry out and jerk his hand back.

He sucks blood from the cut and spits it on the floor, but the page in the sketchbook still bears the mark of what he's done.

"So you finish it then," the boy from the mural says to Miller, snapping the sketchbook shut with a crack.

I gasp awake, the awkwardness of my sleep on the couch making every joint in my body creak as I stagger toward consciousness again.

My mind is swirling with paint and lead and blood-red streaks, and I fight against every instinct racing through me to slow down, to concentrate, to try to make sense of it all. But the pieces are chasing one another, rabbits through a dark forest.

We gave the woods what it wanted. Company.

My uncle, he's the one who always encouraged us to do the creative stuff, even though Jack never really got into it.

If you had a chance to right a wrong, something truly awful. Just paint over it and start fresh. You'd do it, wouldn't you?

The price for that decision was too high. The Doris I know would never have paid it.

We were all supposed to be his sons.

He'll need a jacket. There was a cold snap.

A gasp launches me from thought, my hand covering my mouth, but not before the sudden intake echoes throughout the downstairs, waking a new horror somewhere deep inside the recesses of my mind.

I rush to the jacket on the wall, the one April left despite its incongruence with the room. The one I'd been assuming this whole time belonged to Jack after the first scene the boy in the mural showed to me.

"He'll need a jacket," I say, the words of the mother on my lips almost as horrific as the realization they bring. "Which means Jack didn't have . . ."

I dig into one of the pockets and find nothing but the slippery synthetic lining. But in the other, I feel the round plastic button, the thread still dangling from the tiny holes poked through the middle, the same one I found that first day we arrived at the Carver House. Then I pull out the tiniest stub of a dark lead pencil.

The kind used for sketching.

Jack was the oldest. Then Danny. Then Miller.

"Oh my God," is all I can mutter under the shallow breath that finds its way into my lungs.

I hear the softest thud above me, and I know right away that it came from the room at the end of the hall.

I look to the ceiling above me. "You're not Jack. You're Danny."

April mumbles something in her sleep from the next room. I want to wake her, to tell her the horrible truth I just learned. But she's sleeping for the first time in a century, and besides, where would I even begin?

Another soft thud from upstairs.

I approach the stairs cautiously, trying to remember which steps creak the most so I can avoid them.

A third soft thud. I climb the stairs, determined to be done with this.

A cursory glance at the first two rooms reveals nothing but indeed a cleaner, more put-together upstairs. The pictures on Linda's screen told me that much. But nothing to indicate where the thumping might have come from. Except that upon closer examination, the neatly made beds are missing. Or rather, part of the beds—the mattress and the frilly linens dressing them.

The second two rooms—the one that used to be mine and the first of the twin rooms—reveal a similar picture. Their mattresses are also missing, the remainder of each room undisturbed but for Troy the unicorn lying on his side in the middle of the floor.

I don't even need to look in the second twin room to know what's missing. The last bedroom is almost in view, the only wall visible from my place in the hallway the one with the mural.

There's the painted boy—Danny—his hair angry purple in the harsh moonlight. I scan the rest of the mural for clues to what I'll find once I approach the doorway, as though that might stop my heart from thrashing behind my ribs. I follow his thin arms down to his hands, palms open and exposed, adolescence frozen.

I take a few more steps toward the room, emboldened by the absence of the thudding for several minutes now.

But what I see once I approach the doorway drains me of every ounce of bravery.

The mattresses from each room form a tunnel from the open window straight to the black, open space of the closet.

I struggle to find my breath, but it's buried somewhere under my knocking heart.

And when the humming of that same indecipherable tune begins, even my rabid heart stops to listen, every system in my body slowing to a muddy pace while I search the darkness for the source of the sound.

But I already know where it's coming from. The mouth of the tunnel, where it starts at the window.

I shift my focus to the boy in the mural and am horrified to find him staring wide-eyed at the same window.

The humming grows louder until the sound of it vibrates the depths of the throat it comes from, grating before dwindling to a murky stop.

And then the laughing starts, that horrible, high laugh that sounds too old to be a child's giggle but too high to come from anything else.

I look to Danny for help. I look to him to tell me what to do next. But he's no longer looking at what I'm looking at. His eyes are squeezed so tightly shut the top of his face looks like it might fold over the bottom.

The wind picks up outside so suddenly it scatters the neat piles of papers across the room. A crack of lightning splits the sky violently, and the trees part long enough to let in a sheet of fresh rain, a gift the clouds have been hanging onto for days.

But even through the chaos of wind and rain, I know that whatever was making that sound from the mouth of the tunnel is still in there. I feel the spray of rain reach me all the way from the window to the doorway, but I can't move my hand to swipe away the wetness.

As suddenly as it burst in, the wind and rain draw back on the intake of a breath, leaving the room floating through a void of sound.

That's when I hear sliding, the sound of something heavy but determined, easing its way through the tunnel toward the closet. I can't fathom anything that could make a sound like that, something so heavy it labors, but trails with a fine scratching that sets my entire body shaking, my only movement completely out of my control.

I venture another look at the mural. The grass practically swallows the boy, his hands, dimpled at their knuckles and opalescent in the abrasive moonlight, covering his eyes.

I remember throwing the mattresses back last time. I see my own hands—hands that are not over my eyes but lifeless by my sides—tearing the fort down, exposing the thing that drags behind those mattresses, edging closer to the doorway of the closet, the place the boy in the mural can't bear to watch now that it's been found.

I see my bravery return, over and over, and feeling begins to awaken my hand. It tingles, and I form a fist against that dragging, that horrible scratching edging toward the closet. I can feel the floor beneath my feet.

But just as I take my first step toward that hideous sound, a new one takes its place, and every ounce of blood halts in my veins.

A deep exhale, grumbling so low at first I think it's thunder. But then, the lowest register of a voice utters two words at the tail of that breath: "You're it."

A shriek cracks the air, and the room feels like it might cave under the sound of it.

The boy in the mural refuses to uncover his eyes, but his mouth hangs so low his jaw dips to the middle of his waist.

The mattress tunnel collapses as though the floor has disappeared beneath it. The bed skirts and floral sheets flutter under the wind that whips through the room from the open window. Then, like a wave pulling back from shore, the wind recedes, dragging the curtains and papers in its wake with it before the window slams shut.

Hands on my shoulders whirl me around. Hands on my shoulders shake me. Hands on my shoulders move to my own hands and struggle to pry them from my face. Struggle to free them from my grip over my eyes.

"Penny! Penny, stop! Stop!"

April is yelling over me, but I'm the one shrieking. I'm screaming so loudly my throat is seared.

April's hands are on my head now. She's holding my face still. She's making me look into her eyes, even though my own eyes are still trying to adjust to the darkness of the hallway.

"Penny, my God. What . . . what?!"

But I can't find my voice. I can't believe that was my voice screaming a second ago, but the burning of my throat tells me it was.

"What is this?" April looks at the pile of mattresses. She looks to me to explain it. But all I can do is look to the boy on the wall, whose eyes are once again staring at the closet, though now they could just as easily be staring at the wreckage of the room, the wreckage April thinks I created. The boy's hands are back at his sides, his body unburied from the grass that consumed him seconds ago.

That laughter. That voice.

"Oh my God," I breathe, staring at the boy who won't stare back at me.

"Penny?"

I turn to look at April. I beg her to understand, even though I've given her absolutely no reason to. "It wasn't just a horrible mistake."

April turns me back to her, my shoulders now squared with hers.

"Penny, listen to me. Listen to me," she says, catching my eyes shifting back to the mural. "You have to stop blaming yourself. It *was* a horrible mistake. That's all. A night full of mistakes, few of which you could have avoided. It wasn't your fault. What happened to Rae wasn't your fault. You have to stop this."

I start to shake my head. "April, you don't understand."

But she's pulling me down the stairs, mumbling something about the toilet again, and I know she's pissed as hell because she thinks I trashed the room. But there's no way April could understand what I do now.

Because now I realize what Miller was trying to tell me, what he was so desperate for me to find so he didn't have to say the words. It wasn't just a horrible mistake that all those parents made. It was a decision. And his parents' decision was the most horrible of all.

The brother I've been seeing this whole time on the wall, in my half-waking moments, in Miller's canvases—it hasn't been Jack.

The child Miller's parents traded for their son was Danny. They traded one of their own children for another.

21

Dear Rae,

Here's something I didn't know about me before there was you: I have a ridiculously high tolerance for pain.

I didn't know that until we were sitting across from each other in the vinyl chairs that day and I'd already gotten my ink and you were waiting to get yours. You bit every last fingernail off while you watched me, and when it was your turn, you shrank away from Chewy the tattoo guy every time he raised the needle. You told me afterward that I was insane, but I knew you wished it was me who'd flinched under the pain.

*I think that's why I never understood how you could push
a needle through your vein without even blinking, how you
could smile at me when you did it, like you were so glad I
was on the outside of feeling whatever you were feeling in
that moment. Remember that time you said, "Sweet little
Penny. You're way too precious to sink this low. But I'm
higher than you'll ever be. I'm the only one who can make
a unicorn appear." Everyone else was high, so they thought
you sounded like a poet. But I knew you were just lying
again about winning Troy at the fair.*

*It's just that you always made me so aware of what I owed
you for acknowledging my existence when I first moved
to Phoenix. And it's exhausting to always feel like you're
repaying a debt.*

Penny

I press the notepad to my forehead and hold it there. I
press harder and harder until the pressure of my fist threatens to cave my skull in, and then I press a little harder.

With the pad this close, I can still smell the smoke from
the bonfire that night. The odor makes me light-headed, but
the pain in my forehead keeps me grounded. And it keeps

last night's discovery at bay, since I still can't understand how in the world I'm supposed to process what I just learned about Miller's family.

She didn't believe me when I told her between all the smoke and dust that night that the letters weren't the full story of us that I'd written. Instead, she got the benefit of careful revision and erased pencil marks that formed the words I wanted to say perfectly, but left out all the doubt about what I was writing, which was just as true.

A soft knock on the the open door announces April. Who knows how long she's been hanging out there in her fleece and her practical clogs, the wrong attire for summer anywhere other than chilly, dank here.

"So that's what I'm smelling," she says.

I glance at the notepad, which I've let fall to my lap. "You're smelling the house."

"Yeah, well if I'd ever been able to get a structural engineer to come out and take a look, maybe I could have agreed with you. I'm headed into town to drop in on one today. He won't return my calls, so I'm thinking it's time for an ambush."

"Sounds like a pretty good strategy," I say.

April's mouth tilts into a half smile. "You going to be okay alone?"

Neither of us really went back to sleep after last night. I

woke up feeling mostly guilty for robbing April of the first solid REM cycle she's had in what would appear to be a century, judging by her under-eye bags, her constant companions these days.

I look down at the letter to Rae. "That question doesn't mean anything at all if you really think about it. It's not like anyone ever really wants to hear the answer."

That's exactly the sort of thing I thought I was done saying to April. What bothers me the most is the way it just came out. I didn't even mean to say it. It's that it doesn't occur to me to be careful with her. Not like I am with my own mom, who hasn't called in so long, I'm starting not to feel the loss of her.

"I think they have their own strategy," April says, fully passing over my last comment and returning to the contractors. "I'm sure they have a vague idea of what they're doing, anyway. The gods are against me on this one. The gods and this whole messed up little town. Anyway, I'm not stupid. I know a money pit when I step in it."

She eyes the notepad in my lap, and the bags under her eyes take on the tiniest bit more weight.

"When I was fifteen, I had this friend named Summer," she says, sitting at the end of the bed. "The first thing she ever said to me was that her parents loved her so much, they named her after a whole season, not just one month."

"What a bitch," I say.

"She was," April agrees. "She didn't know that my name was actually Lindsay until my mom died."

I look up. I never knew. Of course, I'm not sure how I would have known. It's hard to know something like that about someone when you haven't ever, *ever* had a conversation like this with them.

She shrugs off all the questions I know I should ask but don't.

"I was two when she passed," she explains. "It's not like I remember. I couldn't really even say my own name yet." She grins this odd kind of grin. "My dad had it changed legally in a moment of grief, and much later on, he told me he never should have done that."

She's still smiling for reasons I'll probably never understand, and I smile too, because I still can't think of what to say, and I'm at least relieved that we can agree on a mutual smile.

"My point," she continues, "was that even if Summer had known about all that, I'm not sure it would have mattered. That wasn't the worst thing she ever said to me. She also told me I was stupid to have a baby at eighteen." She squares her jaw, pulling her ears back. "And I let her say that and worse for six solid years while I called her a friend."

I shake my head. She's trying, and I don't mean to shoot her down, but she has no idea. "It's not the same."

That familiar stone in my throat. I swallow, but it lodges there, and my eyes tear up from the strain, and April mistakes that for making me cry, and I feel even worse because I'm not actually crying.

Even still, she puts her hand on my foot, which is half-tucked under my leg, and she does it timidly, like she's afraid I'm going to snatch her hand off of her wrist and devour it. The one person who hasn't thrown me away, and maybe that's only because she's actually just afraid of me. And who could blame her after my epic freak-out last night?

Still, she keeps her hand on my foot, and even though it's starting to make me uncomfortable, I don't move.

"You can think about all the ways it might have happened differently. I'll let you do that. But I'm not going to let you believe you could have changed the ending," she says.

I've never heard her talk in terms of what she'd "let" me do, and she asserts herself boldly. Maybe too boldly. Which is why I twitch my foot to let her know that I know she's holding it, and then I match her weird smile a little closer than before. She squeezes my foot before letting it go.

"Rob wasn't a mistake," April says, her bluntness shocking me out of my trance for a moment. I try to say something, but every word I could say would be grossly out of place.

"I'm sure plenty of people besides Summer thought so. And I'm sure plenty of people wanted to hear me admit it."

I'm having such a hard time following the direction of this conversation, I decide to stop trying. I'm embarrassed for us both, and I think maybe April's relishing that a little. There are probably many, many things she's wanted to say to me in the years she's been married to my dad, and probably hundreds of additional things in the months since I've been living in a family that isn't fully my own.

"But he wasn't a mistake," she keeps going. "He is one of the only things in my life I don't regret. I'm full of wrong decisions. I have so many stacked up inside of me, sometimes I think I'm not going to be able to see over the pile at some point."

April runs her finger over one frayed edge of a fingernail. It's such a small movement, the only movement I can detect in the whole room.

"I'm not ashamed of my mistakes, though. They go with me everywhere. They're my little buddies." She laughs a raw laugh. "But Rob's not one of them."

I continue to say nothing, and maybe that makes me sound patient, but the truth is I'd give anything to know what to say right now. Luckily, April doesn't make me grapple for very long.

"I'm going to harass the engineer," she says, pulling us both to the surface again. "Wish me luck."

"Give him hell," I say, forcing the smile to stay long enough for her to turn the corner and head down the hall.

The rattling of April's keys chases the clomping of her clogs, and for the first time since my dad remarried, I understand what he meant when he said once that he didn't care if April understood him. He just cared that she wanted to.

And for the first time in four years, I miss my father.

It comes out of nowhere and smacks me squarely in the mouth, and I can almost feel the sting of it as I find his number in my phone, the picture box next to his number blank. I've never chosen an image to put inside it.

Your wife is weird, I type. I stare at the text for what feels like hours before I finally hit send, my brain still trying to catch up with my actions.

I don't expect to get a response, so when I do, I immediately get nervous thinking of all the ways he might have answered a message that didn't even make sense to me.

Miss you guys.

I stare at the words for a very long time, uncertain I enjoy the feeling of relief. It doesn't match the emotions I've allotted for my dad. So I set the phone aside and search out a more familiar feeling.

I pick up the notepad sometime after I hear the motor of April's jeep struggle to turn over before finally igniting.

I read the letter eight more times, then land on the last sentence and let my eyes run over it until they burn. I remember writing those sentences. How forming each *T* and *L* and *R* felt like peeling off layers of clothing, the kind that scratches and chokes.

I trace my fingers over the letters already on the paper, trying to remember the feeling instead of simply picturing it like a scene in my head, a snapshot from some moment in time that seemed so profound I had to capture it.

Then I find my pen on the table next to the bed and make a new sentence.

I let you run away to die.

When the lump in my throat finally clears and a tear resurrects itself from the depths of my cracked heart, my new sentence blurs, and I only see the words *I let you die.*

22

WHEN I WAKE UP, THE letter is in my hand, soft and a little damp from the sweat of my palm. I'd been clenching it in my sleep, the page half torn from the notepad. Sleep deprivation finally won out, even if it came at the wrong time of day.

I look at Linda, whose Cyclops eye is turned slightly away from me.

"I know you're mad at me," I say, nudging her lens toward me. "I'm going to make it up to you. We're taking more pictures of the downstairs today. We'll start on the kitchen."

I feel a little better at the thought of erasing a trace of the puffiness under April's eyes as she walks through the door after her meeting with the engineer, her funky oven I still can't find the charm in glistening with the shine of some powerful scouring, pictures snapped of the ever-important "before" and "after."

Maybe, just maybe, I'll be able to force myself into the same exhaustion that put April into a deep sleep last night. That is, until I woke her up. And maybe for a fraction of a second, I'll be able to erase from my mind the horribleness of what may have happened in these woods ten years ago.

I sling Linda's strap over my shoulder and head downstairs, setting her on the kitchen counter before returning upstairs for the cleaning supplies.

But as I begin to descend the stairs once again, I hear a clicking I shouldn't hear.

It's the sound of Linda's shutter, and as I round the corner to the first landing, I see her flash working on overdrive in the kitchen, the click popping a bright light for every take.

I lock up for a second at the thought of whatever might be training her lens. The paralysis of last night as I listened to that dragging progress through the mattress tunnel begins to seep in.

And then suddenly, the anger I wanted to feel last night— the animal instinct I was waiting for while I heard that horrible voice—kicks in at the thought of Linda in anybody's hands but mine.

My feet move with a force of their own, landing in hic-cupping stops as my boots scuff April's shiny new floors. I round the corner of the kitchen so fast, I'm just in time to see Linda's strap disappear through the open kitchen door.

"Hey!" I scream. "Bring her back!"

I pound down the steps to the dirt that borders the edge of the woods, and a muddy footprint points me down a path that's becoming more familiar than I'd like.

"Bring her back!" I scream into the trees before lunging after the footprints. I can't hear Linda's clicking anymore, but I know she can't be far. I'm moving faster than I have in what feels like months, and the need for exertion, for some-place to put this chaos inside of me, overtakes all.

I crash through the trees with insane abandon, the last of my reason cast in my wake. I push the branches away from my face, the leaves slapping my skin with a little more force than they should be able to.

I've already run too far before I have to stop and admit that I have absolutely no idea which direction Linda could have gone with her thief.

I stand as still as I can on tired, shaking legs. The trees are passing a tiny breeze between them, handing it off from one branch to the next. The ground is damp from last night's rain, and even though I know it can't possibly be true, it feels almost as though the soft ground is absorbing me like everything else.

I shift to a new stance at the thought of it, receiving a scrape on my shoulder from an unseen branch to my right.

"Where are you?" I whisper, my voice buried under the weight of my panting breath.

In response, I see a billow of white, then a flash of long, dark hair. And then, pointed directly at me, a flash from my own camera.

The same girl from the night with Rae. The same girl who led me all the way out past the clearing to the shed.

"Not this time," I say through gritted teeth. "You're not going to get that far."

My patience with the game of chase I've been playing all month has worn so thin, I can see through it. But even as I barrel through the woods to the spot where the girl was standing—her footprints so deeply embedded it looks as though she'd been standing there for half a lifetime—I know that not all the rage fueling me is on my own behalf. I'm feeling their rage, too. These kids. Their insistence on robbing me of sleep every night. Their encroachment into the daylight now. It's their way of being heard, of *making* me hear them. They've been tossed away, traded for what was wanted.

Given over to a greedy place to right a wrong that could never be corrected.

I slow to a walk and edge into the clearing, knowing for certain now that the little girl is bringing me right back to the shed that marks the beginning of the deep woods.

I leave the clearing, brushing past the rope swing with its platform of wood for a seat. I blink away the memory of the boy who was Miller's disposable brother, his feet passing over me as I lay on the ground, drunk and feeling only a fraction as lonely as he must have felt.

When I finally see the back of the shed, I can hear the familiar clicking of Linda's shutter.

"Show me what you want me to see," I say too quietly for anyone to hear. I know they need to be heard, so I'll brave whatever it is they need to tell me. But after this—after I have Linda safely back in my hands—this stops.

After this, I tell April that we need to leave this place. No one should have to bear the depth of what this loneliness brings.

The splintering green door that was shut so tightly the last time I was here is now standing open. Just a crack, but enough to beckon me. Just like Miller's painting.

And while I know I'm expected, I couldn't feel less welcomed.

I see dishes first, and I can't understand why that bothers me.

There's a lot I could have noticed before the tiny round table with four mismatched chairs tucked neatly under the rusted tin belly of the bistro table, but I see the dishes on the table before anything else. They're placed evenly, as if measured by a ruler—a large plate beneath a small bowl at each setting, a fork to the left of the place, pinning a different cloth napkin to the rusted metal table, a spoon on the opposite side. Four chipped, mismatched glasses adorn the upper left corner of each setting, filled with years upon years' worth of rainwater and grime, clouded with the type of organism that grows in water left to stand and wait.

And that's what bothers me, I see now. The waiting.

It's as though the entire table was set in anticipation of something, and it's held its breath ever since.

A newspaper clipping surfaces in my clouded memory. *We'll have more questions for the kids, of course. We'll want to know how they kept alive in that sort of weather.*

A centerpiece bound by once-pliable forest grass now chokes the stems of wood scrub and pinecones, intact only for lack of movement. I know that if I were to touch it, the bundle of foliage would crumble in my hands. But I have no desire to touch it.

I imagine four kids brought here separately, playing house as best they know how in a place that is home to nothing.

I pull my gaze reluctantly around the rest of the small cottage. It's difficult to say what this structure is exactly. It might have at one point been a large equipment shed. Hooks on the walls still hold shovels and rakes. I follow an intricate spider web from one corner of the ceiling to a hook holding a gray chainsaw with a corroded blade and a hand crank for operating it. I see the outlines of more toothed machines from somewhere way before my time on various hooks throughout the little house.

"Stop calling it a house," I say to myself.

There is a doll with a missing arm, seated precariously on the tip of a shovel in the far corner opposite the little table. One glassy eye stares across the room into a corner too dark for me to fully distinguish, the other eye obscured by a lid ending in curled plastic lashes. Her black hair separates in a center part, still coiled into slick braids, though dust has matted her crown. The doll is naked, its cloth body slumping under the weight of such an awkward sitting position.

Then I spot the teal My Little Pony abandoned in a shadowed corner, the one with the pink hair, which I last saw in the Carver House. The one that had no other way to wind up here than to be brought by some intruder. The same kind of intruder who stole Linda.

I look down to find a model car on its side in front of me, the kind that collectors buy now, not for playing with but for admiring from high shelves out of reach of clumsy fingers. Like the one a boy would hide in a box to keep it for himself, a box marked for Christmas decorations. Only this car's wheels are missing.

Upon further examination, I see that the posts on which the little model wheels would spin are still intact, and indeed something on them is still moving. I approach the car and crouch down to see the slowly moving legs of a spider. They writhe and reach for help, and it only takes a second longer for me to see that each of the four spokes that should have wheels attached to their ends instead pierce the thick bodies of brown and black spiders, strategically mounted to the car so that they didn't die, at least not right away.

I pull away in horror before kicking the car over, my brain pushing disgust away long enough to knock the spiders from the spokes and step on them, snuffing out their last moments in four stomps.

My breath dissolves and replaces itself in front of me, white cloud after white cloud of proof that I'm more afraid of this place than I was willing to admit when I chased the girl into the woods.

The girl. She had to have come here. Where else would she have gone?

I walk toward the table. The bowls are filled, and the gnats and flies that circle startle away from the dishes long enough for me to see their contents. Various insects, some alive. Various parts of small animals, squirrels or something similar, fur matted and stained, decomposing or otherwise disintegrating. And up close, the smell is horrendous.

They were just animals, and maybe they were already dead before he . . .

I throw up before I can keep it down, a physical reaction to the confusion I know I'll have to process at some point, but not now. Now I have to get the hell out of here. Now I have to abandon my beloved camera (*Sorry, Mr. Jakes. Your baby's dead*). Because a particular thought has just hatched at the sight of this horrific table setting.

What if these thrown-away kids aren't trying to tell me anything? What if they're simply angry?

Or lonely?

My breath forms another misty cloud in front of me, and I'm edging toward the door when I spot the curl of Linda's strap down a short hallway leading to another space in the nonhouse, a tiny room that isn't even a room. It's more like a large closet.

A few reluctant steps bring me to Linda, battered but otherwise intact, the lens miraculously unscratched, at least from what I can see in the murky dark of the little shed.

Linda in hand, I take a single step toward the door before I hear the clicking, then see the stripe of light that follows. A click, then the light. Click. Light.

It's coming from a crawl space at the back of the little room, guarded by a tiny door. Click. Light. Then the light disappears. Click. Light.

Just get out of here.

But what if I'm wrong? What if they are trying to tell me something? What if they're desperate to be heard, their broken jaws screaming soundlessly into the woods that can't talk back, their lives dislocated, stolen, traded for the value they never knew they had?

Click. Light. Then it disappears in the crack underneath the door. Click. Light.

I open my mouth to say something, to start whatever conversation the little girl might be begging to have. Nothing but a puff of air escapes my lips.

I walk closer to the door and put my hand on its little knob.

The light disappears at my feet, and I wait for the next click, for the light to reappear, but the little room stays dark.

I listen a few seconds longer. I wait for the click. Still, nothing happens.

I pull the knob, and the little door opens easily, emitting not even the faintest creak on its tiny hinges.

The space inside is completely black, and I wait a moment for my eyes to decipher something in the inky darkness. So when the click does return and the light follows, I'm temporarily blinded, my eyes screaming behind my lids before they recover. When I open my eyes again, I see only spots, then the blackness, but something has shifted.

Now I can just make out the outline of the light source. A flashlight. A string hanging from the bottom of the handle.

The flashlight I dropped that night at the edge of the woods before following Rae into the forest.

"Enough," I say, the breath finally parting way for words. My relief is misplaced. I know that, but it doesn't keep me from feeling it. "Rae, I've had it. I told you, I'm done."

But as I squint into the darkness more closely, I see a small, pale hand gripping the handle. And as I follow the pale fingers wrapped around the flashlight, I see they're connected to an impossibly thin arm, nearly translucent in its whiteness, bent at a jagged angle. The swath of pale skin looks almost cracked, as though fractured by its tiny dark veins.

And then I hear singing.

The same song I heard in the house. The same song that led me to the mattress fort and the handprint weeks ago. The same song I heard coming from the fort last night. Before the dragging. Before the screaming.

The soft melody turns again to the tiny girl's giggle, then to the clogged, gurgling choke of something old, something not at all funny.

When a head appears, its mouth is what I see first, a jaw unhinged, a bottom lip drooping so low it practically hits the dirt floor of the crawl space, exposing a cavernous, rasping hole. Pale blue eyes roll upward into whites so enormous I'm not sure I'm looking at eyes at all. The bottom lids droop to the floor, red flesh exposing itself. The singing has turned to humming, but it's vacillating frantically between the child-like tone and the older, gurgling one.

And then the girl drops the flashlight, and the beam falls on the ragged ruffle of a dress, a spindly leg poking out underneath, the same cracks practically splitting her skin apart. The thin, pale hand lands on the dirt floor, dragging long pointed fingers across the ground, and her head lumbers forward, and this thing that might have once been a little girl is crawling toward me.

I bolt around the corner and past the overturned car with its dead spiders and the table set with animal parts, and I practically knock the door to the shed off of its hinges as I flee.

I can hear the singing growing louder behind me. I run back through the clearing with the rope swing and set it swaying on its creaking branch as I sail past. I slap branch after branch out of my way, and I'm maybe halfway through the thicket leading to the house when I hear my own voice, almost unrecognizable in my ear.

"Help!"

Then, suddenly, I'm hoarse, and at first I think it's because I'm out of breath, but soon I realize it's more than that—I'm not out of breath. I'm being robbed of it.

It's the same heaviness from the rest stop. The thickening corrosion that fills me up, slowing every movement, every intake, every pull of oxygen. Soon, I'm only able to sip at the surface of air. The rest of me feels as though it's sinking into the ground. And when I look down, I see that the needles of the forest floor are parting to expose fresh mud.

"Help," I try again, but I can barely breathe, let alone speak. I feel my foot slip through the ground, pushing hard on my ankle. And then I feel something else. Rough fibers close over the bridge of my foot like fingers from under the ground. My other foot sinks in an instant, and the trees suddenly feel taller than they were a moment ago.

"No!" I manage to squeak out despite the burning in my lungs. My heart is throbbing behind my chest, and I flail for something to hold on to.

Through the pounding in my ears as I struggle for breath, I hear it again, the humming of that song on the little girl's voice. The fibers tighten across my feet and tug, and less than a second later, the mud and needles cut across my knees.

The singing grows louder, and soon I hear the soft padding of feet approaching from behind me. I try to twist my body around, but I can't move enough to turn that way. The padding turns to dragging. The song fills my ears, the giggling spilling out of the cracks of the melody, dislocated from the voice that's singing.

"SOMEONE HELP!" I finally manage to scream, but the grip on my feet pulls harder. I brace my hands against the soft ground, but this is a huge mistake. The mud begins to take them, too, and my heart is pounding so hard against my frozen lungs I'm afraid one of them will splinter under the force.

"Penny?"

I almost don't hear her at first.

"Penny? Where are you? Call out again!"

"Here!" I try to say, but it only comes out in a haggard rasp.

More feet padding on the ground, but I can't tell which direction they're coming from. I hunch my shoulders and prepare for whatever it is. I'll do whatever I have to do. I don't have my hands or my feet, but I have my teeth, and I'll bite the shit out of whatever comes for me.

"Penny?"

The padding grows louder, and soon it's a full-on run. I squeeze my eyes shut and let out my last sound, a scream that rips the air in half.

"Penny!"

April is holding my face, inches from me, her pale blue eyes wide and wild.

"Pull me out!"

"What?"

"Pull me the fuck out of the ground!" I scream, jerking my head out of her hands, but she grabs my hands before I can flail, and I look down to see my clothes caked in dried dirt, a thick pile of gnarled tree roots erupting from the ground beside me. She's struggling to keep me still, her eyes searching me for danger when they should be searching behind me.

I look behind me into the woods—nothing. Absolutely nothing.

I look down at my legs again, my boots barely visible underneath their brown shell of dried mud.

"She was just . . . behind, and the ground, there was something under the . . . back in the shed, she . . ." I keep trying. I try to tell her, try to clear that fog of confusion and panic from her face—the fog of fear and disbelief from my brain. I try to remember all that I vowed to tell April as I fled from the little wooden shack.

The camera.

Linda is lying on her side a few feet in front of me, a wounded soldier down. I push past April and rescue my camera by her strap, calling up the menu to advance through the last pictures taken.

Then I see her. See *it*. Or at least enough to know it's real.

"Here," I say, thrusting the camera into April's hands.

April stares at the image, her head shaking slowly at first, then faster.

"I don't know what I'm looking at."

"That's her. Or it. Or whatever. That's what I saw in the shed back there," I point behind me, then drop my hand as soon as I see it trembling.

"All I see is a shadow of someone's hair, maybe a stick or a—"

"Hand," I interrupt. "Her hand. And I've seen her before. I've *been* seeing . . ."

I can't even bear to look at April. The risk that I'm taking in telling her. The one person who hasn't given up. I could be burning my last hope to the ground in confessing to her now. But after what just happened—after what would have happened if April hadn't come running when she did—it's not possible to stay any longer. Whatever these kids want, whatever they're screaming into the vacuum of the woods, we can't stay to hear it.

"There's something out here, April. I just got an up-close-and-personal look, and it's seriously fucked up, and we need to figure out—"

"Come back to the house with me," April says.

"April, we have to leave."

"I know," she says, and despite my dizziness at the effort to regain oxygen, despite the adrenaline and terror still coursing under my skin, I'm surprised to hear her agree so quickly.

But then I catch a glimpse of the shadows that have spread across April's entire face, creeping past the circles cupping the bottoms of her eyes. Her once peachy skin has drained of its former dew. Her chapped lips hide her usual smile, lost somewhere behind a mouth that never laughs anymore.

I think of all those nights she spent shuffling around.

"You know," I say.

April squeezes my hand between hers but just keeps walking.

"Let's get back to the house," she says, and for the first time ever, I trust the authority that's woven itself into her voice.

23

APRIL HAS TWO MUGS OF steaming tea waiting on the side table in the sparkly new living room by the time I emerge from the bathroom by the kitchen, toweling the last drops of water from my hair. The dirt is gone. I watched the tail of a little mud tornado disappear down the drain. But even that set my body trembling as I unsuccessfully pushed the memory away of those roots closing around the tops of my feet. Pulling me down.

"How long?" I ask April, my shaking hands rattling the saucer underneath my mug a little too loudly.

April's eyes search me from the top of her own cup. She lowers it to the table and her eyes follow. "Probably as long as you," she says. "I should have said something. I just wasn't sure if you . . . I didn't want to . . ."

I don't tell her she's right, that she should have told me. I'm not sure it would have been a comfort to know I wasn't imagining it. It certainly wasn't a comfort hearing it from Miller. I wanted to believe it was Rae for so long, I'm not sure how I could have kept from going fully insane if I'd known what I was seeing was real enough for April to see it too.

"The toilet," she says, and I search her face for where she might be going with that. "It wasn't flushing itself." I can barely hear her voice as she confesses her own horrible secret. And even though it looks like she might say more, I don't prod, and eventually, she just lifts her mug back up to her lips.

"There's more," she says after a silence so long I'd almost forgotten we were sitting in the same room.

She sets her cup down with a clink, the sound of it filling the Carver House.

"The engineer," she says, and I rifle through my brain for a connection. Engineer. Engineer. I'm drawing an utter blank.

"The structural expert," she says, clearly noticing me struggle.

But I still can't fathom what could be so important about this stupid house's structural integrity that it would trump what we just shared.

"Wait, you can't possibly be considering staying here after all this, could you? You still want to fix this place up?"

"Wait," she says, her hand groping the back of her neck, her fingers pressing into her skin. She closes her eyes. "You'll understand in a second." She shakes her head, and her hand drops to her side. "No, that's not true. You won't. At least, I haven't been able to fully comprehend it yet."

I want to be patient, but I feel like we have already spent far too much time sitting around in this house in the middle of these woods for me to be delicate.

"April, can we talk about this while we start packing or something? Seriously, we need to leave."

"The engineer refused to assess the house," April says, ignoring my request but picking up speed, her eyes wide open now. "But he was a little less coy than the others. Maybe he felt guilty, or maybe I just got fed up enough at being told no, so I lost it. And he took all of two seconds to crack."

"April, I don't understand, can we just—"

"Your friend Miller told him not to agree to the inspection," she says, the end of her story landing like a hammer.

"What?" My brain is so tired, it's a wonder I'm still able to form words. "What do you mean Miller told him not to? I don't understand."

"See, that's the thing. I understood everything right then. He's been the one this whole time."

April is pacing the floors now, step after step over the same moaning floorboard. She runs her hands through the hair that used to look shiny. Now it looks like straw.

"He got every contractor in town to refuse to do the work. The engineer had no choice but to refuse to inspect the house. I mean, really, what's there to inspect? No work's been done!"

She throws her hands in the air, her voice rising to a level just shy of hysteria.

"I'm two hundred thousand dollars under water, and a nineteen-year-old kid is holding my oxygen tank!"

Her eyes are wild, and while I know I should step in and steady her shoulders the way she's done for me, I am a little afraid to get in her path. I hardly remember the blinding rage I felt before pummeling that girl in the bathroom, but I suspect I might have looked a little like April does now in those sparkling seconds before my anger ignited.

But then her eyes clear of their flames, and she looks like she's shrunken a couple of inches. The boiling fury has eaten some of her already small size.

"I thought I was a better judge of character than that. All because I offended his uncle. What kind of grudge is worth hundreds of thousands of dollars?"

I want to tell her so much. Words push one another out of the way, competing to go first. That his uncle Ripp had nothing to do with it. That Miller isn't protecting his uncle. He's trying to protect us. He knows how lonely the woods are, and he knows that no one should be living in this house, a place so close to a mouth that would devour it.

But I still see that flicker of rage behind April's eyes, and I remember now. I remember how badly I needed that feeling in those first months after the desert's bonfire had diminished to ashes. I needed something to fill the gaping hole that Rae left behind, and though the new flame of anger burned fast—and though it was ultimately destructive—it leveled the ground for me to begin building something new.

To extinguish that flame right now would do nothing to fill the whole of such a massive financial and career failure for April. I would rob her of the only thing keeping her from caving in on herself. The walls aren't mine to take down.

"Don't worry," April says. "I already gave him an earful. Like that'll do anything. I should have put a brick through his window."

I imagine April's murderous anger unleashed in the wake of the bell at Scoot's. I picture Miller standing there, taking the verbal bashing he had to see coming, given what he did.

He knew he would be maligned by the very people he was trying to protect, but he did it anyway.

Except I know the truth. And I can't leave Point Finney before he knows how grateful I am for what he did.

That's when I remember the jeep.

"Shit. The car needs coolant."

"Dammit," she says, forgetting to correct my language. "I meant to do that the other day."

Clearly, April has been dodging her own preoccupations.

"If I go now, I can catch the convenience store before it closes, and you can start packing," I say. "I'll help as soon as I come back."

I leave out the part about planning to call Miller from the gas station. I can't exactly explain how I intend to thank the person responsible for screwing her out of her entire life's savings.

"Besides," I say, "it'll give you some time to say good-bye or whatever. You know, closure."

I look around at the house she's tried to give the love and attention she hoped it deserved. It doesn't occur to me until now that she might be afraid to be in the house alone. I consider the likelihood that she's in danger, that we both are the longer we stay. But my plan works before I can form the rest of my thought.

"Just hurry back. There's more to pack than you might think, and I'll need your help loading it into the car," she says. She's already looking around her brand new living room, beginning her silent good-byes to the Carver House. A place that has meant such different things for her than it has for me.

I'm out the door faster than she can tell me to be careful, and I take the dirt road out of the North Woods far too carelessly, my mind everywhere but the unpaved road ahead. I hit a significant hole and set April's jeep bouncing on its already tenuous tires, the struts feeling a little far south of healthy, too.

Just as long as it can get us out of here tonight, I think. What I wouldn't give to see Alfredo rolling up, all eighties paint and howling wolf, new transmission running him as smoothly as ever. What I wouldn't give to see Rob behind the wheel.

I realize I've come to associate the smell of gasoline with sanctuary as I roll April's jeep into the parking lot, a strangeness I stack against the rest I've accumulated over the past month. The feeling is only slightly diminished by the incessant, mechanical jingle crawling out of the speakers the minute I step foot in the convenience store.

I find the coolant and pay the attendant quickly, but I only make it three steps toward the door before a familiar crew cut pops up from a crouch in the snack aisle.

Ripp lifts his head from his candy bar, his usual discomfort at seeing me almost comfortable by this point.

"So, I guess this is good-bye," I tell him from the end of the aisle.

If it's possible to look relieved and surprised in the same intake of a breath, Ripp does. He holds that breath for a second, maybe to see if it's real, to see if I mean what I say.

"The house won't pass inspection," I say so he can exhale.

He goes back to examining his candy bar, but he does so a little more slowly now, like he can take his time doing it.

"Sorry to hear that," he says, and I think I may have just found a worse liar than Rob.

"No, you're not," I say, but I try a smile with it.

"No," he says. "No, you're right about that. But you may not have the whole story," he says.

I know that's what he must think.

"I've gathered enough of it," I say. We lock eyes from our respective stances across candy bars. "And I'm sorry. For all you've been through. I'm sorry about that."

Ripp's eyes fall to the shelf, and for a moment I think he might tell me to leave him the hell alone. But he pushes away from the rows of chocolate instead and ambles toward me slowly. He never looked as young as the newspaper clipping on the wall in his shop seemed to indicate he was at some stage, but he never looked quite this old, either. Maybe it's just that I'm seeing him out of context now. His brow is heavy with wrinkles and the weight of so much more than I'd ever be able to see, even if I knew him for twenty more years.

"There's a whole range of mistakes out there to make," he says, his eyes growing red and damp. His voice is gravelly, and I wave away the potent memory of a different kind of gravelly voice. "The worst ones are the kinds that stick to you like barnacles. That cover you up so you can barely see your own skin anymore. The worst mistake I ever made was something I didn't have to lift a finger to do. I just . . . let it happen," he says. "But some things can't be papered over."

My memory conjures the hastily hung wallpaper strips that couldn't manage to conceal Miller's mural of Danny.

My breath catches, a tiny punch to the gut.

"He wasn't a bad kid, D—" Ripp starts to say, but to even put it in words—to put a name to the horror that followed him—is something neither of us wants Ripp to do.

"It should never have happened. Nobody deserves it," he says, letting the generality coat the awful taste of what he has to confess.

Then he says, "I could live the rest of my life trying to

change something that ain't never gonna change, or I could make sure that everything I do for the rest of my sorry life is better than what I didn't do in that moment."

I know he's saying this for me. Even though he has no idea what happened that night in the desert or the years before it or the months after it, he knows that I've been looking for something. He knows because he probably tried looking for something of his own. So he recites a mantra he outlived long ago, and he does it just for me.

For me, and for Miller.

I start to back away, but slowly enough to say, "It was nice to meet you, Ripp." Because there's really nothing else to say after the strange moments we've shared.

"Dominic," he says. "People who know me call me Dom."

I hear the door to the restroom swing open behind me, and just before I turn to excuse myself, a familiar voice soaked in bemusement says, "You know, I know a guy who sells candy bars not too far from your shop, Uncle Dom."

I watch Ripp's face light at the sight of his nephew, and it occurs to me I've never seen the two of them in the same place together.

Yes you have. Danny showed you.

And when I turn to face a surprised Miller, I'm startled to see an eight-year-old boy with burnt red hair and pleading green eyes, standing in the doorway of his bedroom, hands empty at his sides.

"You don't sell these," Ripp—Dominic—says from behind me, but Miller isn't paying attention to him anymore. "I'll wait in the car," Dom says. And his uncle pays for his candy and leaves us.

I watch Ripp as he ambles out of the shop and to the curb, his head turning for a moment to study the same boy who has sat in the same place for so long, I wonder if he was simply built along with this sparkly new gas station, a mistake in the plans.

I watch to see if Ripp looks at him like a mistake. But he doesn't. Instead, he looks like a man who has just been reminded for the millionth time that he has a new job in this life, one that won't allow him to stand by idly.

I watch him drop a dollar into the boy's cup before opening the door to Miller's car.

"I think your stepmom might put a hit out on me," Miller says, bringing me back to the shop. His hands are looking for a place to rest. They're as empty as ever.

"Yeah, about that," I say.

"Yeah, about that," he says, and I guess I hadn't considered the possibility that he'd be pissed at me now that he's had ample time to think about what he probably wished he'd said to April.

"Look, she obviously doesn't know why you did it. She thinks it was because she offended your uncle or something. And . . . seriously, it's all the money she had in the world."

"Yeah, well, you know me. I just love ruining people's lives and stealing their money," he says. "It's better than getting drunk and watching the game on TV. It's live action."

It's the first time I've heard sarcasm from Miller. It sounds horrible on him.

"I'm not trying to pick up where she left off," I say. "But I'm starting to regret feeling the urge to thank you for any of this."

This seems to break through because he sighs, his shoulders slumping. He runs a hand through his hair, and when he looks up, I think that maybe I've never seen his eyes look quite this green. My heart pulses a little too hard in my chest, and the rhythm of it brings to mind a ticking clock. It's time to get back to April.

But just as I think that, Miller takes three steps toward me and deflates our distance.

"So you know why I did it then," he says, his eyes searching mine.

"I was planning to call you from here," I say, not stepping back. "I wanted to make sure you knew that I knew."

He nods, and there it is. The dimple in the corner of his

pressed lips, the one that appears when just enough of a smile manages to break through. My heart ticks.

"I'm sorry for what I did. I really am," he says. "All that money. It's not her fault, and she didn't deserve to lose all that. I just . . . I couldn't let you stay there," he says, leaning back on one foot, putting some distance between us again.

"I know that," I say. He doesn't need to tell me why. I already know why. All I want now is to knot that thread, the one that snapped the other night. I think if I can get close enough to him, I might be able to find the end that broke loose.

"And it's not that I don't want you here," he says, edging closer, then backing away again, his hands moving excitedly through his hair.

"I'm glad," I say. I can almost see the thread. If I could just get close enough.

"But it's too dangerous, you guys being out there."

"Miller, I know."

"And I'm almost done. I've almost finished," he says, his eyes locking on mine, his dimple deep and irresistible, and I want to feel what his hands feel like in my hair, too.

"You're almost done with what?"

"My last painting," he says. He's a foot from my face now, and this is the moment. This is when I should be able to see the loose end of the thread. But all I see are those pine green eyes searching my face, wondering why I can't find what he's seeing.

Because he's clearly found whatever it is he's looking for.

Then it dawns on me.

"Painting? You mean a new canvas?"

"I'm almost done. And when I finish, he'll come back," Miller says, but his smile is gone. In fact, everything is gone. The color behind his eyes. The fire above them. The warmth of the store. Everything I thought I recognized in Miller is gone, replaced by the same feeling I had the other night.

"How can you be sure of that? How can you really know, Miller?"

And now he sees, too. He sees that he's been wrong about me the whole time.

"After everything you know now, how can *you* doubt it?" he asks, his voice pleading, but I know he's already giving up on me. "When I paint, things happen. All I need to do is repaint the picture."

We're miles apart. We're years apart. We live in different galaxies. If I'm a satellite drifting, Miller's just the planet I keep bumping into.

I picture the mural in the last room at the end of the hall and its smaller cousins stacked in the gallery Miller keeps in a tower. I've already heard so many awful truths. What's so wrong with believing this could be true, too? This hunch that Miller's molded to gospel, his uncle's lessons for coping warped into a new reality. What's so wrong with thinking it could actually happen? After everything I've seen for myself? That the woods are only as bad as the horrible deeds we bring to them?

"So finish it then."

I think back to one of my first conversations with Miller. It feels like an eternity ago. *"If you had a chance to right a wrong, something truly awful. You'd do it, wouldn't you?"*

"Maybe some wrongs are just too awful to try to make right," I say, knowing that this is the end. "Maybe the best thing you can do is try to build something new out of the pieces. Maybe you just try not to let the rubble suffocate you."

Miller looks at me like he's never known me. I've seen that look before. Rae gave it to me. That night in the desert, as she held my notepad over the flames, the consequences of our shared actions too great for any one person to suffer.

Maybe it's not the consequences I've been so afraid of. Maybe it's the randomness with which they're doled out.

"Then you really don't get it," Miller says, and it kills me to know these are the last things we'll say to each other.

"Maybe I don't."

I take a step back from Miller. "Good luck," I say. And I genuinely mean it.

For a moment, I think he's going to close the gap between us. I think he's searching out the same thread I was looking for a second ago. Then I realize he's looking at my hand. The same hand he held that night in the car as we escaped the rain and I broke my soul open and he didn't ask me for anything in return.

In a million different worlds, in a million different ways, this would be the moment when we kiss. I almost lean in. I almost cast the broken thread aside, put his hand on my heart so he can feel it pound out the words I can't form, and press my lips onto his. I want to feel that space between our lives shatter apart and fall to the floor, even if I cut my feet on the pieces. I want to tell him to tie himself to something other than this wretched past he can't escape.

But he won't do that, and if I'm really honest, I would never forgive myself for asking him to do it.

So I take another step away from him. I widen the distance between us and feel the thread fall away. The tinny jingle sings me good-bye.

Beside the jeep, I pull out my phone and send a text to Rob. **Leaving tonight.** His response is immediate. **Good.**

I add the coolant and get in the car, taking one last look

at the concrete sanctuary, its bright pumps and smooth driveway beckoning me to stay. I look to the boy who sits off to the side of the entrance, his cardboard sign covering his face. His foot taps out the rhythm I can't hear anymore.

I pull back onto the road, still not certain what needs to be done, but I know one thing for sure: Miller is the only one who can repaint his own past, and April and I don't need to be around when it happens. If Miller can really do what he thinks he can do, I don't want to be anywhere near the North Woods when he tries to take one of the children that it's held on to for all these years.

The thought of Miller's anguish over his brother brings a fresh wave of tears to my eyes, and through my blurred vision, I almost bypass the fork that leads me to the Carver House. Lightning starts to backlight the clouds, and I know it's only a matter of time before the sky opens up and these dirt roads turn muddy and treacherous. I hadn't heard it was going to storm tonight, but given my exile in the land without Internet, I'm not sure how I would have heard.

The next flash of lightning blinds me for just a second, and when I regain my sight, I slam the brakes so hard, I hit my head on the steering wheel.

"Oh my God, no. No no no!" I pant from behind the dash.

I don't think I hit him. I didn't feel the car hit anything at all.

I couldn't have hit him. They came out of nowhere. Where did they come from? Where—?

My mind is moving faster than my pounding head can keep up. I fling the jeep's door open anyway, buckling under the pain in my skull. I stumble to the hood, cringing against the memory of what I saw right before I slammed on the brakes. Right before the lightning cleared and the road became visible again. Two boys, one in the middle of the road, enormous eyes, wide and starving. Mouths opened in silent screams.

But the boy who was in the road is not lying on the ground. The other is nowhere to be seen, either. I crouch and check underneath the car, but all I see is a mass of pine needles and a large gouge in the road.

I hear a twig snap beside me and spin too fast, pain crashing behind my eyes. I see the bend of a branch, the flutter of needles.

Lightning dances behind the clouds. The first tap of a raindrop hits the ground, then another. Soon, a light pattering begins. I'm getting wet, but I don't feel a thing.

A pinecone pops, the crunch of it collapsing underneath the weight of someone's foot.

The dense air is doing all it can to stave off the imminent downpour. Drops continue to fall in that light patter, but the otherwise quiet of the woods has me feeling the need to get back in the car immediately. There was no boy in the road. My mind was playing an evil trick on me.

Then I hear the song, clear and even on immature vocal cords. And it's close.

The tone of the song drops, the octave far too low to come from a child's mouth. And then it laughs that horrible, gurgling laughter that burbles from the depths of an ancient throat.

The next flash of lightning precedes a deafening crack of thunder, and the sky splits open to release the downpour it's been threatening.

I can no longer hear the laughter, but I don't need to hear it to know it's too close to be safe. I squint against the gush of rain and throw the driver's side door open, soaked by the time I heave it shut and start the engine.

24

WHEN I FINALLY PULL UP to the Carver House, I barely remember to turn off the car before falling through the front door.

"April!"

I'm answered by a loud slam upstairs. Then another.

"April!"

I fly up the steps and find April pulling the windows shut in the twin bedrooms.

"Get yours and the one at the end of the hall!" she yells. "I've got the rest!"

I follow orders, shocked at my own relief seeing her safe. I hadn't realized I was as afraid for her as I was.

"We're closed up downstairs," April says, brushing her

bangs off her forehead. Her cheeks are dusted with rain spray. I've never seen her look younger, and a renewed sense of responsibility for both our safety leaves me feeling more panicked than ever.

"We need to go," I say, not yet prepared to explain my mania.

"That was the idea, wasn't it?"

"We're not safe here," I say, knowing I'm just repeating myself now. But the sound of that singing from the woods is still fresh in my ear.

"Yeah, well, we're going to have to stick it out through the night," April says, shaking out the dampness in her hair.

"April, we've got to leave tonight!"

"It's too late!" she says, throwing her hands in the air. "We missed our chance! The rain's already turned the roads to sludge."

I know she's right. I could feel the jeep slipping all over the road. I was lucky just to make it back. And with the windows shut against the outside, some of my earlier panic subsides, and I follow April into the room that's never really felt like mine, but I can't sit still, so I pace in front of her while she chews her nails. She doesn't say anything, so I feel like I should, even though all I want to do is sprint out of here.

"I don't think you could have known everything you were getting into with this house," I say, easing into what I should tell her. About the North Woods. The kids who were exchanged for the ones who were actually wanted. Why nobody but Miller would voluntarily revisit a place with such a brutal history. But she doesn't seem to follow, not that she could.

"I just thought I had this one right," she says, staring at the fingernails she's nibbled to jagged stubs. "It was going to be my thing. My winning project." When she looks up at me, I know she's not just talking about the house. She never was. She's talking about me, too. I stop my pacing.

I shake my head. "It's not about you," I say.

"I know. Objectively, I know. I just thought with enough of the right attention, I could build it back up."

I stare at her hands with their rough nails. April's so free-spirited with her easy laugh. But there are jagged edges to her, and sometimes she gets it wrong, and inside, I think there's not much more than some weak glue holding her together, too.

"I think sometimes it's more of a tear-down project," I say, leveraging a real estate term I think I heard her use once.

She smiles a watery smile, knowing she's failed and trying to be okay with it. "So I'm just supposed to watch the whole thing come crumbling down?"

"No," I say. "You're supposed to hand me the controls to the wrecking ball. It's mine to rip apart and rebuild."

We're quiet for a minute. All I can hear is the branch outside my window thrumming its tree fingers on the pane. It takes all I have not to throw the window open to see if there's an actual hand attached to those spindly branches.

Following my gaze, April says, "I think we'll be fine until the storm lets up. We'll leave first thing in the morning."

"And you're sure we can't try—"

She laughs, not hearing me, and only the tiniest hint of humor lights her voice. "The engineer did let one thing slip. The last electrician who worked on the house said the wiring's hanging by a thread. Comforting, huh? We've basically been living on top of a tinder box for the last month. So much for 'minor electrical issues.'"

She shakes her head against my last question. "Those roads are going to be murder, and my old jeep's needed new tires for about a year now. I don't trust it in all that mud. We could wind up on the side of the road."

The thought of having to walk back to the house if we got stranded—the woods all around us—is enough to make my hands start their trembling again. But the recollection of the road—of what happened *on* it—terrifies me just as much.

"But April—"

"We'll be fine for tonight," she repeats, and I get the sense it's more for her reassurance than for mine. "Let's just try to use as little electricity as possible."

"Great," I say. Because spending one more night in this house—one dark night—feels like a living nightmare. But the knowledge that we'll be leaving first thing in the morning sustains me. Which must be apparent on my face, because April pats my knee in a move that feels far too old for her before she stands to leave.

She turns one more time in the doorway, but only offers me a hint of a smile before walking away, apparently deciding she's already said more than she intended to say.

I text Rob back, his "Good" still hanging there in the conversation ether.

Make that tomorrow morning.

When I don't get a response, I know it's either because the last ounce of cell service has swept away with the storm or Rob's worried. Either way, there's no point in saying more.

April and I don't eat dinner. Neither of us even brings it up. After April goes downstairs, I stay in the middle room for the rest of the night packing the Rubbermaid, placing Troy the Miraculous Pink Unicorn delicately beside Linda, only venturing outside long enough to drop the box into the jeep with the rest of the boxes before hurrying back into the house. I can hear April moving around downstairs, doing the same. I know I should go down and help her, but there's one more thing I want to do. I take the notepad and pen from my bag—the only thing I haven't packed—and start writing.

Dear Rae,

I start and stop writing five times. I line through each new sentence as I listen to the rain attack the windows of the Carver House.

I allow one voice from the past few days to remain in my head, unquieted because it's the only one that's actually helped.

April's.

And after I've just about given up on my last letter to Rae, I finally understand what it is I want to tell her.

I don't regret you.

Because there's so much to regret, but ultimately, it wasn't her.

I close the notepad gingerly and set it on top of my bag. Then I tour the upstairs of the house, double-checking each window to be sure it's locked. I snug each latch tighter into place, pulling the curtains of the windows that have them. Not that this offers any additional security, but somehow it still makes me feel a little better. The storm hasn't gotten worse, and I think that we might be fine tonight. I make myself feel the peace that's taken hold after my talk with April. After my final good-bye to Rae.

I tell myself there's nothing out there that can get in here. Not tonight. Because tonight, I know that when we wake up tomorrow, all we have to do is leave, and it'll be over.

"Now I know how to let you go," I say to Rae, but it's meant for any ears listening now.

The room at the end of the hall is stuffier than the rest. Of all of them, this room needs its window open the most, but I don't dare. Instead, I lean against the door frame and survey the room's contents, piled neatly against the walls but never cleaned through, never discarded like they should have been.

I eye the canister on the floor on top of the plastic tarp, the primer April rolled across all the walls but one. The room still smells faintly of paint. I let my gaze travel to the place it always does, to the boy on the wall. Danny.

He stares in his usual direction—the closet across the room. I look like I always do, bracing for what I might find this time. But tonight, there's nothing except the little box of matches, which I pick up now and rattle in my hand.

I cross the room to look Danny straight in the eye. This time, as he stares back at me, I think that maybe I don't see anything at all. For the first time, it's nothing but paint on the wall.

I pick up the roller, pry the canister open, and dip the

sponge cylinder into the paint. I hesitate for a moment, then before I can stop my hand, I'm bringing the roller to the wall and pressing into the farthest corner of the North Woods depicted in the mural.

"Whatever happened to you out here," I tell him, "it needs to end now."

Even though I'm doing exactly what Miller has been trying so desperately to do, this is different. I don't intend to paint a single thing over this white canvas.

I press the roller as hard as I can into the wall, paint dripping down the plaster in milky streams. I roll large swipes of nothingness across the mural. I erase the North Woods and the tiny shed. I erase Danny's empty hands. I cover his crooked smile and his singed hair. And with a fresh dip into the bucket of primer, I look down to blot the excess paint from the sponge. When I return to the mural, I see that I've left his eyes for last.

"Don't look," I tell him, and I run the roller over his pine green irises, tucking him into the forever night of a wall covered in glistening white paint.

I survey my work from the doorway, enjoying the sight of absolutely nothing on the wall. It looks like a barren desert.

Back in the middle room, I find the letter to Rae right where I left it.

I try to think of something to say to her, too, but I know I've already done that. I've been screaming in silence for nine months.

So I take one of the two remaining matchsticks from The Washingtonian box and drag the red end across its edge. I hold the corner of the notepad up to the flame and think about the match's hungry orange mouth devouring the paper. But just before it does, I extinguish the flame and slide the box with its lonely matchstick into the pocket of my jeans.

"Not yet," I say to the notepad. I've let enough walls crumble for one night. I need this last one to stand. Just to get me through the night.

I sit for a long time on the mattress, listening to the tree's fingers toy with me on the glass. I lie down before I'm aware that I've moved. Sleep takes me over, one that skims the surface of comfort, drifting along the tenuous space between waking and dreaming.

And in that in-between place, I hum along to the sound of a familiar tune, drifting to me from somewhere so close I can hear the breath behind it.

25

Hot waves lick the side of my face, a stilted rhythm of thick, warm air.

The snap and pop of a bonfire beats its song in the background, and I look for Rae. Paces away from the fire are the guys I don't know with the girls I only know a little bit, most of them passed out on sleeping bags and blankets stolen from their parents' linen closets. These kids have parents who keep blankets neatly folded in hallway closets. These kids are not like Rae and me.

I see her now, her green Converses with their dragons doodled on the rubber soles. She's staring up at the moon. Stars form a halo over its big, glowing face.

"You're going to freeze out here."

"I don't feel a thing," she says. I narrowly miss crushing the

needle under my foot, and I sit on the other side of her to put some distance between me and it.

"You should come back to the fire."

"There's nothing for me over there."

"I'm over there," I say.

"You're nothing," she says.

"I know." Her words don't sting. I've already felt the venom of them, my skin numb to her bite now.

"You should have just drifted away," she says. "Isn't that what you do when you don't want to be where you are anymore? You just float away?"

"Maybe," I say, staring up at the stars she's staring at. And for the first time, I think we might be able to share them. "But I was afraid if I did that, I'd just drift forever."

I turn to look at her, but her eyes are glass reflecting the sky.

"I have to tell you something," I say.

"Say it then," she says.

"I'm sorry."

"I am, too," she says. "Because it's your turn now." She faces me suddenly, her drooping eyes as white as the moon. "You're it."

The heat on my face shocks me awake, but I don't move. Because even though my nightmare has ended, it left something behind in the room with me.

A gurgling so close, its breath threatens to melt my skin. A pressure on the bed that tells me it's inches away.

When I open my eyes, the ones staring back at me are whited out but far from blind. Pearlescent skin turns almost purple under the sweeping clouds from outside the window, veins so close to the surface they threaten to break through. The gurgling comes from somewhere deep inside the little boy, but it's not emanating from his mouth, even though it's open so wide the blackness threatens to swallow me. The gurgling grows high in pitch, escalating to a maniacal laughter. The skin beneath his eyes sags to the bottom of his face.

I try to roll away, but the sheets twist and bind my feet, ensnaring me. The boy lunges, and his hand is around my wrist, his long, bony fingers with nails like curled, crisp leaves. They pierce my skin under his grip.

I try to scream, but my lungs are thick and heavy, choking the sound back. I wrench my wrist free and disentangle my feet to find my boots still on. I kick the side of his jaw, but it's softer than it should be, and I only succeed in giving him another limb to grab.

With horrifying speed, he rips me from the bed and drags me to the floor, my knuckles scraping wood planks when my fingers fail to grasp something—anything—to hold.

He drags me to the open window, and with a snap of strength from someplace that could never exist in an actual child, he's hoisted himself out the window, his full weight on my leg.

I kick the dry night air, the rain betraying me now as it hides in the clouds. In another second, he'll pull me out of the window with him.

I slide a few more inches out the window. The boy's nails are dragging across my skin, and I feel the searing pain of flesh tearing.

Warm trickles slide down my calf under his unnatural grip, and his long fingers slip to my ankle.

One more wild flail at freedom releases his hold so fast, I fall hard to the floor of the bedroom.

I try to find the air that can't fill my lungs, but my eyes are watering now, and the air in the room is hazy and sweltering.

I slam the sash closed to the threat that found its way in through that same bolted window, and I nearly collapse under the billowing smoke that fills the room instantly.

I crawl into the hallway and see the room with the mural engulfed in orange flames. The pile of mattresses leading to the closet forms a mountain of tinder on which the flames climb, licking the ceiling and spreading like corrosion across every surface, lighting wood and wallpaper and blankets and everything else it touches.

Everything but the wall with the mural.

The flames have melted the paint to oozing streams, the wall bleeding all around the boy's face. His eyes are as white as the primer that streams to the molten floor underneath him, the skin below drooping to the painted grass. His jaw is open in a scream I can finally hear. It sounds like the hiss and wheeze of wood being eaten alive.

Smoke overtakes my vision, and I squeeze my burning eyes, backing away from the room at the end of the hall. But just as I crawl away from the epicenter of the fire, I see through the ripple of smoke filling the upstairs glimpses of those same pearlescent hands and purpled veins wrapping their twig-like fingers around the frames of windows that should be closed. White eyes emerge, bodies dragging toward the doors.

Toward me.

I scramble to my feet and stumble down the stairs. Each gasp for air fills my lungs with a thickness that hardens them against expanding, and I resist the urge to collapse in a heap at the bottom of the stairs.

The screaming from upstairs has given way to the crackle of flame, but I know that those white hands are close. The blood from my ankle puddles in my boot and slicks the back of my heel, chafing the skin.

I round the corner to April's room, and the smoke is so thick it takes me a second to find her. She's in bed in a sleep so deep, I know right away it isn't sleep at all.

"April!" I wheeze, but it doesn't matter. She's inhaled too much smoke to raise her from unconsciousness.

I hoist her from the bed and hook my arms under hers, backing out of the room in time to see a white hand close over the railing at the top of the stairs. With the same speed the boy ripped me from my bed and halfway out the window, this boy takes three lunging steps to the middle landing.

Just above the roiling smoke that billows down the stairs toward us, choking only the living, I see something different about this boy. A purple cap with the head of a wolf emblazoned across the top.

"Danny," I wheeze. It's a whisper, nothing more, but it's enough for him to hear. His mouth, already on its way to dropping to horrifying depths, closes, and his eyes clear of their white. In their place, I see the clearest green.

I see the fog of confusion and anguish clear. The smoke lifts for a single second, and in it I see the same realization in his eyes that Miller's father must have seen when he left him for the woods to take. I see the comprehension fill a face too young to experience a betrayal that deep.

And maybe it's the memory I've forced him to recall that sends the white back over his eyes. His bottom lip drops, his jaw softens, and his mouth opens to a giant, gaping hole as he takes another step down the stairs.

I race to the front door and drop April on the other side before reaching back to pull her car keys from the hook. A veined hand closes over my wrist just as I pull back.

"NO!" I gasp as I pull the door closed hard over the arm attached to the hand. I slam it twice more before it loosens its hold, and I lock it shut against my attacker, knowing that will only buy me a few extra seconds. I hoist April over my shoulder and carry her to the jeep with the same sort of strength I've heard mothers find when they lift cars off their trapped children.

I shove her into the passenger seat and climb behind the wheel, throw the jeep in reverse and come within inches of a tree before shifting to drive in time to see pale arms and legs sliding from open windows, fire devouring what they don't cling to.

My throat and nose burn as I force my shaking hands to grip the steering wheel. April slumps in the seat next to me, and I consider the horrifying thought that I didn't find her in time, that she inhaled too much smoke. I reach for her wrist, but I can't get my hands to stop trembling long enough to find her pulse. I try to pat her face, but I only succeed in tapping the side of her head.

"April? Wake up. Please wake up!" My voice rakes across my throat, but I'm relieved to have something more than a squeak finally leave it.

The jeep's wheels struggle over the still muddy road, the sticky earth even more impossible to drive on now that it's had a few hours since the rain stopped to start to dry. A shudder of lightning illuminates the tree line, and a growl of thunder follows it. I press the gas a little harder.

"Just get to the road," I tell myself, the thought of asphalt like a white knight. "Get to the gas station." It's the only place close enough to civilization that might have a pay phone I can use. I'll call an ambulance for April. They could send a fire truck for the house, but the entire North Woods can disintegrate to a charred mass for all I care.

The jeep finds another hole, and I temporarily lose control of the wheel. Mud clings to the bald tires and they slide over thinner patches of earth as I overcorrect in one direction to nearly hit a tree on the opposite side of the narrow road.

I've almost righted the jeep when I see a glistening puddle of water directly in front of me, the ripple of moon waving to stop me. But I'm too late, and we hit the hole hard, the motor whining as I pump the gas, sending us deeper into the mud.

"Come on. Come on!" I scream at the wheel. But it's no use. The tires spin and spit up mud, and the more I try, the deeper I grind the jeep into the road.

April is still slumped in the seat beside me, but a deep moan emanates from her laboring vocal cords.

"April, wake up!" I hiss, unable to find my full voice.

April moans, then slumps deeper. I have never felt more acutely alone than I do in this moment.

I kill the engine and search the backseat for one of our purses, which would have a phone. But I know I won't find them. I'm positive my purse is still somewhere upstairs in the burning Carver House, and who knows where April left hers. But we're still in the grip of the woods, so it's not like I would get a signal, anyway.

I look out of every window I can. The trees are so close, they tap the top of the jeep, sending tiny shocks of fear through my skin. Still, I don't see any sign of those horrific white eyes.

I open the door slowly and swing my legs out, landing on the ground hard enough to splash droplets of mud across my jeans.

My calf still burns where the boy tore through my skin, but I won't let myself think about that now. I see it's the rear driver's side tire that's stuck, entrenched in a mass of mud that sucks at the bottoms of my boots.

"Leaves," I say to myself, the sound of my voice slightly more reassuring as the rasp of smoke inhalation clears the tiniest bit more. I search the surrounding area for anything that'll provide traction. I scoop up slick leaves and pine needles, even a few sticks from the sides of the road, shoving them underneath the tire at its front.

I stand back, check the road behind us once more, check the tire again. I start the car and feel the tire catch some traction, but not enough.

"Just a little more." My heart quickens. I might get us out of here after all.

And then, just as I crouch to gather one last armful of leaves, I hear the humming. The song emanates from an ancient throat, choking on the melody as it dissolves into a frantic giggle.

I drop the leaves and throw myself at the car door, but I'm too late. Hands encircle each of my ankles and yank, whipping me high into the air and snapping me like a sheet caught in wind. I land heavy on the ground, my hands catching the blow just before my chin makes contact with the forest floor.

"APRIL!" I scream, my voice finally my own, but it's

no use. I see her head lift slightly, but it wobbles on her neck, disorientation still imprisoning her. And while she struggles to regain consciousness, she and the jeep grow smaller, the hands dragging me deeper and deeper into the forest.

I claw at the ground, bringing up handfuls of earth, rotting needles, and leaves and insects. I spit mud from my mouth and grab for branches. But each limb of each tree swats me away, making contact only long enough to slice thin cuts across my reaching arms. My stomach and chest flinch from the friction of the ground, and the hands drag me farther and farther from the road.

I scream, but I already know that these woods are full of unhearing ears.

Lightning cracks the sky open, and thunder follows it within seconds, sending buckets of rain pouring past the tree line and onto the ground. The hands around my ankles slip, and I seize that second of faltering, kicking out of their grip temporarily. But they find me again, grasping harder this time, nails puncturing my skin.

"Penny!"

The sound is so faint, I'm sure I haven't heard right. It could be April, but she'll be too late.

The moon breaks through the tree's canopy long enough

to illuminate the clearing, and I turn my head to see my captor, needles and earth raking my cheek.

Danny.

The little shack with the green door is on my right by the time the hands release their hold on my ankles.

I struggle to my feet and quickly buckle in pain, the branches and the ground having gashed my skin so thoroughly I'm not sure if I'll ever be able to move again.

"April!" I try, pleading with the woods to pass my message along. But I know they won't.

Terror takes hold as I see the little girl in the white dress emerge from her shed, white eyes finding me fast in the darkness. The two little boys from the curtains crawl around the side of the shed behind her, and from my periphery, a purple hat jerks toward me on bent limbs that look too long to belong to a person.

I start to back away, and roots like tentacles twist around my ankles, but they're not pulling me deeper into the woods. They're pulling me into the ground.

I grab for the only thing I can—a gnarled tree root jutting from the mud. But it turns to a decomposing mass in my hand, maggots and worms exploding from its center and covering my skin. I claw at the earth, but the mud betrays me too, turning to soup that slips between my fingers.

"Penny!"

But I can't respond. The roots tug at my ankles so hard, I think my legs might tear from the rest of my body. The mud is up to my chest, and soon, my chin. An apologetic moon is the last thing I see before the woods take me completely.

The dark swallows me whole, and now I know I'll hear what those silent screams have wanted me to hear this entire time.

Earth fills my lungs, fast and without ceremony. I struggle to regain the breath I only just got back from the smoke, but I know that the North Woods are greedy. They'll take me if they want me.

I land in a hollow place, debris floating before me, a kind of pocket below the depths of the forest, but darker than the sludge above, the sludge that still coats my insides.

I peer into the murkiness of my grave and search. I know I'm not here alone. I can hear something breathing even above my own dying lungs.

I see the eyes first. White like the moon, but these eyes aren't apologizing. The mouth next, with its wide open gape, a scream silent but desperate to be heard. I'm not looking at either of those, though. I'm looking at its hands. I'm looking at what it holds.

My notepad. The story of Rae and me.

I look up and see for the first time the purple curls pinned above those horrific white eyes.

I see veined hands hold the pad above a blazing fire, the smoke curling into the desert sky, choking the night around us and blurring the memory of a friendship that was never what it should have been.

Curled nails like brittle, dead leaves press against the pages.

I see my own handwriting: *I don't regret you.*

My throat closes around its last plea for breath, and then, just as I think my lungs will burst under their hardening shell of mud, I remember.

I thrust my hand into the pocket of my jeans, and it emerges with the matchbox I put there last night after I refused to burn my farewell to Rae.

I strike the last remaining match, thrust the flame underneath the notepad's edge, and ignite the paper.

A piercing scream rips through the murky underbelly of the North Woods, and the roots' hold on my ankles drops.

Rae's eyes fill again with color, their icy blue turning royal, the lashes around them rich and thick. Her jaw lifts slowly, raising her bottom lip to join the top, red the color of her unsmiling mouth. Her diamond labret twinkles at me in the murky darkness of the woods' black heart. And then one eye closes over her radiant blue iris, black fringe lifting in time to see a tiny glint of light emerge from that eye. The root that held me before wraps its embrace around Rae's stomach instead, pulling her from me, but she doesn't fight it. Instead, she puts her own arms across the root and for the first time in all of her months haunting me, she smiles with her entire face.

The root carries her into the darkness, her body small and frail in its grasp.

I watch until she disappears before panic seizes me, my lungs screaming for air. I kick and claw in the cavernous space, my feet finally finding a tapestry of tangled roots that no longer try to hold me. I use my last ounce of strength to reach the surface, pushing my head above the earth, pulling a breath of air so deep it cracks the shell around my lungs. I drag my body out of the ground and pull myself to my hands and knees, vomiting the mud and leaves I'd swallowed.

There in the clearing by the shed, under the light of the helpless moon, stand four throw-away children. A girl in a white sundress, her face so much clearer now than her grainy picture at the rest stop depicted. Two anonymous boys wearing shoes with broken laces, shoes that probably never fit quite right.

One brother, different and disturbed and never the brave eldest nor the vulnerable youngest.

Their faces glow pale, but their eyes and mouths close tightly against the exposure from the moon's light. They do not watch me go. They do not scream silently into the soaked night.

They do not wake as I leave them to sleep in these lonely woods that will never truly let them rest, those woods that have taken one more unwanted soul.

Rain pounds the woods and trees, and the second I'm able to, I run. The trees whip under the fierce wind that's fanning the storm, and I can see the distant glow of the Carver House on fire. But the wind carries another sound, too.

"Penny! Please!"

I run too fast at first, stumbling and falling to the ground, but the feeling of the earth that close to my face sparks a terror that pulls me back to my feet and sets me running even faster than before. I'm far from steady, but I push the trees aside, despite their insistent reach. I see their high roots in time, leaping over them and landing on unsteady legs that carry me all the way to the edge of the woods and back to the road, where I crash into April hard enough to make us both stumble.

She holds me so tightly I think she might break me in

half, before shoving me into the passenger seat and climbing behind the wheel.

We're at the hospital before we say another word, and even then, the only sounds we utter are responses to the most basic of questions from nurses. Our only request is that we're kept in the same room. And even after April is treated and cleared, she never leaves my side. Not for a single minute.

26

Mr. Jakes is late, but I don't mind. I was hoping for a little more time with Linda, anyway. I washed the strap three times in the washing machine before April finally suggested I try sticking it in the dishwasher. All the mud and dirt are finally out of the cloth. There isn't much I can do about the scratches on the corners but smooth the frayed plastic down and apologize to Mr. Jakes for scarring his baby.

But that's not why I want the time with her. Holding the camera as high as my arms will reach, I turn her around and angle the lens at my face. I tilt my head up and click. Then I return Linda to my lap and advance to my picture. I still flinch a little each time. It's going to take a while before I'm not bracing myself for what I might find.

My hair has gotten a little longer, and I now have to tuck pieces behind my ear. The points of the stars are still there of course, but I can't see them as clearly anymore. Wrapped around tough neck muscles and skimming the tops of my shoulders, they're a part of me, but folded away, sheltered but not forgotten.

The light in the room casts a purplish shade over me, and I look sleepier than I used to. Or maybe that's what calm looks like on me. Either way, Linda always did make me look a little different than my mind's eye saw me. This time, I don't mind what I see.

This time, I recognize myself.

"Why does every student take the self portrait on the last day?"

I turn to see Mr. Jakes standing in the doorway, blocking some of the purple light from outside.

"I'm not your student anymore, remember?"

"So you made clear the last time you came to see me," he says, and a smile seems to sneak up on him, taking him off guard. He clears his throat. "You've brought Linda home." He reaches for the camera before recoiling in genuine horror. "What in God's name have you done to my child?"

I was prepared for this. "She's given me some amazing images," I say, which is truer than I'd like it to be.

"From where did she give you these stellar images? The bottom of a bunker?"

It's true, she and I have been through a kind of war.

Mr. Jakes takes Linda gingerly from my hand. I remember learning once that you should never pick up a baby bird that's fallen from its nest, no matter how much it calls out for help. Touching the chick would make its mother abandon it, the scent of human an offense the unassuming creature could never disguise.

After he's done examining her, he pushes Linda back into my hands. "I don't even recognize her anymore. She's not mine."

"Look, I'm sorry, okay? She still works just fine," I start to say.

But he shakes his head before I can finish, his lips pinched against the mere thought of reclaiming her. "She's not mine."

I hold her closer. I cradle her, the strap a little softer than it used to be after four thorough washes.

Then something in Mr. Jakes's face shifts. He doesn't look so pained. His lips loosen their hold on each other.

"I'm teaching three more sections in the fall," he says. "One of them is 101. A lot of the same material we covered in the class you took, stuff you've already heard. But a lot of the stuff you missed, plus some history of photography, which you need."

"You as in the general you, or you as in me?" I ask.

"You," he says. "You'll suck without it."

"I see," I say. "So does that mean I don't actually suck now?"

He doesn't answer. I'm not even sure he heard me. "It's a transferable credit," he says. "It'd count toward a major. If you wanted it to."

I wasn't planning on telling him that my proposal for an independent study of photography was accepted by my guidance counselor on a probationary agreement. It's awkward to explain that I'm a sort-of independent senior, so long as I can keep my GPA above a 3.0. I feel like he might be disappointed in me for cutting it so close grade-wise. I still don't think I'll tell him that part, but I can at least answer him about the class.

"Okay," I say, and I make sure he sees me nod before I look down at Linda. I know I owe it to the reluctant mentor looking completely uncomfortable in front of me right now. And when my heart jumps a little at the thought of pointing the camera in plenty of new directions, I let myself enjoy the feeling.

"I will," I say. And I mean it.

Outside, I feel my phone vibrate in my purse and find my mom's face on the screen, her weird downturned smile looking ready as ever to mock me.

"Your father wants me to tell you he's going to be in Boise until Thursday now."

386 · CARLY ANNE WEST

"Why couldn't he just call me and tell me that?" I ask. "And wait, you and Dad talked?"

I think back on their conversation from March. The amicability of their relationship has been low on my list of things to care about since the summer, but now the thought of them chatting casts enough of a shadow for me to feel the chill of confusion.

"Yes, Penny. We do that on occasion, considering we share a daughter and all. That is, unless you've decided on a more suitable replacement for me."

It has been almost a full week since Mom has not-so-subtly suggested I have swapped her out for April. She's improving as far as I can tell, so I give her a pass.

"So what was on the agenda for this conversation?" I ask.

"Many topics that are none of your business, aside from that one detail," she says. "He'll be on project sites from today until he gets home. I assume he's told his own wife, but you might consider mentioning it to her when you see her."

She's having a bad day. Two April mentions in one phone call means a worse than normal day. And though I pull in the deepest breath I can, I refrain from sighing loudly enough for her to hear me.

"Did he say anything else?" I ask. "For me to know, I mean."

"No. Just that he loves you, blah blah. The usual," Mom

says, which makes me glad I've managed to keep my cool for as long as I have. I guess I'm improving a little too.

"Well, if you talk to him again," I say, "tell him I love him too."

"Sure. Glad to be the bearer of so much warmth," she says.

"Hey," I say. "I got into that program for seniors. The independent study. On probation. My grades aren't high enough yet. But if I do really well, you know . . . ," I say, deciding to add, "I haven't told anyone else yet."

There's a long pause, and I pull my phone away to make sure the call hasn't dropped. Her face on the screen is still there, her hair looking a little grayer than I think it did a second ago, which is of course impossible. Mostly.

"Well, hon, you'll get them up. You're smart."

Now it's me who doesn't know what to say. It's the best she can do, so I try to feel like it's enough.

"This call is costing me a fortune," she says. "You went over your data allowance again this month. Seriously, Penny, what are you doing, watching documentaries over the wireless?"

"Bye, Mom," I say.

"Good-bye, Penny."

Before I turn the corner onto my dad's street, I pass the house with the garden gnome mooning passersby. I uncap Linda and take a picture of him.

"That's some sage advice, my friend" I tell him.

Back at home, Rob is pulling something out of the oven that was likely meant to be cookies. Burnt sugar has the kind of cloying odor I've smelled in those really cheap candle jars they sell at the ninety-nine-cent store.

"It's only been eight minutes. The recipe says ten. What the hell?"

"You need more butter in the batter," April says. "And language."

"In the batter?" Rob asks.

"As in watch it," April says. "Save it for when I'm not standing right next to you helping you bake cookies for your new girlfriend."

"Aha," I say, and they both look up. "I was going to ask. And no offense, Rob, but I wouldn't even let you pour cereal for me."

He looks genuinely panicked. "Look, you missed a few things this summer," he says. "I'm more than just soccer and surprisingly insightful advice for my age. I'm in a *relationship* now."

I will not look at April. If I look at April, I will see the look she's dying to give me, and Rob will never be able to erase the sound of his mother and stepsister laughing at his declaration of sudden maturity.

So I take a cookie from the tray, and despite its steaming,

charred edges that smell even sweeter this close to my face—
and despite the stamp of heat it presses onto my tongue—I
nod my head and give him an air high five.

"Gwen had better appreciate you," April says, and finally
I feel brave enough to glance up at her. She's looking right
at me, something I didn't expect given this should be a
moment between her own son and her. But Rob is too busy
sliding burnt hockey pucks from the cookie sheet to see the
look April offers me. A smile that seems to thank me, though
I can't imagine what she would have to thank me for. Still,
I feel grateful, and I find myself hoping my face somehow
reflects that.

In my room, eight-by-ten-inch black-and-white photographs
paper my walls. Every surface mirrors back the glossy image of
a mistaken picture. Overexposed renderings of streams and
trees, the unfocused capture of what was probably a toad leaping from a rock. A close-up of a man I thought was interesting
on the street, but when I printed the picture, he felt hollow
somehow. Mr. Jakes's classroom recycling bin is full of these
types of shots. Ideas gone wrong, meandering inspiration that
got caught up in barbed wire along the way.

I keep each and every one, though.

At the end of the summer, after April and I came home,
after the fire inspector decided it had to be old wiring

that caused the blaze—a fire inspector who plays poker with Miller's electrician friend two nights a week—April decided she had no choice but to take a loss on the property. She could have fought to keep it. It was, after all, legally hers. But after it was condemned and the inspector added it to the long list of investigations he would eventually get to, April reflected back on the summer's failures and told the fine folks at Pierce County that they could choke on the house for all she cared. She was done.

And only because I was standing there when she threw her phone after hanging up did she also hear the breath escape my mouth. The one I think I might have been holding all summer.

"Good fucking riddance," she said to me.

In that moment, for the first time ever, I saw where Rob got everything. His compassion and speedy assessment of the problem, his unmuddled advice. His confusion at why I might be so grateful for the honor of his understanding.

Faced with that new revelation and a comfort knowing that there are two of them in my life, I offered April only one observation from the events of the summer.

"I think some destruction is just too massive to repair."

I never told her what happened that night we fled the house, and she never asked me.

Instead, she took a job with the Seattle Historical Society after two months off for internal reflection and an unexpected boost in luck after the investigation on the Carver House closed. The official cause of the fire: faulty wiring. The result: a substantial payment on insurance, enough to erase over half the devastating debt April thought she'd incurred.

Her new job specializes in, among other things, restoring old houses. Her first project is a 1912 Victorian in Pioneer Square. There was some competition for the position, apparently, but not even a spotty track record could keep April from cajoling her now boss into hiring her.

"It's three stories, with a basement and an attic!" she said after the deal closed. "And it's a total mess."

She's been giddy for weeks. I've agreed to take her "before" and "after" pictures on this one, too, but only because I think it might be fun to spend weekends with her. Plus, it'll give me a little more practice behind the lens.

My gaze rests on the only image that survived the summer. I've hung it on the back of my bedroom door so I see it right before I go to bed at night, and it's the first thing I see in the morning. It's of a silver cloud, bloated with the light of the sun it's hiding, dusty rays extending from the edges.

The phone in my purse vibrates, and when I pull it out, I see only a phone number, no name or face to accompany it. But it's a number I remember, even after two months of not seeing it.

"It didn't work."

I barely recognize Miller's voice. I could blame the horrible reception. It sounds like he's calling me from the bottom of a well, just like the very first time I heard his voice. But the crushing anguish is what distorts his tone now, fracturing each word so it sounds like they're falling in pieces from his mouth.

"What didn't work?" I ask, but it's only to make him keep talking. I already know what he's going to say.

"The last painting. I finished it, recreated it just the way it happened. The day they took him away. Just the way it *should* have happened. I thought . . ."

"Miller, I'm so sorry," I say. It's the only thing I can say, but it's all wrong. Miller knows I'm not really sorry. Danny belongs to the woods now, just like the rest of them do. No one ever should have come back. Miller has finished his tragic landscape, and it didn't work, and now he's broken. And even though I didn't want him to be right, I never wanted him to feel what it was to be wrong.

"You were right, though, Penny."

"I didn't want to—"

"It's okay. I'm not saying—" He stops himself, and I feel horrible. He's agitated, and I know he's probably looking for people to hate. It makes me sick to think I'm that person, but I'm willing to serve the purpose this one time.

"I'm trying to say that you were right. It doesn't have anything to do with him. Any of them. It's the woods. It's the goddamn woods, Penny."

His voice pitches high, and I brush off the thought that he sounds a little hysterical. Of course he would be after what he's been through.

"He wants out, Penny. Don't you see? He wants out, but the woods . . ."

I feel cold suddenly, and I press my palm to my skin to find some warmth. But none comes, and I listen more closely to Miller's voice to try and locate the source of the chill I can't escape. I think I can hear traffic, but I'm not entirely certain.

"Miller, where are you?"

"Penny, you told me once that you were a throwaway. That your parents didn't see the purpose for you. Do you still believe that?"

I hesitate while I try to parse out what Miller just asked me and the increasing frenzy in his tone.

"Because I don't believe it," he says before I can answer. "I don't know if I ever told you that, but I should have. I think everyone has a purpose. We *all* serve a purpose."

"Miller? I can barely hear you."

But in the pause between our breaths, I hear something else, something I couldn't quite place earlier. Now I recognize the source of the chill under my skin. Deep in the background of wherever Miller is, I hear the faintest sound of music. The tinny sound of a melody I used to struggle to place. But not anymore.

"I finally understand now," Miller continues. "You helped me see."

"Helped you see what? Miller, you—"

"I have to do it, Penny. I have to make it right. But it's okay. It's all going to be better once I make it right."

"Miller!" I don't realize I'm shouting until I hear April calling to me from the kitchen.

"Miller?" I ask my phone, but when I pull it away from my ear, I see nothing but a blank screen. He's gone.

April's in my room now.

"Is that who I think it is?" she asks, her eyes looking like they're ready to ignite.

"Hmm?" I ask, hunting for my most casual expression. "Oh, it was, um, my mom."

April crinkles her eyebrows, but she doesn't question me once I've invoked my mother.

"Oh, hey, can I borrow your car?" I ask, using every ounce of willpower to maintain my fake calm. "I was hoping to get to the frame shop before it closes."

"Now? Sorry, no. I need to see a guy about some vintage wallpaper."

I give her a look.

"It's important. It's for the new house," she says, almost pouting. "And why am I explaining myself to you? It's my car."

I debate how not to give away my conversation with Miller but still get the jeep from her.

"Tomorrow," she offers. And before I can object, she leaves the room.

I stare at my walls the entire night, awash in a sea of black and white and shades of gray. I stare until my eyes give out and I fall into a haze so deep, I forget where I am. I wake up in a room I swore I'd never have to see again.

"No," I tell Danny, his eyes staring at me from the wall, blinking slowly enough for me to know he has one last message to convey. The grass beneath him is gone, the ground nothing but piles of black char. Instead of the swirl of paint dust that used to

envelop me, tiny black flakes dance like confused snow in the air between us.

He walks away, and I follow him because all I want to do is wake from his horror once and for all. All I want is for him to finally let me go.

A young Miller stands beside Danny, smoke from a cigarette between his older brother's fingers making Miller's eyes water. He rubs at his nose and scrunches his face, then leans unconvincingly toward the cigarette.

"Can I try?"

"Give it a rest," Danny says, and he looks at Miller like he might ruffle his hair. Or punch his back. Instead, he does neither and reaches for his lighter, flicking it. He watches the spark ignite over and over, until he finishes his cigarette and stomps it into the dirt.

They're standing behind a building I recognize, staring at a wall I stared at through a rain-soaked windshield by the light of a dying streetlamp.

A wall coated in graffiti I saw later in a sketchbook.

"I have to tell you something," Miller says to his brother.

"No," Danny says.

"I have to tell you," Miller persists.

"Don't say a fucking word," Danny says, his eyes broiling behind their green facade.

Then Danny looks away, his eyes fixed somewhere beside the Dumpster behind Scoot's.

"I heard it fly into the window," he says.

Miller looks confused, but he stays silent, a practice he seems to understand he's supposed to follow.

"I was clear across the store when I heard. Sounded like a rock or something. I got all pissed, thinking someone was messing with us, you know?"

Miller remains silent, but his eyes continue to search for what they're supposed to be seeing.

"But then I saw this little spray of feathers on the glass, and I knew what happened. I went outside, and it was just lying there in the rocks. Except its eyes were moving around. Like it knew it should be dead, but it still needed to see what was going on."

The young Miller and I find what it is Danny's talking about.

A bird, a crow by the look of it, the kind that's always digging through Dumpsters and screaming about what they've found.

"I was going to kill it. But then something else happened. Another crow, this big angry fucker, it flew down and stood between me and the other one. Actually stood there between us. And it started making all kinds of noise. And I knew if I got any closer, it would do its damndest to peck my eyes out. So I walked away, and I listened to it squawk all day long. Until finally it just stopped.

And when I went out there to check on it, there it was. Dead as a fucking doornail."

Then they're both silent for a while.

"Are you sorry about it?" Danny asks Miller, the question pointed directly at his younger brother, and we both know he isn't talking about a dead crow.

Miller nods dutifully at the ground.

"Say it, then," Danny says, his voice rattling with the anger from before.

"I'm sorry," Miller says, sounding older than he should.

But he still doesn't look at his brother.

There they stand, two brothers who never lived up to the first, watching a dead bird until the other crows come for it. And they walk away before they see what it is that crows do when one of their own dies.

But I see it.

Even though it's still dark when I finally pull away from the house in April's jeep the next day, I reason that five a.m. is officially morning time, and if April were awake, I'm sure she would agree.

The radio would normally be blaring, but my mind is already too cluttered with the sound of Miller's frantic rambling from the day before, and images of crows and sprinkled ashes from a dead forest. In the few hours of sleep I did manage to cobble together, Miller's voice hovered over the surface of my consciousness.

"It's all going to be better once I make it right."

I'm crossing onto WA-16 in half the time it would normally take me to get from Seattle to Point Finney, and I slow as soon as I reach the exit I swore I'd never take again. Only now do I understand that despite my hurrying to get here, I'm in no way ready to see whatever it is I think I'm going to find.

I slow to a stop at the gas station, its lights still on even though the sun has begun to push through the clouds. The massive expanse of concrete yawns before me as I open the jeep's door and emerge to hear what I already knew I would.

The melody that I couldn't place all summer, the tune that emanated from ancient throats, that chimed in the background of Miller's call yesterday.

The melody that I can now place.

That tinny jingle piping from the speakers above the metal awning covering the gas pumps. And when I reluctantly lift my eyes to the entrance of the convenience store, the boy with the cardboard sign is nowhere to be found.

I approach the fork in the road slowly. The choice at my right will take me into the North Woods to desperate trees that may or may not still be standing. I slow to a stop while my heart struggles to keep pace with the engine. With each acceleration, my pulse takes a cue, so I cut the wheel to the left and tell my heart it's okay. We'll get this over with soon.

I pull into the shared dirt lot between Ripp's and Scoot's. At six thirty in the morning on a Saturday, Ripp's should be open, but it's not. In fact, I'm the only one in the parking lot, the jeep's engine rippling the sudden quiet of its surroundings. I pull to the far corner of Ripp's, angling toward the entrance but positioning far enough back to snug the car into a space that allows me to see into three windows of Scoot's, all of which are unshaded even though the CLOSED sign faces out.

I turn to Ripp's windows, looking for the posted hours, thinking but not believing that maybe he'd changed his weekend hours since I was here last. To my right in the passenger seat, Linda sits patiently where I left her after seeing Mr. Jakes yesterday. I use her now to zoom in on the hours stenciled on the glass door of Ripp's, which still claim the café opens at six every morning.

And then a sign above the door catches my eye.

Hastily written on a piece of white notebook paper torn from its spiral binding, the squared-off lines of a fat Magic Marker explain where Ripp and presumably others are.

Shane Michael Rawson

Age 15

4'7" 97 lbs.

Help us find Shane, last seen 9/14/14 at the Gas 'N Drive off Exit 122. Search party meets at 6:00 a.m. in front of Point Finney Public Library. Call Ripp's cell to meet up: 253-555-8812. Any information, call the Sheriff ASAP!

Taped below the description is a glossy Polaroid, the kind of picture taken in institutions that still keep Polaroid cameras around. I recognize him, but he looks different without his khaki jacket camouflaging him against the wall behind him. His hair—closely cropped and standing in tiny, shocked stubble on top of his head—frames a thin face and a smile that looks like it had second thoughts right before the shutter snapped. His ears are massive. His eyes pierce the lens, challenging it to a fight. But his shoulders sag on a neck that looks too thin to hold such a heavy weight, and that's how I know that Shane Michael Rawson was once someone's problem.

The faint sound of a screen door bending on its hinge pulls my attention from the handmade sign on Ripp's door and toward Scoot's. There, standing in the dawn light at the front of the alley leading to the trash cans and the back of Miller's family store is a boy who isn't a boy anymore.

There is nothing about his body that indicates his age, but his face betrays the years his body refuses to confess, years that surpass Miller's age, but not by much. A patchy layer of stubble spots his jawline and cheeks and upper lip. His hair is a little too long, smoothed back by a thick-toothed comb but with some areas unattended to, like he just woke up from a hard, unmoving sleep. Like he woke up with a struggle. A flannel jacket I recognize as Miller's fits loosely around his body, and I remember with a piercing clarity the way the lining felt against the wet of my skin in Miller's car.

He folds a worn purple cap tightly in his hands. Unfurling it, he slides it over his fiery, unforgiving hair. And now the picture is complete, the portrait I watched take shape all summer.

As if summoned, Miller joins Danny at the top of the alley—an orphan and his traded sibling—and they find me parked in the farthest corner of Ripp's, my camera angled in their direction. Their matching green eyes and burnt hair catch a sudden ray of sunlight, one brave stroke of the sun clawing its way from behind overlapping clouds. But the clouds win, snuffing the light before it's had a chance to catch, and Miller turns his brother around toward the store. The bell follows them inside, and the CLOSED sign slaps the glass of the window.

I sit in the dirt parking lot for several more minutes, Linda fixed to the same location, her lens searching for whatever it is she thinks I want her to capture.

When I finally lower her and return her to the seat beside me, I leave her confused. I haven't let her blink on a single image. And as I drive away, I imagine the blur of color her shutter would close around if only I would hold her up to the rear window.

But she would struggle too hard to find a clear image, and I won't do that to her. I'd rather face her forward.

I'd rather see what she can show me ahead.

ACKNOWLEDGMENTS

I wrote *The Bargaining* during countless personal transitions. Some were beautiful. Some were dark. All were necessary. And there were a lot of people who guided me down paths and around blind corners.

To my agent, Steven Chudney, thank you as always for your spot-on insights and tireless advocacy. You somehow manage to find that space between where the writing ends and the business begins, and you create a harmonious place for the two to exist. I don't know how you perform such amazing magic, but every author should be so lucky to be the recipient of it. Thank you a million times over to my brilliant editor, Michael Strother, for your passion and enthusiasm for the macabre, and for sharing that with me through our journey. When I doubted myself, you helped me remember why I was writing the story. You helped me remember the seeds and nourish them into the work I hoped to create. My wild and unrestrained gratitude to the entire Simon Pulse team for your continued efforts on this book's behalf: Patrick Price (I hope your bag still smells of coffee!), Mara Anastas, Mary Marotta, Lucille Rettino, Carolyn Swerdloff,

Teresa Ronquillo, Siena Koncsol, Jennifer Romanello, Jodie Hockensmith, Faye Bi, Kelsey Dickson, Christina Pecorale, Danielle Esposito, Rio Cortez, Victor Iannone, Kayley Hoffman, and Sara Berko. Great big hugs to Jessica Handelman for once again creating such beautiful cover art and to Hilary Zarycky for a gorgeous interior. Very special thanks to Annette Pollert as well, for your invaluable notes in the early stages. I am so, so grateful.

Writing group. Ah, my beautiful ladies. I have come to rely on you more than ever. Lizzie Brock, Laura Joyce Davis, Nina LaCour, and Teresa K. Miller, together and individually, you make sense of this writing thing each month, reminding me when and what to question, when to celebrate and when to mourn, when to bear my soul and when to bear my teeth. This book wouldn't exist without you, and at the risk of sounding a little dramatic here, I might not exist in my current state. I love you.

Thank you for your continued mentorship and support, Kathryn Reiss.

Mom and Dad, somehow the drive to make you proud has grown in a time when that need should be receding. Maybe it's because you've spoiled me by offering it so fully. Thank you for saying it when it shouldn't be necessary anymore. Nikki, Ella, Hannah, and Payton, your love and support inspire me every day. Matthew, when we were little and I had nightmares, you taught me how to face down fear, to understand how to find humor in it. You were maybe the first one to teach me that. Aunts, uncles, and cousins, my God, how did I get so lucky? Lizzy-biz, you are my sister. You know that. Grandpa Phil, the loss of you is still fresh, but the joy of you grew over ninety-five beautiful years. Rick, Jan, Bethany, and Sheldon—I get to call you family, which is wholly unearned. I stumbled into another family, and it was such dumb luck I still can't believe it. Thank you for calling me yours.

Simon, you are everything I aspire to be. Your reckless imagination is limitless in its travels. I hope you never find its outer walls, and if you do, I know you'll be strong enough to demolish them. You are wondrous. Benny, you are still walking that edge between what I see and what I think I might see if I would just stop looking so hard. You have a transcendent vision. I suspect you always will.

Matt, thank you for being the one at the end of every dark passage. Thank you for the security in knowing that you'll always be the one at the end. You aren't my light, and you aren't the one who hands me the candle; you're the one who reminds me that it's been in my hand the whole time. And when my hand shakes, you help me hold it steady until the match strikes the box. It will always be you. Always. You are my love.